MOTHERS

AND

OTHER

STRANGERS

ADVANCE PRAISE

"Whom do we really belong to and why? This dark, gorgeous jewel of a novel probes the secrets we keep and the complex ties of family, love, and loss. Shattering and brilliant, this marks the debut of an astonishing talent."

— CAROLINE LEAVITT,
New York Times–bestselling author of
Cruel Beautiful World and *Pictures of You*

"*Mothers and Other Strangers* is a memorable first novel, a delightfully twisty gothic with the strange and eerie urgency of a fable or a dream."

— DAN CHAON,
author of *Ill Will* and
You Remind Me of Me

"A young woman's investigation of her mother's mysterious past uncovers disturbing revelations about love, family and the fragile bonds that both connect us and tear us apart. An absorbing, sensitive novel that confirms the troubling reality that it's often the people closest to us who do the most harm."

— ELIZABETH BRUNDAGE,
author of *All Things Cease to Appear*

"From the first shocking sentence of Gina Sorell's *Mothers and Other Strangers*, I was hooked on the twisting ride of a woman who receives an inheritance of secrets, debt, and the mess left behind. With stunning prose and the danger of a thriller, Sorell reaches deep into a broken heart and finds what's still beating. I am a fan!"

— SUSAN HENDERSON,
author of *Up from the Blue*

"This compelling debut reveals the astronomical cost of harboring family secrets. Somehow Gina Sorell has managed to craft both a meditation on the messiness of mother-daughter bonds and a mystery that will keep you turning pages until the wee hours of the morning."

— MICHELLE BRAFMAN,
author of *Bertrand Court* and *Washing the Dead*

"A stunning debut, *Mothers and Other Strangers* grips from page one. It's a perfect weave of suspense and of insight about how people love and hurt one another, and sometimes heal, and sometimes cannot. I highly recommend this novel and look forward—impatiently—to Gina Sorell's future work."

— ROBIN BLACK,
author of *Life Drawing*

"Gina Sorell has written a complex mystery of the human heart in her poignant debut novel, exploring how the emotional riddle of our parents shapes our lives well into adulthood. To paraphrase Philip Larkin, they screw you up, your mom and dad. Sometimes they intend to hurt you as deeply as they've been hurt. The quest in this wise novel is to realize that the path to healing a childhood wound passes through understanding the strangeness of one's parents, and accepting it, or not. This book is a must read for anyone who has struggled to understand their own parents."

— ROBERT EVERSZ,
author of *Shooting Elvis*

Published by Prospect Park Books
2359 Lincoln Avenue
Altadena, CA 91001
www.prospectparkbooks.com

Distributed by Consortium Book Sales & Distribution
www.cbsd.com

Library of Congress Cataloging-in-Publication Data
Names: Sorell, Gina, author.
Title: Mothers and other strangers / by Gina Sorell.
Description: Altadena, California : Prospect Park Books, 2017. | Includes bibliographical references and index.
Identifiers: LCCN 2016031392 (print) | LCCN 2016039800 (ebook) | ISBN 9781938849893 (pbk. : alk. paper) | ISBN 9781938849909 ()
Subjects: LCSH: Mothers and daughters--Fiction. | Mothers--Death--Fiction. | Family secrets--Fiction. | Canada--Fiction. | South Africa--Fiction. | Psychological fiction. | Domestic fiction.
Classification: LCC PR9199.4.S6987 M68 2017 (print) | LCC PR9199.4.S6987 (ebook) | DDC 813/.6--dc23
LC record available at https://lccn.loc.gov/2016031392

Cover design by David Ter-Avanesyan
Book layout and design by Amy Inouye, Future Studio
Printed in the United States of America

MOTHERS

AND

OTHER

STRANGERS

BY GINA SORELL

PROSPECT
·PARK·
BOOKS

For my parents, Denny and Leonie,
never strangers, always friends.

And my loves Jeff and Grady,
home is where you are.

My father proposed to my mother at gunpoint when she was nineteen, and knowing that she was already pregnant with a dead man's child, she accepted.

The dead man was actually my real father, Leo, a handsome young playboy my mother had managed to tame. She had loved him since she was a girl, their family farms neighboring each another. She had watched as he had grown from a boy to a man and had felt her heart breaking when he began to play the field with older and more sophisticated girls. For a time, her worship of Leo seemed hopeless. Until one day, he no longer looked at her like a kid sister, but as a woman he wanted to take. She had waited for him without him ever knowing, and when he had fallen hard for her and professed his love and desire to make her his wife, she knew the wait had been worth it.

And then everything changed.

In a second, all that she had longed for was taken from her, and with it any chance of true happiness. On a starless night, a silver Jaguar crossed the two-lane road that wound through the mountains and met my parents' car head on. And in a spectacular explosion of metal and glass, all lives were taken. All except my mother's and, as it would turn out, mine. Sometimes I wondered if I was the only real survivor that night, my mother forever altered and hardened by her loss.

It was Howard, Leo's older brother, the man I called Papa and the one who raised me as if I was his own, who nursed my mother back to life after the crash, healing all of her but the hand that had clutched Leo's fingers as he lay dying on the side of the road. She had tried to keep him alive, tried to breathe life into his failing body, but it was useless. As she cried and waited for help, she gripped Leo's hand, her grief so intense that she claimed she was unable to uncurl her fingers properly ever again. For as long as I could remember, her left hand lay at her side, a withered little fist with crinkly skin that she often kept tucked behind her dress or curled at her waist. I had never understood how a hand could be deformed by grief, but my mother insisted it was so.

Howard had adored my mother since she was a child. He was ten years older and crippled by polio, and he used to enjoy watching her run and play with his younger brother. And as she matured, so did his affection. After his brother died, Howard's love was a secret he no longer needed to keep. And so one night, he took my mother for a ride in his new car, and as they came to the end of their dirt road he pulled out his revolver and held it to his head. In exchange for my mother's hand in marriage, he promised her wealth and fidelity. He also promised that he would kill himself if she refused. He loved her with all his heart, and any love that she could give in return would be enough.

He must've hoped that she would learn to love him eventually, that she would forget his brother, and that in time he could slowly take Leo's place in her heart. But my mother didn't care about her heart; it was broken, and now she needed something more than the fantasies of an idyllic future with a dead fiancé: she needed security. And she knew that this was the best offer she would get. Having a child out of wedlock wasn't an option in those days, not with the Dutch Afrikaners around blaming women for their problems. Every time there was a drought or a bad bunch of crops, the local newspaper would report that it was because women wore skirts that were too short, ran around without their husbands, and drank liquor. She could only imagine what her neighbors would say about an illegitimate child. The last thing she needed were those militants knocking on her door to curse her. And so she agreed, and when my mother announced to Howard a month after they were married that she had gotten pregnant with his child on their wedding night, Howard never suspected for a moment that she was lying and I wasn't his. Together, they moved to the new life he had been building for them in Johannesburg. A life where they could start fresh.

This is how the story goes, at least according to my mother. And now, thirty-nine years old and returning to Toronto to bury her, I still didn't know if it was true. Like the cancer that had claimed her a week earlier, my mother had been like an illness to me, and eventually I'd had to cut her out. We had been estranged for years, and still I hadn't stopped yearning for the relationship we never had. There would be no deathbed reconciliation like in the movies for us. It's hard to reconcile with a stranger. Not only did I not know that my own mother was dying, I had no idea she was sick.

The story of my paternity was just one of many secrets and half-truths my mother burdened me with as a child, repeated enough times that eventually it became true, even if it wasn't. I had no way of knowing, no proof, and my mother wasn't about to give me any. I wondered if my real father would have swung me in the air until I was dizzy, held me in his arms when I was scared, and loved me the way my mother never had, understanding all the things I longed to know, before I even said them. When Howard was still around, I had asked him once about his brother, but he said he didn't have one. For years I had looked for evidence of my real father's existence, but I never found any, and eventually I gave up trying.

I don't know why I had held out hopes of finding proof that my father existed among my mother's things in her little one-bedroom apartment in Toronto when she died, but I did. I sent up a prayer to anyone who might listen, that there would be a photograph, a love letter, some souvenir of his life. I wanted to know if I did in fact inherit his long legs, straight nose, and sad eyes, like my mother said I had. Of all the things she had told me over the years, the story of my real father's existence was the one thing that I hoped was true. That my true roots lay not with my mother, but in a man who at one time really did exist, to whom she had given the best parts of herself. I found my heart beating a little faster with every piece of yellowed paper I found in the shoeboxes that contained evidence of my mother's complicated existence, an existence that began long before I was born, in Africa.

Africa. It seemed like some distant memory, a story that belonged to someone else. We left Africa when I was six and moved to Canada, and even though I'd spent the last decade living in LA, I guess I still thought of Africa as home. In truth, I'd never really felt at home anywhere, except with Ted, and now we were divorced. One more branch removed from my ever-shrinking family tree.

I longed to fill in all the missing pieces that made me feel unrooted, floating through time and space, the wind whistling through the holes history had left in me, threatening to carry me away and toss me aside for good.

CHAPTER ONE
1987

I slowly pulled the car into the driveway of Dalewood, my mother's apartment building, and rested my head on the steering wheel, my whole body aching from fatigue. The dreams of fire that used to haunt me as a child were back, and I hadn't slept more than a few hours since my mother had passed away. Days spent sorting out her affairs had left me dazed, my skin sensitive to everything it touched. I took a deep breath. Soon this would all be over and I could move on.

My mother had willed her apartment to me, but it made more sense to sell it. For the first time in a long time, I had a plan. A plan that involved actually living again, rather than sleepwalking with the disappointments that somewhere along the way I decided were my destiny to carry with me. My mother's death had changed all of that. It had shaken me awake and out of the depression that I had fought on and off since adolescence. Happiness had always been hard won for me, but I'd won it once, and I was determined to do so again. She was gone now. And it was time to send all my heartache with her.

In the mirrored walls of the elevator car, I noticed for the first time how exhausted I looked. My long, wavy brown hair hung in a mess around my shoulders, and I scooped it up and twisted it into a knot at the back of my neck. My brown eyes seemed even sadder now, fatigue and age dragging the corners of them down. I sighed and took it all in: the lines around my eyes, the soft freckles on my pale skin, the lips that were always slightly red from my licking them. I had examined myself a million times in this elevator on the way to see my mother, and the conclusion had always been the same. She was the beautiful one, not me. No matter how many times I'd been told otherwise, I had always felt plain in comparison to her. It was a belief that my mother had done little to change. I took a deep breath and exhaled. I needed to stop worrying about what my mother did or didn't think of me. I would pack up her things, sell her place, and use what little money was left to open my own dance studio. The thought of it made me smile. My name on the door, and a room full of bright-eyed children, all nimble limbs and easy smiles, bursting with the same joy that I'd known as a dancer. Teaching was an idea I had abandoned long ago in pursuit of other things. But now I longed for a life full of purpose and passion, and I hoped that if I planted enough bits of happiness in my heart, they would grow into a love of life again.

As the elevator opened I saw Vincent and some of my mother's neighbors clustered around the door of her apartment.

"Elsie, I am so sorry," he said, running his big hands over his wiry white hair, his eyes wide.

"What happened?"

"A real estate agent came by to take a look at the apartment. He left his card at the desk and got the key from the lockbox."

"But I spoke to Diane this morning, and she didn't say anything about anyone coming by." Diane was the agent who handled all the sales in the building.

"I don't think she knew. Mrs. David came home and heard the noise in your mother's apartment. She knocked on the door, and he bolted past her."

I started down the hall and locked eyes with Mrs. David. She was clutching her arm and talking to a man in uniform. I quickened my steps and felt Vincent right behind me trying to hold me back.

"Elsie, wait...."

"Oh my God." The apartment looked like it had been hit by an earthquake. Except that this wasn't Los Angeles, and the only earthquakes here were of the human kind. The couch had been torn open, the stuffing pulled apart and thrown around the living room. Broken picture frames littered the floor, along with the contents of every cupboard. Her red lacquered jewelry box had also been destroyed, presumably smashed to pieces when the intruder discovered it had only costume jewelry inside. I heard myself gasp as I noticed that even the pages of her beloved books had been ripped from their bindings and tossed aside. I bent down to pick them up.

"Ma'am, please don't touch anything."

"This is my mother's apartment."

"And your mother is?"

"Dead." I took no pleasure in saying it, and I felt a huge lump in my throat that made it almost impossible to swallow. "She left me the apartment. I was getting ready to sell it."

"I see. I'll need you to tell me if you notice anything missing. Jewelry, art, anything valuable."

"She didn't have anything like that," I said, looking around me. "She made me executor of her will, and I can tell you this is it." I wasn't being entirely honest; there were also debts, and secrets, and questions that I would never have answered. My knees started to buckle, and he grabbed me before I could fall.

"Here, take a seat." He picked up the small painting stool that my mother used as a side table and sat me down on it, and it was then that I read his nametag: *Officer Dixon*.

"What happened?" I looked over at Mrs. David.

"It didn't sound like you," said Mrs. David. "I know the difference between packing things in boxes and throwing them around the living room. I kept knocking, and then he opened the door and pushed me down as he ran away."

"Did you see him?"

"Not very well."

"Are you all right?"

"I'll be fine." She paused and looked me straight in the eye. "What was he looking for?"

"I don't know."

"Do you have any idea who would want to do this? Did your mother have any enemies?" asked Officer Dixon.

I could feel Mrs. David and Vincent's eyes on me as they waited for an answer. My mouth was dry and my head was buzzing. It was one thing for me to go through my mother's things looking for clues to her past, but this was something horrible. This wasn't looking, this was ransacking. The fact that someone was able to tear through her apartment with such violence hit me square in the gut and I heard myself start to cry.

"I wouldn't know." Once the tears came I couldn't stop them. There hadn't been many since she passed, only an overwhelming fatigue and numbness. I may have been angry with my mother, but I didn't want to deface her, trash anything and everything that had held meaning for her. It may not look like much, but it was all she had, it was all I had, and it had fit into these five hundred square feet. I was sobbing now and having trouble catching my breath. It wasn't just the shock of the break-in, or the exhaustion that I'd felt since coming back to Toronto to deal with my mother's affairs, that made me weep—it was admitting that any hidden hope I'd had of us having an actual relationship had now died along with her.

"It's okay." Officer Dixon put his arm around my shoulder. I stiffened at first, but his grip was steady and I crumpled into the side of his body.

"I am so sorry," said Vincent.

"It's not your fault. How could you have guessed that somebody would do this?"

"I'll be downstairs if you need me." He squeezed my hand and left the apartment with Mrs. David.

I nodded and took a deep breath. I had soaked Officer

Dixon's jacket with my tears and gingerly pulled my face away from his side. I searched in my pockets for a Kleenex and then gave up and used my sleeve to wipe my face and my nose. I couldn't imagine that there was anything of value to anyone here.

Officer Dixon pulled up a chair and opened his notebook. His rosy, round cheeks made his face look young at first, but the deep lines at the corners of his eyes gave his years away.

"I'm sorry, ma'am, but I have to ask, did your mother owe anyone money?"

"I don't know."

"Was anybody looking for her?"

"Yes. I was."

CHAPTER TWO

I stood in the middle of my mother's apartment and tried to make sense of it all. Who would break in and why? Someone had singled out her place. It felt personal. Or was it? Maybe this was a professional criminal who robbed homes of the recently deceased with prestigious addresses? I didn't know. I lifted my mother's clothes off the floor and carefully refolded the silky blouses and tunics that she favored, checking the pockets and feeling foolish every time my heart leapt at finding something, only to discover it was a rumpled cough-drop wrapper or bobby pin. I was struck by how small she was. She'd always been a slender woman, but she appeared to have shrunk as she'd gotten older. And as I stacked the fragile, tiny tower of tops into a box marked for charity, I told myself not to cry, and took a deep breath and moved on. The floor of her closet held only a few items: a couple of sweaters, wool pants, several shawls, and a dark down coat and boots that I moved into the box as well. In his fury the intruder had done the hard work for me, spilling my mother's belongings out in the open, saving me the pain of going through each of her drawers one by one. As shocking as it was to see her things so violently thrown about, it forced me into action. I needed to tidy up this place quickly and get it sold. The real estate agent, Diane, had warned me that apartments took longer to sell in the winter, especially ones that needed work. My mother had downsized from the two-bedroom that I'd grown up in and moved to this small unit long after I'd left. I was shocked to learn that she had taken out a second mortgage and that the bank still owned most of it, even though she'd been there for almost two decades.

I sat down on the little love seat, smoothing out one of the many afghans hiding cracks in the leather. Looking around the apartment, with its yellowed, incense-stained walls, old wooden coffee table, and threadbare Persian carpets, I tried to see it the way I knew Diane would see it, the way anyone who didn't know my mother would see it when they walked through the door. When first purchased in the late sixties, the hand-carved wooden furniture, batiked bedspreads, collections of crystals, and pictures of Indian saints and Hindu gods would have made this small space a groovy pad. The lamps draped in silk scarves and the over-stuffed throw pillows on the floor next to stacks of books on philosophy, art, and religion would have announced to anyone who entered that this was the home of a new age, forward-thinking hippie, a woman who lived life on her own terms. But now after years of use, with nothing having been replaced or updated, the décor simply announced that the owner's glory days were behind her. It seemed that every item was covered by a thin, sticky layer of dust that had settled for good, as my mother had lost first her cleaning lady, and then her own interest in cleaning.

I hadn't seen anything that I thought warranted a break-in. I began to stack my mother's books in another one of the empty cardboard boxes that I'd brought. There were coffee-table books on art and sculpture, architecture, and philosophy. I thought of all the times I had seen my mother stretched out in her favorite reading chair, poring over these pages, a notebook and pen at the ready to take notes. I flipped through the pages hoping to find something of my missing past, a love letter from my father, a photograph of him and my mother, anything that could prove that the existence of my father, Leo, had been real, and not some twisted fiction my mother concocted, either to excuse her seemingly easy dismissal of Howard from our lives or to cover an unplanned pregnancy by a stranger. But there was nothing. And then I saw a stack of glossy flyers from every dance company I'd ever worked with, souvenirs of wonderful performances that my mother had never witnessed. She had attended only one of my shows, but I'd kept her on the mailing list just the same, hoping for the day when I might look out into the audience and see her sitting there, beaming with pride. That day never came, and I continued to believe she didn't care about my dancing career. But if that was true, why had she kept track of it? And why hadn't she said anything to me? I sorted through the pictures that had been tossed from their broken frames, self-portraits in front of famous monuments, the Eiffel Tower, the Taj Mahal, Big Ben. Photographs she must have taken on her trips with the Seekers, the strange cult-like group she had joined twenty-five years earlier, but none with any of the members themselves. Why? And where were the pictures I remembered of my mother as a young woman, sitting on the beach and smiling at the camera, or of me as a chubby little toddler resting under a huge tree in our backyard? They were nowhere to be found.

I picked myself off the worn Persian carpet in the middle of the living room, unfolding my legs and listening to my knees crack like popcorn. My previous incarnation as a dancer had left my joints much older than they should have been, and living in California had made me soft to the cold Canadian winters. I'd become like so many other fair-weather Canadians: I loved my country, but not in the winter. My mother hated the cold too. I asked her once why on earth, if she hated the cold so much, did she pick Canada when we left Africa? She said it was because Canada would take people like us. Ironically enough, she had wanted to live in California.

My stomach rumbled, and as I placed my hand across my belly, I saw on my watch that it was already six o'clock. I opened the little shuttered doors that concealed a galley kitchen and began rifling through the cupboards. I saw stacks of paper napkins wrapped in rubber bands and Ziploc baggies full of salt and pepper packets. I pushed them aside, knocking over bottles of homeopathic remedies and supplements and neat piles of jams, butter, and sauces that seemed never to expire. I made my way through most of the soup crackers and, with nothing left to eat, removed a packet of blackberry jam, peeled off the seal, and licked it clean. The sugary sweetness of the jam made my mouth water and my stomach lurch.

I had expected to find her shelves lined with the packages of fine teas, biscuits, and chocolates that she had always favored. But those luxury tins, now empty of their original delicacies, were stuffed with the kind of condiments that could be taken off the counters of coffee shops. Never much of a cook, my mother used to buy her groceries and meals at the fine food shops that were within walking distance. I once saw her spend in a week what the average person would spend in a month. But nothing about my mother was average, and that seemed to be the point that she'd been trying to make her whole life.

As a child, I loved the fact that my mother was different. With her long hair, designer outfits, and love of philosophy, she wasn't like any mom I had ever met. We didn't have set meal times, or even a dining room table. We ate our meals at the coffee table, sitting on cushions on the living room floor, listening to records. There was no list on the fridge that detailed when things ran out and needed to be replaced, no specific day for laundry and cleaning, not even a time to go to bed. She said we should eat what we wanted when we were hungry and sleep when we were tired. She spent her days doing as she pleased and her nights lost in her books. She said it was because she'd rather have her time dictated organically by her desires than adhere to the rigidity of an artificially imposed structure, a structure that I had to adhere to, as I was in school. A structure that my best friend Arden and her family had.

Arden Douglas was the first friend I made in Canada. I was six when we met, in a dance class run by her mom. Two years older than me, with long, jet-black hair hanging below her waist and not one but two earrings in her left ear, a stud and a dangling feather, she was the coolest person on the planet, and I followed her everywhere. A gifted dancer, with long limbs and delicate bones, she lit up the stage and wasn't afraid to share her spotlight with a young girl who had a strange South African accent. Arden had always been one of those dancers who got choreography on the first try, picked up routines easily, and after a full day of dancing still had enough energy to do it all over again. Unlike myself, who over the years would earn every inch of flexibility through hard work and determination, Arden had limbs that seemed made of Plasticine. She flew across the stage effortlessly and gracefully, defying gravity. Dancing wasn't work for her, it was play, and she infused all her movements with such joy it made you want to dance alongside her. What I struggled to accomplish she was blessed with.

Arden and I spent all of our time together, her family quickly becoming mine. I had never known parents like the Douglases. Arden's mother would greet her after school with a hug and a kiss, sit down at their kitchen table with her, and ask her about her day. She'd send her to her room with a snack for when she did her homework, and call her down when dinner was ready, and the whole family would eat together. When I got home from school, I was greeted by an empty apartment in need of cleaning, my mother's belongings strewn everywhere. I'd pick up after her, do the laundry, and wait for her to return. Sometimes she'd come in with one order of takeout for us to share and a new coffee-table book that we had to read together immediately. And sometimes she came home long after I'd fallen asleep with some of her friends, and they'd turn on all the lights, play records, and pick up in the middle of whatever heated debate they were having. I'd wait as long as I could, hoping they'd leave, until I couldn't take the noise anymore, and then I'd reluctantly wander out to the living room and remind her that I had to be up early for school. She'd sigh and tell her friends that they'd better go, and I'd feel terrible for breaking up her night, wishing that I was at Arden's, asleep on the top bunk, just an arm's length from my best friend. Eventually I just went home with Arden after school, and when dinnertime rolled around, I would take the extra place at the table that Mrs. Douglas had set out for me. She never asked if I wanted to join them or made me feel like I was a guest, and after dinner I'd clean up along with everyone else and hang out in Arden's room listening to music and doing my homework. On nights when I knew that my mother was around I'd sleep over so that I wouldn't get in her way, and if she was out I'd go home. I bought groceries with the money she left me, learned to make my own meals, and washed my own clothes. I did my homework when no one asked me to, put myself to bed, and set my alarm to make breakfast and get ready for class. It wasn't that my mother didn't care, I told myself; it was just that she didn't respond to structure.

I slumped against the counter and decided to call it a day. I had made little progress, and yet I was too exhausted to continue. Exhausted and angry that she'd left me all alone, full of unanswered questions. I left with my trophies for the day's work: two garbage bags to be dropped down the building's chute on my way out. I grabbed my parka and messenger bag and shut the apartment up for another day. I locked the door, stood in the hall, and took a deep breath. I heard Mrs. David's door unlock and started to walk away, dropping one of my garbage bags and thwarting my quick getaway.

"Need a hand?" She picked up the dropped bag and started walking past me.

"I'm all right, thanks." I reached for the bag, but Mrs. David kept going in the direction of the chute, forcing me to keep pace with her.

"This is garbage, right?"

"Yes."

She opened the garbage chute at the end of the hall, threw the bag down, then took the other one out of my hand and did the same with it.

"You look tired," she said, putting her hands into the pockets of her purple double-faced knit cardigan. "Then again, maybe this is just how you look. It's not as if I have a lot to compare it to. You weren't around that often."

The way she said it was more a statement than a judgment. She stood there staring at me, her blue eyes clear and sharp in her wrinkled, papery face.

"No. I suppose I wasn't."

"Can't say I blame you." She tilted her head to the side, reminding me of a parrot, with her shock of white hair and her sharp, pointed beak. She put her hand on my shoulder for a moment, and then turned and walked back toward her apartment. "Good night," she called without looking back, and disappeared into her home.

Can't say I blame you. Tell that to my dead mother.

I put on my parka and rode the elevator down nine floors to the lobby. Vincent had left his desk and was standing in the entranceway, staring out the glass doors.

"Looks like it's gonna be a bad one, Elsie."

"How can you tell?"

"Well, just look at how that snow's starting to circle up the driveway."

"I mean, how can you tell it's me? You never even looked." I knew that my reflection couldn't be detected in the glass all the way from the elevator.

"I can always tell." Vincent turned to face me, and for a second a smile crossed his face.

"Uh-huh."

I had known Vincent for over thirty years, or rather he had known me. There was very little that anyone actually knew about the man who had watched the desk of this old, elegant apartment building for nearly five decades. After I left home, I returned for a visit many times over the years but often failed to make it past his concierge desk. I was either too chicken or too angry to go upstairs and see my mother, so I just stayed in the lobby and talked to Vincent instead. His constant presence behind the desk in his uniform of gray wool trousers and navy blazer was comforting, making him seem as much a part of the furniture as the desk itself. I had often tried to imagine a life for him outside of the co-op and couldn't. He was always working, and it seemed impossible that there were enough hours in the day for him to take care of the needs of all the tenants and himself as well. He was the eyes and ears of Dalewood, and one could only imagine the things he'd seen and the stories he knew. I had asked him once, while avoiding a visit with my mother, what was the strangest thing he had ever witnessed, and he answered by asking me how much time I had. It was funny, but it wasn't true. Even if I'd had all day, Vincent wouldn't have revealed a thing. As far as he was concerned, it wasn't his place to say.

"You should get some rest. You look tired," he said.

"So everyone tells me. You don't look so great yourself." His hair was thinner than ever, and his brown skin looked slightly yellow. There was even a trace of gray stubble on his face, something I'd never seen before.

"I'm allowed, I'm old."

"Yeah, well my mother died, and someone ransacked her apartment."

"Still using that one?"

We laughed a little before stopping ourselves. There was nothing to laugh at, we both knew that, but we had always shared a morbid sense of humor, and I was more grateful for it than ever. It was always this way with us, an easy exchange between two people who may as well have been invisible to those around them.

"Don't forget this—it arrived for your mother, but she hadn't opened it yet." He walked over to his desk and came back with a large envelope of forwarded mail.

"Why she needed a P.O. box in addition to Dalewood is a mystery to me," I said. Vincent just shrugged as I took the envelope.

I leaned my head against the glass, closed my eyes, and sighed. I hadn't had any contact with my mother in years, and yet here I was, cleaning up her mess now that she was gone. I felt Vincent's hand on my shoulder and opened my eyes.

"Night, Elsie. Bundle up."

"Night, Vincent."

I pulled the synthetic fur-lined hood up over my head and snapped it tight under my chin. I reached into my pockets for my gloves and as usual found only one and put it on. I waved goodbye to Vincent as he held the door open for me, and ran clumsily against the snow that was whipping in the wind. I found my car and gently turned the key in the door. I had already snapped off one key inside the lock and didn't need to waste another call to roadside assistance. I jumped inside and started the engine, rubbing my bare hand against my jeans as I did so. It had been only fifteen or so steps and my hand was frozen. I blasted the heat on high but quickly turned it off when only cold air came out. I hated the cold, always had. A chance to escape the cold and soak up the California sunshine was a big reason why I had let Ted talk me into moving to Los Angeles with him.

I hated LA at first. It was the optimism. The relentless, baseless optimism that everything was going to be all right. No matter what that *everything* was, or what the odds of it working out were, everyone but me seemed to be convinced the universe was unfolding as it should. The universe. How could anyone know what the universe should or shouldn't be doing? It was too similar a philosophy to my mother's responsibility-shirking talk about karma, and it drove me nuts. That and all the driving. But even now, ten years later—five more than people had told me it would take for me to really fall in love with Los Angeles—I figured I liked it as much as I was ever going to. On a scale of one to ten, I'd give it a six-point-five. And yet when Ted and I divorced, three years ago, I was the one who stayed while he returned to Toronto. I liked to say I stayed for the sunshine, but it was also far away from Dalewood, and my mother. Living in another country allowed me to pretend that it was just physical distance that kept us apart.

The snow was really flying now, and I was thankful that I had only a short drive home. I carefully wound my way away from my mother's building, past the brick mansions set far back from the sidewalk and lit by old wrought iron lampposts. One of the oldest neighborhoods in Toronto, Rosedale was full of old money, and little about it had changed, with the exception of a few co-op buildings near its entrance. Unlike my mother, most of the tenants of her co-op building had at one time or another resided in the neighboring estates before passing their homes on to their children and opting for a smaller yet still prestigious address. It was the address, and the way people reacted to it when she said it, that attracted my mother. She could have lived in an apartment five times the size for the same money, but then no one would have treated her differently. No one would have assumed that she was one of them. Every day she'd leave the building dressed in her best overcoat, silk scarf and leather handbag slung across her body, her fashionable urban attire a far cry from the bohemian image she projected for her friends from her spiritual group. Like a chameleon, my mother would change her appearance to suit her surroundings, adapting and working her environment to her best advantage. She could play any part, for any audience. The only role she ever seemed incapable of performing was that of mother, to me.

With her salt-and-pepper hair teased and smoothed into a low knot at the nape of her neck, her piercing eyes framed in gray shadow, and lips stained with a glossy beige lipstick, she'd start out on her forty-minute walk to downtown. My mother didn't drive. After her car accident she refused to learn. She could fly or take subways and streetcars with no problem. But if she had to get in a car, you could see her anxiety rise and her breathing grow shallow. She'd stare straight ahead, gripping the handle of the door like she was ready to jump out at any moment. And when I'd suggested that maybe if she took lessons and got her license, it would help her get over her fear, she'd snapped that she would never get over a car crashing into her and taking the life of Leo and two other people. She told me that she had felt helpless as a passenger, but she could only imagine what the other driver must have felt, veering into oncoming traffic and knowing that he was moments away from killing everyone.

Keeping a brisk pace in her Italian leather walking shoes, she would walk through the winding streets nodding and smiling, as women decades younger settled their already-soft bodies into their luxury cars. She loved the fact that she was fitter than women twenty years her junior. She had worshipped her body, and as a result others had done the same, making pilgrimages and bringing gifts along the way.

"My body is my temple," she would say.

Yeah, yours and everyone else's, I'd think bitterly to myself when the boys I brought home in the hopes of noticing me would notice her instead.

I crossed onto the bridge and made my way slowly along it. Mine was one of the only cars on the road tonight, proving that everyone but me had taken the storm warning seriously. The windshield wipers were working overtime, and yet I could barely see more than a few inches in front of my car. I just had to make it across the bridge and then I could take side streets. My little Honda was being pushed around by the wind, and I stupidly slammed on the brakes, sending the car spinning. I had forgotten how to drive in these conditions. In Los Angeles, people didn't even like to go out if it rained; nobody knew how to drive in anything but traffic, and it seemed I was no different. My car swerved as it hit a patch of ice, and I gripped my hands tightly on the wheel and prayed to anyone who was listening not to let me die yet. After all, my mother had just gone and it hardly seemed fair that I should have but a week without her. Someone somewhere obviously agreed, and twenty minutes later I made it back safely.

The front path was dark, and I tried to remember whether or not I had left the light on. I probably hadn't—I wasn't used to it getting dark so early. But then again if I had, it could mean that someone had turned it off and was waiting inside for me. I was being ridiculous—why would anyone be waiting for me? Unless whoever it was that was looking for my mother had come looking for me. My heart started to pound loudly in my chest and I held my breath, trying to walk as quietly as I could. Thankfully the salt that I'd sprinkled on the ground in the morning had long since melted, so there was no crunching beneath my boots. I held my one gloved hand out for balance, willing myself against the wind, determined not to fall, and crept up the front steps. I made it to the door, quietly let myself in, and felt along the wall for the light switch where I knew it to be without even looking. It had once been my house, after all. I snapped the light on and let out a warning yell as I quickly looked around and found nothing. I was alone. I took off my boots, hung my coat in the house's shared entranceway, and headed upstairs.

Ted and I had bought the house right after we married. We had spent a long and unemployed winter turning the left side of the duplex into two apartments that we could

rent out while we lived in the other half. We rented the
first and second floors to a couple of musicians who toured
a lot, and the third floor was sort of a guest room/office
that we left for ourselves and friends visiting from out of
town. When we split up, Ted found directing work back
in Toronto and returned to our house. Knowing that I had
earned almost no money after we moved to LA, he had
offered to buy me out and I had gratefully accepted. My
part-time bookkeeping job would never have been enough
to live on, but with the sale of my share of the house I
was able to stay in our small rent-controlled apartment by
the beach, and I had been carefully living off my savings
ever since. When my mother died, Ted offered me the attic
apartment to stay in while I took care of her affairs. He'd
recently bought a house in the suburbs, using the apartment mostly as an office now and as stomping grounds for
our cat, who did not get along with Ted's live-in girlfriend.
It was a good deal: I had free lodging for as long as I needed
it and in exchange, I'd look after Shadow. He would have
offered it no matter what, but I liked to think that I was
helping Ted out for a change.

The attic apartment was the warmest place in the whole
house. It was the only place I'd ever stayed in Canada where
I wasn't freezing in the winter. The heat rose to the top and
got trapped under the A-frame wood-beamed ceiling. The
hardwood floors were only slightly worn, and the light-yel-
low walls that we had painted to look like sunlight had
held up well. It had a bathroom with a big soaker tub and

a kitchen that opened up onto the rest of the apartment and boasted top-of-the-line appliances from ten years ago. There was even a tiny balcony off the top, large enough for a chair and a plant, with a ledge just the width of a coffee cup. It was the nicest apartment in the house, and it was definitely an apartment for one.

"Hello, Shadow." I scooped the cat up and cradled her in my arms like a baby, her head in the crook of my neck. I buried my face in her fur and closed my eyes, listening to her purr. She was the closest to a child we had ever come, and I'd let Ted have custody. I turned on the stove, heated up some soup for me, some milk for Shadow, and pulled out the two wooden stools at the counter for each of us. Shadow hopped up, cleaned her paws and waited. I grabbed the large manila envelope Vincent had handed me and turned it over. It was packed to capacity, and I ripped off the clear masking tape that held it together. I cleared some space on the counter and emptied out the letters, ar-ranging them into two categories, business and personal.

The milk was starting to bubble, so I transferred it to the small ceramic bowl that she liked to drink out of and put it in front of her. I opened a bottle of week-old red wine and gave it a whiff. It wasn't vinegar yet, so I filled a glass, fixed myself a bowl of split pea soup, and sat down next to Shadow. It was nice not to eat alone.

"Why do I have to open all the mail?" Shadow just ignored me and kept licking her bowl.

There were a lot of handwritten letters, although as I looked at them closely I realized that not all of these were meant for my mother. Only some of them were addressed

to Mrs. Robins. But there were also letters addressed to a
Mrs. Robi and a Ms. Rabino. Obviously someone at the
mailbox store had made a mistake and thrown in the wrong
mail. Great. I'd have to trudge out in the snow tomorrow
to return someone else's mail. The very thought of it made
me want to collapse. I decided I'd done enough for one day
and shoved the letters back into my bag. That's when I saw
it. The letter addressed to Devedra. I stared at the envelope,
my hand tightening into a fist and my jaw locking.

Devedra was my mother's initiation name, given to her
when she joined her secret new-agey group the Seekers.
She had always been ahead of trends. She was a vegetarian
when everybody else was a carnivore, a follower of homeopathic and natural remedies long before it was popular, and
a devotee of yoga when it was still considered the pastime
of old Indian men and Sikhs. She had always been drawn
to whatever was just beyond the grasp of ordinary people,
delighted when she defied conventions and entered worlds
where others weren't brave enough to go. When she became
a member of the Seekers, she'd been singled out by the
group's leader and given a new name, Devedra. I remember the first time I heard it. I was fourteen and unpacking
groceries that I'd once again paid for with my babysitting
money. My mother had a habit of spending her money on
everything but the necessities. She had been feeling ill and
was lying in her bed giving me orders for where to put
things when the phone rang.

    "Hello?" I answered.

"Yes, may I speak with Devedra please?" The voice was soft and mellow, a slight French accent barely detectable.

"I'm sorry, I think you have the wrong number," I said as my mother sniffled and blew her nose loudly.

"Is this not 416-555-4843?"

"Yes, but there is no Devedra here, only Rachel, sorry." I went to hang up the phone but my mother stopped me.

"Elspeth! Give it to me." She bounded out of bed, grabbed the phone, and went back into her room and closed the door.

From the other side of the door I could hear her clear her throat and apologize.

"I'm so sorry Philippe, the girl didn't know."

The girl. Not my daughter, not Elspeth, but the girl. Just some hired help like she had years ago in Africa.

I felt Shadow's paw on my arm and turned to her and smiled. I was sure that cat could read my mind.

"I'm okay." I put my hand to my cheek and felt my face flush at the memory. I didn't know what shocked me more, that my mother had a whole other identity and friends I never knew existed, or that my own existence was a secret to them. I remembered how I had unpacked the rest of the groceries, lingering in the kitchen longer than necessary so that I could listen to the sounds of her muffled laughter on the phone. That night, like so many others, I had waited in my room for her to apologize or explain. But she never did.

Devedra. Just seeing the name in print made my chest tighten a little. Like a secret handshake or a nickname among sorority sisters, it was meant to convey one thing only—that she was special and I was not. The writing on the front of the envelope was small and precise, as if it had been written by an architect or draftsman, all capitals at exactly the same height. I turned the letter over and ran my fingernail under the piece of tape that held the envelope closed. I pulled the pale-blue paper out, half expecting it to be one of those donation forms for which you tick off the amount you want to give. My mother had always insisted her group wasn't a religion, it didn't have tithing, but over the years they had passed a plate that never seemed to fill, no matter how much she gave.

Our beloved soul sister, the thoughts and prayers of all of your soul family are with you as the strength of your spirit and devotion are tested.

I crumpled up the paper and threw it on the floor. Sister, family...didn't they know that I was her real family? Probably not. My mother had always had an easier time with strangers. I used to marvel at how easily she could talk to anyone and how people warmed to her. She could listen patiently for hours, genuinely fascinated with what was going on in their lives, offering advice and sharing her own made-up experiences in an effort to help them. *Call me if you ever need someone to talk to*, she'd say, writing her number down, and they would. But when it came to me, she acted more and more as if she belonged to some secret club that I was privileged to even know about. Whatever

I knew about her life was an honor she afforded me rather than a right. Never mind that she was my mother, and that to most that would mean she had a responsibility to me. It felt like she saw it the other way around, as if my being born had been a huge burden to her, and my life's mission was to somehow repay this debt.

I grabbed my glass of wine and drank half of it in one easy gulp. It burned going down, and the ache in my throat was comforting. I slumped over the counter, put my head on my arm, and nudged the rest of my pea soup toward Shadow. I was still hungry but I was too tired to eat, and I polished off the wine instead. Shadow stared at the soup, swishing me with her tail.

"Finish it, I'm done."

I dragged my body across the attic to my bed and flung myself down. I was so bone-tired that just inhaling seemed to hurt. I'd do the dishes in a few minutes; I just needed a nap first. It was only 7:30 p.m., but it felt like midnight, and outside the snow whipped against the dark sky and rattled the windows. Shadow finished my soup and sat in the old recliner opposite my bed. The heat coming off the radiator wafted over me, wrapping me in a blanket of warmth and pulling me deep into a fiery sleep.

CHAPTER THREE

The dreams always end in fire. Snapshots of memory mixed in with sleep, they lure me in like an old home movie, bringing me along on a ride that starts familiar and true and ends foreign. It had been decades since I'd had them. As a young girl after we moved to Canada, I would awaken from them in the middle of the night calling out for Lafina, my beloved nanny we left behind, her name caught in my throat between sobs. My mother said it was because I missed her.

She told me that the fire represented change, and that once I embraced my new surroundings, the dreams would stop. And when they didn't stop, she warned me that dwelling on bad things *made* them happen. That did it. From then on, I went to bed every night determined to dream of something else, and eventually I did. But ever since my mother's death, the dreams had returned, stronger and stranger than ever.

In the dreams I see myself as a small child, no more than five years old and sitting under a tree with Lafina. The tree is an enormous, leafy, green umbrella that stands tall, shading me from the sun and cradling me up onto its lap full of roots that break through the dry ground. The sun is bright, and the heat moves in waves across the earth. I am chatting away, scooping out bread from the center of the fresh loaf that Lafina has baked. I pass the loaf to Lafina and she does the same, all the while nodding, her face serious as she listens to me. Lafina was a tall, strong, wide woman to whom my complete care had been entrusted. Not yet in school, I spent my days alongside her, keeping her company as she did the washing and cleaning for my parents. When I got too tired to follow her, she'd hoist me into a sling on her back, and I would hang there with my head on her shoulder napping in the afternoon heat as she hung the washing on the clothesline. Sometimes, even though we weren't supposed to, we'd eat lunch out back by her living quarters with the gardener and the houseboy. They all came from the same township, and every week they'd go home and spend Sundays with their own families. But from Monday to Saturday, Lafina would insist that she and the rest of the help were each others' family, and then she'd squish my cheeks and say that meant me, too, and I would crawl up onto her to listen while they gossiped and swapped stories. And each afternoon before Howard returned home from work, before my dinner and my bath, Lafina and I would sit under a tree, eat our freshly baked loaf of bread, and talk. I don't remember what we talked about because I was so young, but I remember feeling safe and happy.

We are both staring straight ahead at my family's house

off in the distance, and then a car pulls into the driveway, the sky turns dark, and Howard and my mother get out of the car. I feel like something bad is going to happen, like I am waiting for it to happen, and there's nothing I can do.

Lafina runs her big hand over my curls and pats my back in a soothing circular motion. "Come on now, get your shoes."

I go to look for my shoes from behind the tree where I thought I left them, but they're not there. Lafina wipes my face with her skirt, arranges my wild hair into two little bunches on either side of my head, and smoothes down my dress. She leans down and kisses me on the forehead, and I reach for her, but she is gone, and then the sound of an explosion thunders out, sending me to the ground. Lafina runs out of the house covered in flames, screaming my name. I try to move, but I can't.

Once again, I was awakened by the sound of a scream caught in my throat. Soaking wet, with rivers of sweat running down my back and chest, my clothes stuck to my body, I covered my face with my hands and took deep, slow breaths. Shadow meowed and hissed at the window next to my bed.

"It's okay, Shadow, she's gone now, she's gone." I peeled off my shirt and tried to mop myself dry. My skin felt hot to the touch, and I was surprised to find it wasn't actually burnt. I couldn't stop sweating and decided to take a cool shower as Shadow stood guard by the door. I had heard cats were once considered protectors and used to guard the tombs of pharaohs. After what happened in my mother's apartment, I was grateful Shadow had taken up my far-less-glamorous cause. The water felt cool against my skin, and although it was just in my head, I washed my hair to rid it of the smell of smoke that was trapped inside my nostrils. I don't know how, but I knew that these dreams that end in fire are not just about my mother, but *because* of her.

It had been a long time since I thought about where I was born, and now every night I returned there in my dreams. All I had of my time in Africa were bits and pieces of stories that my mother had told me, none told as often or as clearly as the story of her gunpoint proposal. I had often wondered about our life before Canada. What happened to our family? According to my mother, she had no family. Her mother died in childbirth, and her father disappeared into his grief and passed away just before I was born. There were no aunts and uncles. No cousins for me to reach out to. And as for Howard, the answers about him always changed. For a long time, my mother told me that Howard didn't want us anymore and so we left. Another time she told me that she had wanted a fresh start and seeing as Howard wasn't my real father anyway, there was no point keeping in touch. But I didn't care if he was my real father or not. He was the only father I knew. And though I didn't remember much, I remembered that we'd once been a family: my nanny Lafina, who adored me, and Howard, who'd mess my curls and let me ride on his horse with him. It was more than we had in Canada, so I kept asking questions.

And finally one day when I was ten years old, my mother, tired of me asking if I could write to him, told me he'd died of a heart attack. I was devastated and sobbed that we had no family. She said family's what you make it, and I should be grateful for what I had. I wanted to be grateful, I did. But I longed for what I thought was a real mother, a real family, and a real home.

Even though I'd grown up in Canada and lived in America, somehow Africa was home to me. But how could I long for a place that I hardly remembered? I knew it was more than just because it was where I was born; I knew it was because it was the last place I could remember being mothered, by Lafina. *Those are your roots*, Lafina used to say, pointing at my feet as I curled my toes into the dirt in our backyard. My roots. Was home where your roots were planted? And if so, did part of me remain severed there, my growth stunted by my leaving all those years ago? I had been searching for home for years, desperately trying to find it in the company of others—as a child with my best friend Arden, and as a young woman with the dancers I'd toured and lived with. I thought I'd finally found home when I married Ted, but all that changed when we got divorced.

I was jolted from my thoughts by the sound of Shadow yowling. I turned off the water and pulled back the shower curtain to look for her, but she had left the bathroom. Her cries intensified and I quickly wrapped myself in a towel and went to find her. She was on the balcony hissing at something off in the darkness. I opened the door and pulled her inside, the air freezing against my skin and wet hair, and grabbed a blanket for the two of us.

"You crazy cat," I said, bundling us up. "What were you thinking?" Shadow was prone to getting into fights with other cats and the occasional raccoon that she was bold enough to taunt, but it was so cold, I was sure there were no other animals outside. She kept hissing loudly and I felt my whole body start to tremble as I realized that I had just pulled my balcony door open to get her. I was sure I'd locked that door. I always did. But if I had, how could she have gotten outside? I scanned the apartment, looking to see if I was alone. I checked under the bed and in the closet, and when I found nothing, ran downstairs to make sure the front door was locked. It was. My heart was pounding in my chest, and I saw that the porch light was out. I flicked the switch on and off from inside the house and it lit up again. *It was an old house with old wiring*, I told myself, but that did little to comfort me, and I ran back upstairs and locked my door. Shadow had stopped hissing, but she wouldn't come away from the door to the balcony. I crouched down to her level and tried to find what she was looking at, but whatever it was had gone. And I knew that tonight there would be no sleep for either of us.

CHAPTER FOUR

The next morning, I headed off to the mailbox store, downtown near one of my mother's favorite coffee shops. It was one of those chains that has tiny little brass boxes with numbers and keys, a couple of photocopiers, and bored staff slumped over their desks in their company-issued khakis and polo shirts. I shuffled up to the counter, hit the little service bell, and waited as puddles formed around my snow-covered boots. Slowly a young man got up from his computer station and came over.

"Can I help you?"

"I hope so. I got a package in the mail for a Mrs. Ray Robins, and there's mail in here that doesn't belong to her."

"Are you sure?"

"Yeah, I'm sure. Her name was Robins." I took off my glove, opened the package and handed him the incorrect mail. "Not Robi, not Rabino. Robins." I sounded it out slowly.

"I see. Let me check our log."

He took the envelope and looked at the post box number.

"Two two seven." He pulled out a black binder and opened it to number 227. "Yeah it's the right number."

"I'm sure it's the right number, but it's the wrong mail."

"No, it's not. These names are all registered to the P.O. box." He turned around the log to face me and there, next to Mrs. Ray Robins, were all the other names.

Of course they were. *Why stop at one name and one credit card*, I thought.

"Thanks." I took the mail and stuffed it back into the large envelope.

Great. More for me to open.

Outside, the cold air hit my wet skin and made me shiver. I got to my car just as a parking officer was leaving a ticket under the windshield wiper.

"Oh, come on, it's only been three extra minutes," I yelled, pointing to my watch.

"Sorry."

"Shit!" I watched as the officer crossed the street to ticket somebody's car that double-parked in front of a little vegan restaurant. That was why my mother had chosen this particular mailbox store; it was across the street from one of her favorite lunch spots. I felt my chest tighten at the sight of the hand-painted sign that read *The Willow*. My mother and I had eaten there once, but like most things that she enjoyed, I had tried not to. It was her restaurant with her people and her kind of food, and she'd made a point of showing off just how much of a regular she was and how many people she knew. I felt like a party crasher, sitting quietly as she addressed the staff by name and talked animatedly to the people at the table next to us. I wasn't her guest so much as her audience, a lesson that took me years to learn. Eventually, I excused myself and left, and she carried on as if I'd never been there.

That was years ago, and now there would be no more lunches with her, terrible or otherwise. I decided it was stupid to let a restaurant make me feel bad and crossed the street to go in for coffee.

"Sit anywhere you like," said the tall young man behind the counter.

"Thanks." I chose a spot on a bench by the window and took off my coat. The restaurant was pretty, with soft yellow tones and dark wood tables accented with beautiful linen pendant lights. It was an upscale vegan joint, frequented by the kind of health nuts who had life coaches and no trouble spending twenty dollars on a lunch of vegetables and wheatgrass shots. Los Angeles was full of places like this, and I did my best to avoid them. I could never understand why anyone would want to talk about what came out of their body while putting food in their mouth. Not to mention I couldn't afford to eat someplace where I'd leave the table hungry. And I was sure that the obligatory staff of young, good-looking professional backpackers wouldn't be able to afford to eat at these places either if they didn't work there.

"What can I get you?" the young man shouted over the music. It was one of those Putumayo mixed CDs, African or Brazilian, world music for people who liked the sounds of other countries but knew nothing of the artists. My mother had a collection of them.

"Coffee with milk, please."

"I've only got soy."

"Black, then."

I started sorting the letters that had been addressed to my mother's aliases. It was more than half her mail. I knew from experience that the thin white envelopes with the clear plastic windows and typed names and addresses were collection notices, utility bills, and magazine subscriptions. There was one from a local bookstore that had let her treat it like a lending library, taking books she had special-ordered and making small payments every few weeks. There was a yoga center for which, it turned out, she had never paid for classes, and dry cleaners, hair salons, and loans from people she had never paid back. Some of them wondered if she had returned from her trip abroad to Europe, Africa, South America. Others had recently discovered that she had passed away; those always started out with, *To whom it may concern, my sympathies for your loss. Please forgive my timing but I am afraid that I still haven't been repaid the loan for....* And then there were the overdue statements from credit card companies, second and third notices, addressed to Mrs. Robi and Mrs. Rabino.

It didn't surprise me that my mother wouldn't bother opening her mail. Opening mail was a boring chore, and boring chores were always left for someone else. What surprised me was that she had debts. I'd always thought of her as a woman of means. Although she often reminded me that her resources weren't unlimited, she had never worked a day in her life, and didn't have to, or so I assumed. I had no idea where her money had gone or how she'd been supporting herself all these years. She had closed out her bank accounts, leaving just her checking account, from which she paid her mortgage and maintenance fees. And judging by her records, she kept little more than that to live on. Now that I knew all those names, and therefore all those credit cards, belonged to her, I had a better idea how she was getting by.

"Here you go." The waiter placed the coffee down in front of me. He was tall, with long, wavy blond hair, his forearms tattooed with koi fish and lotus flowers. "We don't serve lunch for another hour, but we've got some baked goods."

"Do they taste like baked goods?"

"Not a fan of the vegan muffins?" He cracked a smile and tucked a loose strand of hair behind his ear.

"Not so much."

"Strange choice of restaurant then, wouldn't you say?"

"My mother used to come here, it was one of her favorites. I was just in the area."

He reached down and picked up a letter off the table and read aloud. "Robins? Ray Robins?"

"Yeah."

"Man. You said 'was.' Did she pass away?"

"A couple of weeks ago. You knew her?"

"Oh, yeah. Ray was a regular. But I hadn't seen her since I got back from India. She told me some great places to go. That's too bad. I'm so sorry."

"Thanks."

He nodded and walked away, shaking his head. I started to open a letter when he returned.

"Here. On the house." He set down a date square and another cup of coffee, and then plonked himself in the chair opposite me and extended his hand. "I'm Josh. Man, I can't believe I didn't get to say goodbye." He took a sip of the second cup of coffee and looked out the window.

"You're not alone." I tore off a piece of the date square and stuck it in my mouth. It was sweet and delicious. "That's not vegan."

"Don't tell." He smiled and helped himself to a bite. "Look, I don't know how to tell you this but...."

"My mother owed you money."

He looked surprised to hear me say it and answered. "Yeah. It's not much, but we kind of let her keep a tab. She hardly ever had to use it. Most of the time people paid for her, but you know, the few times that didn't work out, we'd float her." He smiled and gave a small chuckle.

"What do you mean people paid for her? Like a beggar?"

"Oh, God, no, no, nothing like that." He reached across the table and squeezed my hand. I kept my fingers still and wondered if it was rude not to squeeze back. I wasn't used to being touched; I'm not much of a hugger. "No, not like a beggar, like a celebrity. You know, always getting free stuff?"

"No, I don't know." I flattened my hand on the table and slid it out from underneath his.

"Your mom could talk to anybody, and she always had great stories. She used to come here alone and strike up conversations with people and before you knew it, she was eating lunch with them and telling them about her travels and they'd pick up the tab. Sometimes, she'd even add something to the bill and they wouldn't mind. A couple of the older suits would pay her tab whether they ate with her or not. You know, guys who wanted to be all spiritual and whatnot, but were still really just bankers who did yoga on the weekends. I think they liked that your mom could always give them advice and that she was the real deal."

I thought of that day we had come together and I had left, my mother charming the table next to us, talking about art and philosophy and debating with the two older gentlemen next to us. She'd been trying to find a way to pay for our lunch and I had no idea. My cheeks burned at the memory.

"Are you okay?"

"Yeah. I'm fine. How much did she owe you?" I snapped, busying myself with the letters on the table.

"Uh, I'll check." He went behind the counter and returned with a little notepad. "Two hundred and twenty dollars."

"Put it on my card. The date square too." I handed him my Visa and turned my attention back to the mail. I didn't find the idea of my mother conning customers for meals charming. And I didn't like that until recently I had no idea that she had to. I found a letter from a store not far from here and, after reading it, decided to go there. I finished my coffee, paid the bill, and left a twenty-percent tip, to make up for my mother.

❋

I checked the address on the envelope with the number on the door. It was the right place, but the sign read *By Appointment Only*. It was written in gold pen in cursive writing on a scalloped piece of paper and hung from a ribbon. The effect was vaguely Victorian, mirroring the dusty rose-colored furniture that lay behind the thick glass doors. Inside, the lights were on low, and I thought I could see someone leaning over the counter. I pressed my face to the glass, trying to get a better look, and rapped on the window, hoping to get their attention.

"We're closed," a woman's voice called out; she waved her hand, shooing me away.

I knocked again, and again.

"I said we're closed! You'll have to make an appointment."

"I don't want an appointment. I want to ask you about this letter you sent." I waved the gray envelope in my hand.

I had gotten her attention and watched as she grabbed glasses that hung from a chain around her neck and put them on. She snatched her keys off the counter and made her way toward the door. She must've been at least a full foot shorter than me, and tiny. An older woman, she was stooped at the shoulders, with her head hanging forward at her neck. She was wearing a Chanel sweater set and a pleated black wool skirt that stopped just past her knee. Everything about her clothes and her antique-pearl earrings and choker announced that she was someone who invested in her fashion wisely. Everything, that was, with the exception of the heavy black orthopedic shoes, which seemed to be the only thing keeping her weighted to the ground.

Snow was coming down heavily now, and I was sure by the way she arched her eyebrows and pursed her mouth as she gave me the once-over that I was not cutting an impressive figure.

"You sent this letter to my mother, a Mrs. Robins, uh, Robi?"

"And?"

"Could I please talk to you about it?"

"Have your mother call me."

"I can't...she's dead. Two weeks ago." I was getting good at just blurting this out. I might as well use it while I can; it would lose impact as time went on. She stopped and studied my face, as if to see if I was telling the truth.

"Please, it's freezing out here and I'm soaking wet."

Finally she lifted her huge ring of keys, undid the lock, and let me inside.

"Stand there on the rug, and take your shoes and coat off. You're dripping."

I did as she said and hung my coat on the door handle, where it could drip onto the doormat, and removed my boots.

"Wait." She walked over to one of the large clothing racks that filled her store and took a huge shawl off the hanger and handed it to me.

"Thank you." I wrapped the thick wool shawl tightly around my body and followed her directions to sit on the pink velvet chaise that she pointed to. "I'm Elspeth, Ms. Robi's daughter."

"Mildred. I'm very sorry about your mother. I didn't

know." She walked into a small back room, emerging moments later with two cups of tea.

"How did she die?" She handed me the tea and sat in the high-back armchair opposite me.

"Cancer."

"I see. What kind?"

"I don't know. She waited until it was too late and it was everywhere. So much for knowing my family medical history."

She sipped from her teacup and set it down on the ottoman between us.

It was a small store, packed with neat racks of expensive-looking clothes that had been arranged by designer. Calligraphied signs in little frames sat above the racks, proudly announcing Chanel, Oscar de la Renta, and Valentino, among others. I had passed by the shop times but had never thought to stop in, the prices being well beyond my reach. In truth, I'd never even had occasion to wear anything other than blue jeans and hand-knit sweaters.

"Your things are lovely. I can see why my mother liked your store."

"Well, she had acquired quite a collection, and it was in excellent condition. That's why she came here."

"I don't understand."

"We're consignment. Ladies sell their designer clothes here, and my clients purchase them at a generous discount. Of course, they have to be well taken care of, so no one will guess that they aren't brand new."

"You mean these are all secondhand?"

"Previously loved."

"I see." It was my turn to sip tea and avoid the awkward silence, and I took my time doing so.

"I take it you and your mother didn't share the same taste."

I could feel Mildred's eyes taking in my own previously loved clothing-swap sweater and jeans.

"I love secondhand clothes." To my surprise she smiled, and we both relaxed a little more into our chairs. "According to your letter, I understand that my mother had an outstanding account?"

"Yes, let's see." She stood up and returned with a leather journal. "Well, I owed her four hundred dollars for a Chanel sweater set and scarf, and she owed me six hundred for a Yves Saint Laurent winter coat, so her balance was two hundred dollars. I think everything else was settled up. Now, I can take a check, or if you like, in light of the circumstances, I could just wait until the rest of the jewelry is sold."

"The what?"

"The jewelry. Your mother told me that she no longer had any use for it and that there was no one to leave it to."

"I never wear jewelry." It just came out. It was partially true. I never wore it, because I never had any, and I never knew my mother did either.

"Oh, well that explains it."

"But still, if you don't mind, I should take another look. Maybe my, uh, sister...would like it."

"Of course. I never knew that your mother had two daughters."

Neither did I. But admitting that my mother didn't

even think to leave me her jewelry was an embarrassment too large to take on my own, so I invented one.

"She was very private." I smiled and smoothed my frizzy hair behind my ears.

"Yes, the British usually are."

I coughed and sent tea spluttering down my chin. "Excuse me." I wiped my face with the back of my hand and returned the teacup to the tray on the ottoman.

My mother may have taken elocution lessons as a young woman to soften her South African accent, but she was hardly British. She had always disliked the hard, guttural sounds associated with the Dutch Afrikaners and had taken great pains to not be confused with them. Hers was a lovely low voice with a slightly more exotic than usual accent, her South African heritage only revealed in her use of expressions like *shame*, meaning poor thing, and the occasional *ya* instead of yes.

I leaned over the jewelry counter as Mildred turned on the little interior light. It was packed with heirloom pieces, mostly gold with brightly colored stones. The kind of jewelry that older wealthy women wore to advertise how well their husbands were doing. A few pieces were understated and elegant—still expensive-looking, but in a much more subtle way. I was particularly struck by a gold bangle and a small white gold brooch with a cluster of tiny little rubies that looked like flowers. I was shocked to learn these pieces belonged to my mother.

"Could I please see them up close?" I asked. Mildred removed both the items from the jewelry counter and placed them on a little black-velvet pad.

The only jewelry I'd ever worn were things that people had given to me. Silver earrings and the occasional beaded necklace made up the entirety of my collection. With the exception of my wedding ring, a beautiful round sapphire-and-diamond setting that once belonged to Ted's grandmother, I'd never owned anything of much value. I'd loved my wedding ring but chose to return it to Ted during our divorce, so that maybe one day he could give it to another, hopefully more permanent, wife.

"These are really beautiful. I don't think I've ever actually seen them before. At least I can't remember if I did."

"I see. Well, the diamond pin is a vintage piece from Van Cleef and Arpels. She said she got it in Paris. And the gold bangle is the last one from a stack that she had brought in. I believe it's stamped," said Mildred, turning it over and checking the inside. "Yes, eighteen carat. 1950."

"I don't suppose you could check your book and tell me how many pieces she had sold?" I never knew my mother had so much jewelry.

"I won't be able to track them down for you, if that is what you're thinking," she said firmly.

"I'm not. I just...." I felt Mildred's eyes burrowing into me and decided to just be honest. "I don't have a sister. I had no idea that my mother had any of this jewelry, and I certainly didn't know that she was selling it. I just wish I could ask her why. But I can't."

Mildred's face softened and she sighed. "I don't usually disclose personal details about my clients, but seeing she's...." She stopped for a moment and then opened her notebook and turned it to me. There, across two pages, was a list of all the pieces my mother had sold over the years, the date and price written neatly in red beside each one. I ran my finger down the list, quickly adding up the numbers for each year. I suddenly had a much better idea of how she had been supporting herself.

"She used to call it her severance package. I didn't push. I just assumed there'd been a nasty divorce."

I closed the book and shook my head no.

"I see. Well, there was one more thing. She brought it in separately, about a month ago."

She reached into a drawer underneath the jewelry case and removed a small felt bag. She untied its drawstring and took out a large ivory and diamond ring.

I placed it on my ring finger, and in spite of my small hands, it fit.

"It's a very unusual piece," said Mildred, "not the kind of thing that I would normally sell here, so I suggested we get it appraised before I put it in the showcase."

"And did you?"

"Yes." She paused. "I had someone take a look at it, and he wrote up an appraisal for her. She was supposed to come and get it, and let me know, but she never did. And now I realize why."

I closed my fingers tightly around the ring and brought it up to my face for closer inspection. The ivory was cool and smooth, and the gold thread that wound through the ring shone as it caught the light. The center of the ring was carved with some sort of insignia, and a large diamond rested in the middle of it. I wasn't an expert, but I'd seen enough sparklers on the hands of wealthy Angelenos to know a good one, and this one was amazing.

Mildred slid the sealed appraisal along the counter toward me, and I tucked it into my pocket. "It looks good on you. If it really is a family heirloom, you may just want to keep it."

CHAPTER FIVE

I left Mildred's with my head full of questions. She had called the ivory and diamond ring a family heirloom, but my mother didn't have any family, except me. *And the Seekers.* I felt a chill run down my spine as I thought of the letter they'd sent, *Our beloved soul sister, the thoughts and prayers of all of your soul family are with you as the strength of your spirit and devotion are tested.*

Could this ring really be so valuable that the Seekers would risk breaking into her apartment to get it? I reached into my pocket for the appraisal and tore the envelope open. *$150,000. Flawless, 3.5 carat diamond ring. Hand-carved antique ivory.*

My mouth fell open. What on earth was my mother doing with a ring like this?

I stuffed my hand and the ring deeper into my pocket and tried to clear my head, letting the cold air freeze my face and thoughts. The sidewalks were icy and covered in salt, leaving little white rings around my boots and soaking the hems of my pants. It had been a long time since

I'd had to deal with winter, and as much as I loathed the never-ending cold in my bones, I welcomed the opportunity the gray skies and slushy streets gave me to scowl at the world. In Los Angeles, where the sun never stopped shining and everyone answered "the weather" when asked why they lived there, it was a lot harder to justify my misanthropic attitude. It was as if somehow the fact that it was sunny all the time could make up for the rest of life's disappointments.

"I hate this fucking weather," said a young woman trying to navigate the small lake that had formed at the edge of the sidewalk.

It was the kind of thing that Torontonians said from November until April, and it always made me smile. I'd missed Toronto, but didn't realize how much until I was actually back. It wasn't like New York, which you raved about no matter where you lived. It was more like the underappreciated, always-striving-to-do-the-right-thing older sister of the popular and pretty girl, the one who is overlooked in movies by the leading man for her lack of exterior beauty. But in the end, after the popular girl breaks his heart, or the flashier city breaks his spirit and bank account, he returns to the plainer sister and sees her understated elegance and integrity, and finally values what he has taken for granted all along.

Still, the weather stinks.

By the time I arrived at my car, my pants were soaked from the knees down, and I was freezing. My head was spinning, and with the exception of a mouthful of a date square, I hadn't eaten anything since the night before. I was all out of groceries, but the thought of going into a store and being surrounded by regular people going about their daily lives made me want to scream. I decided to ignore my empty stomach and grab a coffee from the coffee shop on the corner instead. It was an old bad habit, not eating, but a familiar one, and with no one around to keep me in check, I found myself returning to it when things got out of control. Nothing made sense right now, and somehow the gnawing in my stomach was strangely comforting. I headed back to Dalewood and spent the rest of the afternoon packing my mother's apartment in a kind of fog. I went through the motions of sorting her things into piles, packing and labeling boxes for the different charitable organizations I'd arranged pickups with, my mind questioning each item's possible appeal to someone else. Until learning of the jewelry, I didn't think my mother had anything of value to steal. Now I wondered what else she had hidden from me.

"Hello in there," said Mrs. David as she rapped loudly on the door, making me shriek.

"Just a minute," I said, undoing the chain on the door.

"Sorry to startle you."

"No, that's all right. I'm just a little jumpy, that's all," I said, my heart racing.

"Why don't you join me for dinner?" She turned and left without waiting for me to reply and walked back into her apartment, leaving the door open.

My stomach felt like it had started to eat itself, and I knew that nothing but cat food waited for me back at my place. I stuffed the appraisal deep into my purse, removed the ring from my hand, and tucked it into the front pocket of my jeans. Wearing it would hardly go unnoticed, and I didn't want it to raise any questions. Questions that I couldn't answer. I hit the lights and made sure I locked the door, double-checking it before walking away.

"Help yourself. I won't be long." Mrs. David gestured to the open bottle of red wine on the dining room table and went into the kitchen.

"Thanks." I poured myself a big glass and took a large sip. The wine warmed my cheeks, and I felt my shoulders relax a little with the next sip. Mrs. David had her back to me while she tossed a salad, and I took the opportunity to take in my surroundings.

It was a beautiful apartment. Floral fabric couches with matching wingback chairs made up the living room, and the dusty pink wall-to-wall carpet matched the heavy, tasseled silk drapes that framed the windows. Everything, from the china cabinet to the ornately carved side tables, was polished to a high sheen. It was definitely the interior of a once much larger Rosedale mansion, and its current incarnation as a two-bedroom apartment gave off a feeling of elegance and refinement.

"Your place is beautiful."

"It's colorful, that's for sure. But spending most of my life working in black and white, I guess I needed a change."

"These are yours?" I moved closer to the framed black-and-white photographs that filled the walls.

"Some of them; there are hundreds more. But I ran out of room."

The pictures were exquisite. I didn't know much about

photography except to know what I liked, and I loved these. There were photos of what I guessed were family, portraits done in living rooms: parents, children, and the pet. The settings were grand, with everything in its place and staged just so. They were the kind of photos people attached to cards and sent out at Christmas announcing how well everyone was doing. The kind of cards I would have loved to have sent out if I'd had a family. Then there were pictures one might see in a coffee-table book about European vacations: Greek Islands, Venice canals, the Spanish Steps in Rome, places I had only heard about or seen in photographs like these. But there were also candid shots of strangers: an old man feeding pigeons on a park bench, a young girl looking at her reflection in a puddle, people caught in a private moment, unaware of a photographer's lens. These were my favorites.

"Those are my favorites too," said Mrs. David, as if reading my thoughts.

"They're wonderful."

"Yes. The others were about work, and these were just for me."

"I didn't know you were a professional photographer."

"Why would you?"

"True."

"Come, sit down." She led us back to the dining room table, which was set for two. "It's nothing fancy. Just quiche and salad."

"It's more than I would have made."

"I figured." She gave me the once-over in that way that only women do, unabashed about commenting on the weight of someone they hardly know.

I took my seat next to the head of the table where she sat and let her dish up for me.

"It's mushroom. I didn't know if you were a vegetarian like your mother."

"Thanks."

I waited until she sat before stuffing an enormous portion in my mouth. It was delicious, and I ate half my plate before complimenting her on her cooking.

"Thank the Everyday Gourmet. It has been a long time since I actually cooked anything. Not much point when you're just cooking for one."

I knew what she meant. "My mother used to love that place."

"I know. I'd see her there sometimes." Mrs. David smiled and went back to eating.

"How well did you know my mother?" I pushed my plate a little farther away, for fear of inhaling the whole thing.

"Not well. But one lives next to somebody for years and, well, you get to know them a little."

"So you never became friends."

"Your mother was there for me when my husband was ill. It was a long and horrible death, and she would sit with him so I could shower or go to the store. I had nurses, but she would read to him, and he loved the sound of her voice. And when he died, she sat shiva with our family."

"Shiva? My mother? That doesn't sound like her. She disdained organized religion. She insisted that group of hers was a philosophy, not a religion." Although I didn't know of any other philosophy that asked for donations.

"She said as much. And yet she told me that she found the whole ritual strangely comforting, and that I was very lucky to not have to hide what I believed."

"Oh please, she chose to hide her beliefs. She was always very secretive about her group. She kept them hidden from me until I was fourteen."

Mrs. David paused for a moment and then smiled knowingly. "Well, she was definitely an interesting woman."

"That she was." I took a big sip of my wine and let her top off my glass. The idea of my mother being so kind to a stranger stung, although it shouldn't. She did best with strangers.

"I'm sorry about your husband."

"Thank you. I was happy to return the favor when she was ill."

I looked at Mrs. David and felt my jaw tighten. "I didn't know she was sick. We weren't exactly on good terms. By the time I found out, she was already in the hospital. It was too late. She should've gone in earlier." I wished she'd gone in earlier. It might have given us more time. I might have been able to say goodbye.

"She didn't want to die in the hospital; she said she wanted to go back home."

"Here?"

"Africa."

Africa. The word hit me. My mother had never called Africa home. Why now? Why would she want to die there?

"Why are you telling me this?" Josh at the vegan restaurant, Mildred, and now Mrs. David. Everyone knew my mother better than me. I stood up from the table and gripped my wine glass tightly. I was afraid I might crush it or scream or both.

"Because you weren't there. I am not blaming you. I can't imagine a woman like that would be easy to have as a mother."

I waited to see if she would elaborate, but she didn't. She didn't need to. Judging by her photographs it was clear that Mrs. David knew what a family looked like, and in ours, I wasn't in the picture.

"You have no idea."

"I think you should know what happened. I've thought about whether or not to tell you since you came back. But I think she'd want you to know. Please sit down."

I loosened my grip on the glass and sat back down in my chair. I wasn't hungry anymore, just exhausted and raw.

"Know what?"

"That she was sorry."

"For?"

"I don't know. She just kept saying that she was sorry and that she needed to make things right. That she wanted another chance. She called someone, and I heard her say, 'we're coming back,' and then she collapsed."

"What do you mean *we?* Who did she call?" My heart was racing. Was it someone from the Seekers? Or someone back in Africa? And why didn't she call me? I was always the last person on her list. I leaned back in my chair and tried to calm my breathing.

"She was in a lot of pain at the end, and she wouldn't take any medication for it. She was suffering on purpose.

She said she deserved it. She said it was her karma. Do you
know what she meant?"

"That sounds like the kind of crap that she'd say after a
meeting with her cult."

Mrs. David sat back in her chair and looked at me.
"And I thought I was angry when my husband died."

"Except you weren't angry at your husband." I took a
breath and continued, "I'm sorry. It's just that my mother
didn't share her life with me, okay? And I am trying to
move on, I really am. But she sure isn't making it easy for
me."

"No, she isn't."

"She had plenty of time to apologize while she was
alive." I wondered if my mother had lain in her hospital
bed full of remorse, her hand outstretched in apology. I
would have taken it and held it tight. I would have listened
to her stories like I did when I was a little girl, long before
she stopped telling them to me. Long before she gave up
being my parent.

My skin was flushed and my cheeks were starting to
burn. I needed to get outside as quickly as possible or I
might scream. "Thanks for the dinner and sorry about
yesterday." I grabbed my coat and headed for the door. "I
think I know what they were looking for, but they didn't
get it."

"No they didn't."

I stopped walking and turned to face her. "Excuse me?"

"Please. Wait here."

My body went rigid and my feet felt glued to the floor.
I watched as Mrs. David went down the hall and returned

with a wooden box.

"She asked me to keep this safe for her."

"Why didn't you tell me?"

"I didn't know what I was keeping it safe from, until yesterday. I needed to be sure."

I took the box and held it in my hands. The size of a shoebox, wooden and carved with little jewel-like pieces of colored glass inlaid into a flower design, it was heavier than it looked. There was a big brass latch on the outside, but no key.

"I don't know what's in there. I think that's for you to find out."

I nodded and my eyes filled with tears. "Thank you."

"And this is also for you. I took it of your mother during her last days, before the pain. She was really beautiful. This might help you to remember that." She placed a brown envelope in my hand. My mouth opened, but nothing came out. It was too much, and with tears streaming down my face, I turned and left.

CHAPTER SIX

I needed to see Ted. It was late, but I knew where I could find him. He was on night shoots at a studio by the lakeshore all week. He had left behind a note with his production schedule for me at the apartment. It was his way of letting me know where he was if I needed him. Nothing pushy, no invitation to get together—he'd let me decide when I was ready. The same way he let me decide when our marriage was over, even though he hadn't wanted the divorce. I drove past the empty security booth, parked on the lot, and ran toward the buildings ahead. I suddenly felt foolish. Where was I running to? There were so many soundstages, and I didn't know which one he was on. I looked around for his car and then realized that I had no idea what he drove anymore. Maybe if I looked inside the cars, I'd recognize something of his, but it was dark in the lot and freezing, and I couldn't just go around peering into every car. I started to cry. I didn't know what to do, I just knew that I needed to talk to him. I needed somebody who had known us both to tell me I wasn't crazy, that the woman I had been hearing about all day wasn't the same woman he had met.

"Excuse me ma'am, can I help you?" A young man in a security uniform walked toward me.

"I'm looking for Ted Brennan," I said, wiping the tears from my face.

"Is he expecting you?"

"No, but I have to see him."

"This is private property, you can't just wander around."

"I'm his wife. Ex-wife."

He looked me over, taking in my tear-stained face and disheveled hair. "I'm afraid you'll have to leave."

"No, I need to talk to him."

"Ma'am, you have to leave now," he said, reaching for my arm. I moved out of his way and started to walk back to my car when I heard another voice through his walkie-talkie.

"Everything okay out there?"

"Someone here looking for Ted."

I looked back at the security guard, and pleaded. "Please, can you just tell him that Elsie is here. Please. It's urgent."

He took a deep breath and sighed. "Somebody find Ted. I need to ask him something."

I waited on a small leather couch in Ted's office. A piece of paper with his name and the title *Director* was taped to the door. The office itself was nothing more than some plain drywall and a concrete floor, a place where a film could set

up shop for a few months and then move out for the next
production, but still, it felt like Ted.

I recognized the vintage steel tanker desk that we had
bought together in LA to celebrate his very first directing
job, an indie film that paid him little more than the cost
of the desk, and the basketball hoop that he always hung
on the back of a door. Stacks of entertainment and polit-
ical magazines sat next to a tower of moleskin notebooks,
an old steel lamp, and his favorite mug that read *Yes! But
first coffee.* Even the beat-up couch with its old Hudson
Bay blanket felt like him, and I thought of all the times
I'd curled up under it while I helped him work on a script.

"Elsie, are you all right?" asked Ted, rushing into the
room.

"Sorry to bother you, I just...." I looked at the security guard who'd been watching over me, like I was some
criminal.

"It's okay Bill, I got it, thanks," he said, walking him
out and closing the door.

It had been three years since we broke up, and two
since I'd last seen him.

"I'm sorry," I repeated.

"Don't apologize. Else, what is it? What's wrong?"

I took him in. His shoulders were a little rounder now,
but he still looked like the kind of guy who climbed mountains and sailed boats and wore Irish cable-knit sweaters.
He was a city boy who looked and moved like a country
boy—calm, measured, confident. And even though he was
one of the hardest-working people I had ever met, he gave
off the appearance of the regular, easygoing guy next door.

It was why they'd loved him in Los Angeles as an actor. He never seemed like he cared what anyone thought of him, and in many ways he didn't. "Not everyone has to like me," he'd say, and so naturally they did.

"Me. I was wrong. I never knew her. I had no fucking idea." I was crying again and having trouble catching my breath.

"I know. I know." He sat next to me, close enough that I could touch him, but far enough away that I didn't have to.

"No, I don't just mean we weren't close. I mean she had a whole other secret life...."

"She always did, Elsie."

"Not just the Seekers, Ted. Aliases. Credit cards in fake names that she racked up, and jewelry that she was selling off in order to get by. And she has this ivory and diamond ring that I think the Seekers are looking for. She was broke and owed money, and I never knew. I always thought she was fine. I thought that she just didn't want to share her life with me, but I think she was hiding something."

"Slow down. What do you mean?"

"She had a box, a secret box. And I don't know if I can do this. I don't know if I can open it."

"It's okay, Else, it's okay," he said, turning to look at me. He ran his hand through his hair and exhaled deeply. "I am right here." He opened his hand toward me, like he had so many times. And that did it, the floodgates opened.

I met Ted at a fundraiser for my dance company. It had been a variety night and Ted was a last-minute fill-in for a missing actor in his friend's sketch-comedy troupe. He didn't know the lines and was terrible, but the audience liked him anyway. He was great looking, extremely charismatic, and a good sport about being the butt of the other performers' jokes. At the open bar afterward, he introduced himself and assured me he wasn't nearly as bad an actor as I had just witnessed, and if I agreed to go for a drink with him, he promised to never perform at a fundraiser of mine again. He was handsome and confident, worked steadily in film and television, and certainly didn't lack for admirers, judging by the women who had gathered around him after his performance. I, on the other hand, was really only comfortable around other dancers, people with whom I had a common wordless vocabulary. But when I tried to decline, he smiled and said, "It's only drinks, Elsie. I know better than to ask a dancer out to eat." I was shocked and, after laughing, agreed.

He was so sure, so steady, and I loved spending time with him. He made me feel secure and smart and interesting. He made me feel beautiful. Not plain in comparison to my mother, or beautiful in my own way, which I had gradually allowed myself to believe I was, but really beautiful. And when he said that he'd rather spend time with me than anyone else, I believed him. I had never been anyone's first choice before, and when he asked me to move in with him after only a few months of dating, I said yes. For the first time I felt what it was like to share my life with someone. After a long day of rehearsals, Ted would pour me a glass of wine, run me a bath, and sit on the tile floor next to the tub while I recounted stories about my day. When

I was sick, he'd make me soup and bundle me in bed, and together we'd watch movies until I fell asleep. I read scripts with him, helped him memorize lines for auditions, and programmed the timer on the coffeemaker so he always had coffee when he got up, even if I was still in bed. I finally knew what it was like to love fully and be loved back. I didn't have to wonder or ask, I didn't have to find ways to earn his love; it was simply there, day in and day out, as steady as the sunrise, and for a long time he filled all the unfinished spaces that had been left in me. When I was forced to stop dancing, when I was unable to find work as a choreographer, when I fell into a depression so deep I couldn't get out of bed for months, he had been there.

My depression had crept up on me in the eighteen months that my career as a professional dancer was quietly ending. Or maybe I had just ignored the signs until it was too late. My mother used to refer to it as one of my "moods," a pervasive funk that would seep into my flesh and greet me upon waking. I'd lie in bed and open my eyes, and the very act of being awake would tire me out so much that I'd want to roll over and fall back asleep. When I was younger, I'd tell myself that I was just worn out from dance rehearsal, and schoolwork, and from living with a mother who was exhausting to be around, even on a good day. I'd drink more coffee, dance harder, and keep my body so busy that my brain didn't have time to think about the dark shadows that were creeping around its edges. For a long time after I moved in with Ted, the sadness stopped, and I allowed myself to believe that our love for each other had cured it. But eventually the sadness returned, quietly at first and then louder and louder. It got worse when age and injuries stopped me from dancing. Without being in constant motion, my mind demanded I take notice of it, holding me hostage in my stillness.

Ted was the one who told me that I needed to pay attention to it, needed to deal with it, and after pleading with me to try to fix it, I agreed to see a therapist. For a long time, getting to the root of the problem only made me feel worse. I had too many loose threads, and it was dangerous to pull at them. But Ted was patient; he insisted that we could fix me, and I wanted him to be right. I wanted the happiness that we'd had when we first moved in together to return, so when he suggested that maybe a child of my own to love would make me feel complete, I agreed.

I loved the idea that I could rewrite my history with my mother by having a child of my own. Because I had no role model for what actually makes a good parent, I worried about whether I'd be qualified. Ted would say that I'd already proved I could be a great mother—I had raised myself. I began to let myself daydream about what our child might look like and all the things we would do together as a family. I'd notice pregnant women on the street and look at them longingly, eager for the day when I'd be one of them. Getting pregnant became our purpose. It was my entire focus for years, and when it turned out I'd never be able to give Ted the children he'd always wanted, he still stayed. He told me he would always love me, no matter what happened. But it was clear that what he hoped would happen was a baby. That we would find a way, that one day we would be parents. I tried not to blame him for wanting more for us—I saw how much it would hurt him to give up that hope. Instead, I felt guilty, told myself that I didn't deserve his love, that I was too much work and too great a disappointment.

So I ended it. Unable to watch Ted struggle through a life that my depression and barren womb had made miserable for both of us, I demanded a divorce, and always one to give me what I wanted, he agreed. I wasn't being a martyr, I was being selfish. Seeing my failures reflected back at me in his eyes was too much. He always tried to be positive and reassure me that things were going to be okay, that we were going to be okay, but we weren't. My sadness was exhausting, and soon it would have sunk us both. I wanted to save him, sure, but I also wanted to save myself; it was too hard to be depressed *and* racked with guilt. If I didn't have to see what my depression was capable of doing, I could ignore it and pretend it wasn't as bad as it was.

There was a knock on the door, and then a production assistant opened it and looked in.

"Ted, they're almost done with the next setup—we'll be back in ten."

"Got it. Close the door." He stood and waved off the assistant, who did as asked.

"Shit. I'm sorry. I am not your problem anymore, Ted. I shouldn't do this." I wiped my face and stood to go. "You've got Julie to worry about now."

"Julie doesn't make me worry." I laughed in spite of myself, and Ted laughed along with me. "I take it you're still not dating?"

"What gave it away?" I watched as a smile spread across his face and tucked my hands deep into my pockets to stop myself from grabbing him.

"Come on, thirteen years together. That means something, no?"

"Yeah."

"So why don't you sit back down and start from the beginning and tell me about Pandora and her box. Okay?"

"Okay."

I told him everything that I knew, as quickly as I could, and when I was done he waited a few moments before speaking.

"Some inheritance."

My mother had always been a sore spot between us. Ted was the one guy she hadn't been able to win over with her charms. I remember the first time they met. My mother was leaving town for six months and had called on the pretext of letting me know and having me keep an eye on her apartment while she was gone. She'd gone away lots of times in the past and never felt the need to call before. It wasn't like we'd been keeping in touch. With the exception of the obligatory birthday calls and the odd guilt-induced visit, I'd managed to successfully avoid her for months at a time. But that was before I had my picture in the paper and a glowing review for the opening night of my dance company's new season. Before Ted, now a recognizable actor on a well-known TV show, was quoted as saying that as far as he was concerned, his girlfriend's company was the best new dance company in Toronto, and yes he was biased.

We had celebrated the end of my company's opening weekend with a bottle of champagne, a midnight feast of Chinese takeout, and a night of lovemaking that lasted well into the morning.

"That was some celebration," he said. He rolled over toward me in bed, scooped me in his arms, and pulled me against him.

"You're welcome," I said, making him laugh.

He nuzzled his head in my hair and I grabbed his hands, squeezed them to my chest, and smiled. It felt good to be wrapped up in Ted, cocooned in his naked body and shielded from everything around us. The warm September sun was streaming in through the open windows, and outside, the little bird feeder that he had built was full of sparrows yammering away.

"I don't know whether to kiss you or spank you for building that bloody feeder. God they're noisy."

"Spank please," said Ted, propping himself up on his elbow and fanning my long hair out against the pillow.

"I'm serious. I mean it's nice and all, but not first thing in the morning."

He turned over the little alarm clock that we had accidentally knocked on the floor. "I hate to tell you Else, but it isn't first thing in the morning."

It was already noon.

"Noon! Time for mimosas," said Ted, hopping out of bed and crossing the apartment to the kitchen.

"Isn't it a little early to be drinking?" I squinted against the light, my head fuzzy from the night before.

"It has orange juice, so it's *civilized*," he said in a bad British accent, returning with a glass for each of us. "Besides, it's not every day that my girlfriend gets a five-star review in the paper. Shall we read it again?" He tucked back into bed next to me and grabbed the paper.

"No, don't, too much praise will go to my head. I'll get conceited." It was something my mother would have said to me, and I recognized it the second it came out of my mouth.

"That's ridiculous," said Ted, laughing.

I swatted his arm and grabbed the newspaper, my heart skipping a beat over words like *daring, breathtaking,* and *original.* "I still can't believe it."

"Believe it. Are you going to tell your mom?"

"I'm not sure she'd care." I hadn't told him the whole story about my mother. In fact I'd said as little as possible about her. He knew we weren't very close and that I'd grown up thinking that my mother would rather have been anywhere else than with me. Having amazing parents himself, Ted was sure I was exaggerating.

"Oh come on, my mother would buy a hundred copies of the paper and mail it to all her friends if this was about me."

"That's *your* mother," I said, taking our champagne glasses and putting them on the floor next to the bed. "I don't want this weekend to end."

"It doesn't have to," he said, climbing on top of me, when the phone rang.

"Don't answer it," I said, wrapping my legs around him.

We waited for the phone to stop ringing, and when it didn't, Ted yelled out in frustration, "And this is why we should have gotten an answering machine!" He sighed, picking up the receiver. "Hello?"

He turned to me and made a face, as if to say he had no idea who it was, and mouthed the word *coffee* to me, not really paying attention to the other voice on the line.

"May I ask who is calling? Rachel? Oh, Elsie's mother." He sat up straight. "Ms. Robins. Nice to finally meet you. This is Ted. Elsie's boyfriend."

I sat up in bed and pulled the sheet toward me. I hadn't told my mother about Ted. I tried to let her know as little about my personal life as possible. I was safer that way.

"Yes, sure, I'd like that. Hang on, let me see if she's home." He cupped his hand over the phone and passed it to me.

I shook my head no, but could see in his eyes he was hoping that this would be the moment he'd hoped for me, my mother calling to congratulate me and tell me how proud she was. "Just talk to her," he whispered.

"Fine." I sighed heavily as I took the phone. "Mother?"

"I didn't know you had a boyfriend."

"It's new." Ted and I had been together for almost a year, but she didn't need to know that.

"And already living together? Must be going well."

"Is everything all right?"

"Yes, of course. I'm just going out of town for six months with the Seekers and I thought you should know. If it isn't too much trouble for you, I'd appreciate it if you were able to look in on the apartment."

"What about Vincent?"

"If it's too much of a bother, you can just say so," she snapped.

"Okay, I'll do it." I waited for her to mention the article. "Is that the only reason you called?"

"Why? Is there something else you haven't told me?"

I held my breath. I wasn't going to play her game.

"Have a great trip, Mother—"

"Elspeth," she interrupted, "it would be nice if you could make time in your schedule to see me before I go."

It was just like her to put it on me. I hadn't heard from her in months and now I was the one with the schedule that was too busy to accommodate her.

"What's your week like?"

"It would need to be tonight. I leave tomorrow morning and I still have to pack, so an early dinner would be best. It won't take up your whole evening, and you can bring your friend. It would be nice to know who my daughter is living with."

I felt my heart pounding in my chest and clamped my jaw shut.

"What is it?" whispered Ted. He'd been perched on the edge of the bed, staring at me the whole time.

"She wants to meet for dinner. Tonight. Both of us."

"Great! Looking forward to it," he said, loud enough for my mother to hear.

We were to meet in the lobby of Dalewood at 6:00 p.m., but when we arrived Vincent told us my mother was running late and had asked that we go upstairs. The whole elevator ride up my stomach kept doing flip-flops, and I squeezed Ted's hand hard.

"Relax Else, it's going to be okay. Dinner will be quick and painless, and then you won't have to see her for another six months." He kissed the top of my head and I smiled. I was glad he came.

"Nothing's ever painless with her."

"I'm here," he said as we exited the elevator and made our way down the hall to the apartment.

"It's open," yelled my mother.

I took a deep breath as I opened the door.

"You'll have to excuse me, I was just finishing my exercises."

There she was in her white leotard, standing on her head. I heard myself gasp, and I shut my mouth so tightly I accidentally bit my tongue.

Slowly she came down from her headstand, bent over, and rolled up her yoga mat.

"I thought we were meeting at six?" she said. She calmly turned and smiled at us. I looked over at Ted; his mouth hung open, but no words came out.

"It's a quarter after six, Mother." It came out kind of strangled, and I swallowed hard.

"Is it? I completely lost track of time." Her hair and makeup were done, and as she faced Ted, she pulled her shoulders back a bit farther. "Forgive me. You must be Elsie's friend."

"Mother, this is Ted. My boyfriend."

"Pleased to meet you." She extended her hand to him

as if he should kiss it, and he grabbed it in a firm hand-shake instead.

"Ms. Robins." His voice was tight, and the expression on his face was wooden. It took a lot to throw Ted, but the sight of my mother braless in her skintight leotard and nothing else had apparently done the trick.

I watched as the smile faltered on her face for just a moment.

She leaned into him and placed her hand on his arm. "Please, call me Rachel. I assure you I don't normally meet Elsie's friends in my leotard, but I'm traveling tomorrow, and I just could not get on a plane without having gotten my practice in." She paused for a moment, waiting for him to respond, but he said nothing.

"Well, why don't I quickly get dressed and we can be on our way." She went into her bedroom and minutes later emerged in leggings, sandals, and a tunic. The three of us rode the elevator down in silence.

My mother spent the short walk to the restaurant talking about her upcoming European trip and the wonderful work she was doing with the Seekers. She wasn't talking about it for my benefit; she was showing off, trying to get Ted to ask her more about herself, but he didn't. By the time we got to the restaurant, though, I could tell by the way he was looking at her that he'd recovered. Instead of shock, he wore a slightly curious expression, like he was watching some animal at the zoo that he'd never seen before.

The waiter seated us at a little table in the back of an

old Victorian house that had been turned into a Middle Eastern restaurant. Ted pulled out my mother's chair for her and then sat down next to me. It was a simple place with worn hardwood floors and little wooden tables with bright red cloths. Along the whitewashed walls hung family photographs and children's drawings, making it feel as if you were in someone's living room rather than a restaurant. In fact, I was pretty sure the family that ran the place lived on the second floor of the house. I'd been here a couple of times with my mother before, and if it hadn't been a regular place of hers, I would have come more often.

We ordered, and my mother spent the fifteen minutes until our meals arrived flirting with Ted. She asked about his acting, complimented him on his leading-man looks, and laughed too loudly at his jokes. She leaned forward when he talked, and confessed that of all the performing arts, she found his the most impressive, for it used one's body and mind. She behaved like a teenager, running her hands through her hair and touching his forearm for emphasis when she spoke, and it made me cringe. I was so embarrassed I wanted to die, but when I looked at Ted, he was acting like it was the most delightful conversation in the world. The entire time she barely looked at me, and I felt myself sink deeper and deeper into my chair.

"So, Rachel," said Ted after the waiter placed our falafel plates in front of us, "did you see Elsie's glowing review in the paper?" He threw his arm around my shoulder and gave her a big smile.

"No, I didn't." She seemed taken aback, and she took a sip of her water before looking at me. "Why didn't you say something, Elspeth?" She kept her voice light and airy, but there was a tightness in her smile that I recognized.

"I, uh...."

"It was on the front page of the arts section this weekend," said Ted, smiling at my mother.

"Really? What a shame—I've thrown the paper out already."

"That's okay, I have it right here." He reached into his jacket pocket and took out the clipping.

I stared at him in disbelief. I had no idea he had the article on him, and I could see on my mother's face that just as Ted had underestimated her, she'd done the same with him.

"I thought you'd want to see it," he said sincerely, pushing the article across the table. "It's incredible, isn't it? I am just so proud of Elsie." He leaned in and gave me a kiss, and I saw her fidgeting uncomfortably. "You must be too."

"Indeed." My mother pursed her lips and quickly skimmed the article. "Congratulations Elspeth. I would have loved to have been there, had I known."

"Elsie, you should really put your mother on your mailing list," said Ted sweetly. I squeezed his leg under the table. He knew I sent her a catalogue every season. If she wanted to come, she could have.

"Don't worry, Rachel, it runs for two more months."

"Yes, but I'll be in—"

"Paris. Right. Sorry, I forgot."

I looked at the two of them staring at each other with their tight, polite smiles. Ted was probably the first person my mother had met that she couldn't win over. I could only imagine how unbearable she was going to be for the rest of the meal.

I was rescued when she recognized an older gentleman friend of hers entering the restaurant alone and insisted that he join us. Unlike Ted, he found my mother endlessly charming and couldn't hear enough of her stories. After only a few mouthfuls, I asked to take the rest of the food to go, and Ted, understanding how uncomfortable I was, announced we had a prior engagement and had to leave. He apologized for our hasty exit, paid the check, and whisked me out, his hand firmly against my back. As we left, I snuck a glance back at my mother. She no longer seemed concerned about getting home early to pack for her trip, and she sat there comfortably, laughing and talking.

"Fucking unbelievable," said Ted when we were out of earshot.

"I'm sorry," I said, choking back tears and clutching my takeout container.

"Don't you be sorry." He stopped and faced me, taking my shoulders in his hands. "Don't you dare apologize for that woman. She's the one who should be sorry. What kind of mother flirts with her daughter's boyfriend? What kind of mother ignores the achievements of her only child, only to ramble on incessantly about how fucking interesting her own life is?"

He was so angry that he was actually squeezing my shoulders as he spoke, and the tears that had welled up in my eyes fell down my face.

"I'm sorry. I'm sorry you saw her, and that I thought it would be no big deal," he said, hugging me tightly.

I buried my face in his chest. I heard his heart pounding, and it felt good to know it was beating so strongly for me.

"*I'm* sorry you had to pay for dinner," I said, starting to laugh and cry at the same time.

"*I'm* sorry that I had to see your mother in a leotard." He lifted my chin and looked me straight in the eye. He softly kissed my eyes and nose and then my lips. "Now please take me home. I need a shower," he said, making me love him even more.

That night I told Ted all of it. If ever there was a time for him to see just how much crazy was in my family, the night he met my mother was it. I didn't want to keep any more secrets on my mother's behalf; I was tired of protecting her, and tired of worrying how it would reflect on me. Ted lay next to me in bed as I talked and cried and talked some more. And when I was done, he held me for a long time before saying anything. When he finally spoke, he said the three best words I could ever hope for.

"Forget about her."

Ted would never forgive my mother for all she had put me through. And early on he made it clear that if there were sides to take he, was on mine. When I'd falter in my resolve to keep my distance from her and went for a visit, he'd be by my side, coming along to make sure I was okay. He'd sit next to me, an arm wrapped around my shoulder, a hand on mine, presenting the picture of a united front. I loved that he was there to protect me, and I loved that my mother could see it, too. Occasionally a get-together would go well and I'd find myself in my mother's light, privy to her thoughts and feelings, answering questions about myself that she took the time to ask. I'd get my hopes up and wonder to Ted if things might be different with her now that I was an adult. I'd reason that things had changed, that I had changed, and he'd listen silently and bite his tongue. Inevitably things would go back to the way they were, and I'd blame myself for being stupid enough to believe otherwise. Ted would hold me and reassure me that there was nothing stupid about wanting a parent's love and approval. Finally, after years of managing the damage she did to me, he begged me to acknowledge that Rachel would never be the mother I had hoped for, and to cut my losses and move on, for both our sakes. And I had.

"Jesus, even dead she's messing with you." He paced back and forth across his office and ran his hands through his hair.

"You're angry."

"Of course I'm angry. All she's left you is her mess to clean up and a box that may or may not contain her deepest, darkest secrets."

"Maybe it's a box of chocolates." I wanted to hear him laugh again. No such luck.

"Look, Elsie, if I know you, you're going to open it, and if I knew your mother, whatever you find will only lead to more confusion and questions."

"What would you do?"

The door opened wide and Julie stood in its entrance.

"Babe, they need you." She nervously glanced at me and looked away. She was just as I remembered her, only prettier. Julie was a much younger and less complicated version of myself, and I was happy for Ted that he had her. It hadn't taken him long to find someone else. Not because he was a player, but because she had always been there. Julie had been Ted's assistant since we arrived in LA It was her first job out of college, and I used to tease him that judging by the way she doted on him, I bet she hoped it was her last. He would assure me that I had nothing to worry about, and I didn't. Julie wasn't that kind of girl, and I knew it. But it was clear that she adored Ted, and after seven years of working alongside him, she could read his moods and anticipate his needs. And what he needed when we broke up was something easy with someone uncomplicated, and Julie was there to give it to him. She loved him. And after everything that we had been through, I was glad that she'd been the one to pick up the pieces.

"Hi Julie." I tried to smile at her, to put her at ease. It couldn't be easy watching your boyfriend rush off to rescue his ex.

"Hi Elspeth. Ted told me your mom died; I'm really sorry." She looked sincere, and I believed her.

"I should let you guys get back to work." I turned to Ted. "Thanks for listening."

"Burn the box, Else. Sell the ring, take the cash, and move on. You have spent your whole life trying to understand that woman. She's gone. Let her go. She's done enough damage."

"Okay."

"Okay?"

"You're right. What good can come of it?" We stood facing each other for a moment, unsure of how to part ways. Ted moved toward me, and I folded my arms in front of my body and moved toward the door. I couldn't hug him, not in front of Julie, although I wanted to. I wanted to more than I thought I would. I gave them both a small wave and a weak smile as I left. "I'll see myself out."

CHAPTER SEVEN

The box sat in the middle of my bed, and I sat in front of it. Something in me knew that if I opened it, there would be no going back. Ted was right: it had taken me a long time and several thousand miles to try to get over my failed relationship with my mother, and in one day I realized I had no idea who she was. I placed my hands on top of the box and wondered what was so important that she needed to hide it in a neighbor's place. And how bad were things that a neighbor was the person she felt she could trust the most?

I looked at the black-and-white photo Mrs. David had taken of my mother. She shot it as the sun was going down. In it, my mother in her robe stared out the window, her hands on the glass, her hair loose down her back. Her face was thinner from age, the long lines of her nose and cheekbones even more pronounced than usual. She was looking at something far away, unconcerned with the photographer's lens, her face deep in thought. She had the same deep groove that I did between the eyebrows, a long line that came from worrying. I held the picture close to my face. She was exquisite, and, like I had so many times before, I felt a longing to know what she had been thinking, a desire to be included in her private thoughts. And here was my chance.

Shadow hopped out of my lap, turned to face me, and meowed loudly.

"I'm sure, Shadow. I'm sure."

My heart was pounding, and my hand started to shake. I gently lifted the latch and slowly opened the box, and there was the photograph of myself as a toddler under the big tree in our backyard in Africa, and a letter addressed to me in my mother's handwriting.

Elspeth,

I've written this letter a hundred times since finding out the truth. But there aren't enough words to explain how we got here. And yet here I am again, wondering if I should tell you what you are better off not knowing.

I'll be leaving soon, but you still have so much living to do. I hope you'll do it. I hope you'll find a way. I know that I haven't paved much of a path for you, but the road is still long, and I pray that you'll find it leads to a better place than this one.

We all have secrets, and this box holds mine. The choice to bury them along with me or uncover them is yours to take. You don't owe me anything. That is one thing I am sure that we can both agree on.

Out of the darkness and into the light. But

*remember, light can be blinding too. I hope that one
day, you will be able to see that.*
Mother

I held the letter gently, its light-blue paper delicate
in my hands. More secrets. But this felt different to me.
This was the closest to an explanation or apology that I
would ever get. I may have hoped for a simple declaration
of motherly love, but I knew my mother well enough to
know that nothing was simple with her. All my life she had
claimed a superiority, a moral high ground, and here she
was essentially admitting that she had been wrong. Wrong
about what? Ted was right. I should bury the box with
her, but as I lifted the letter to my face, I could still smell
the scent of her rosewater talcum powder. She must have
written this just before she died, and I was moved by the
thought that at the very end, she had been thinking of me.
For once, she had extended an invitation to know her, and
I was going to take it.

Inside the box was a small photo album held together
with an old rubber band. I rolled it off and ran my hand
along the album's cover. Gold leaf lettering that had since
faded and peeled away, leaving only the indentation of the
letters, spelled out *For Ray*. I opened the cover and recognized my mother's slanted handwriting. *This book belongs
to Rachel Mills, Age 15.* On the first page was a black-and-
white photograph of a man, a woman, and two children
standing in front of a small brick house that backed onto
a large field.

I looked at the photo closely and could recognize my

mother's face in the older child. I'd never seen the other people before. I turned the photo over and read the back. *Africa, 1943, Mama, Papa, Ray, and me.*

I'd never met my grandparents. My mother had told me that her mother died in childbirth and her father passed away just before I was born. She'd never mentioned any siblings, and until now I had no idea that my mother had a sister. She had a large birthmark on her cheek and looked to be five or six years younger than my mother. If that was the case, my aunt would have been only around thirteen when my mother got married and fourteen when I was born. Why was it that I had never met my aunt? The room felt like it was spinning. Family. I had family, or at least I used to. Who knew where they were now, or if any of them were even still alive. There were more photos. I forced myself to take a deep breath and gently peeled them from their pages and laid them out on the bed according to the years written on the back. There was one for each year, each with the same pose of the family in the foreground and the house and farm in the background. The only thing that changed were the ages of the people in the pictures, their faces affixed with tight smiles that the photographer had probably called for, until 1950. *Papa, Isaac, me.* Ray, my mother, was gone in this photo, and this time the younger woman held a small baby. My grandmother was also absent from the photo, and something told me that she had died delivering *this* baby, who must've been Isaac. My mother had always said she was an only child, and now here were two siblings. For the next few years the pictures stayed the same, until 1953. This one had only *Isaac and me*, no Papa.

I looked back at the face of the young woman, my mother's younger sister, in the photo. She appeared so much older than the one before, her expression serious as she clutched the hand of her brother Isaac, now a chubby little toddler, and stared straight into the camera, and straight into me.

Me. There was no other name given to this person in the photos, and with my mother gone I had no one to ask. I looked closely at my mother's younger sister in the photograph. With the exception of the titles of the pictures themselves, there was little else that would connect my mother to these people. She didn't look exactly like them, her fair hair and lighter skin setting her apart. That and the distance that she seemed to place between herself and the others. She was like the plus one in an RSVP, accounted for but not necessarily invited. And yet she kept these pictures, which had either been left to her or sent to her by the *me* in the photos.

I had to find *me.* My hands were trembling, and I squeezed them together to make them stop. Carefully, I flipped through the book to the next page of pictures. There was one of my mother with her hair long, parted to the side and draped in front over her collarbone. She is lying on the sand, propped up on her elbows and wearing a halter-top one-piece swimsuit. The sun is in her eyes and she is smiling at the camera. Sitting straight up next to her is a man who looks to be at least ten years older. He is in shorts and a short-sleeved button-down, and he is staring at her, a small smile on his face. *Howard and Rachel,*

Muizenberg Beach, 1947. The next photo was taken on the same day, and my mother is waving at someone off in the distance and laughing, her hair wild in the wind. In this one, Howard stands tall next to her and stares at the person she is waving at, a strange expression on his face. My mother had always described Howard as a cripple, but I saw no evidence of that in these photos. Why would she lie? Did she think it made her seem more sympathetic to be married to a man who was disabled? I took a deep breath before turning the page, although I knew I'd find who they were looking at: Leo, my real father. And there he was. I held my breath as I stared at him. Tall, tanned, and shirtless in his swimming trunks, his slender frame leaning against his surfboard. His chin was tilted upward, and he had a devilish grin. He was young and beautiful, and I drank in every freckle on his sun-kissed face. *Leo, Muizenberg Beach, 1947.* There were more, the three of them in their summer clothes, waving flags at a parade: *Here comes the Queen!* At an outdoor café, Leo in a summer suit, kissing my mother tenderly on the forehead, her head on his shoulder, arms thrown around his neck. There was Howard, sitting at an outdoor table littered with empty champagne bottles and flutes, a highball glass in front of him and a faraway look in his eyes. The pictures told a story of two brothers in love with the same woman, and I wondered how hard that must have been for Howard. But more than that, I wondered why he had lied to me about never having a brother. I looked again at the picture of Leo. It was like looking at myself in a mirror, the face familiar, the eyes sad even when smiling. I inhaled sharply and wiped a tear from the corner of my eye before it fell onto the photo. I wish I had known him. I would have wrapped my arms around his neck and held my face against his, nestled myself between my parents, and smiled for the picture.

I gently returned the picture to its page holder, running my finger around my father's face as I did so. This was my mother's life before me. Why had she told me nothing of it? Why had she kept her family hidden? I turned to the last page. It was a group picture: my mother and her younger sister, the woman called *me*, standing between Howard and Leo. They were all dressed up, my mother stunning in a strapless gown, with a simple wreath of flowers in her hair. The picture was taken at the entrance of a spectacular mansion, with people milling around with cocktails in the background, and my mother glowed as she smiled at the camera. *The Robins' Annual Spring Fling Party, 1947.* I wondered who had taken this photo and what caused my mother to have hidden it in this box. I slowly unfolded the old newspaper clippings, careful not to rip the fragile little pieces of paper. They were death notices. The first was for a Hannah Mills, 1950, died in childbirth. *Hannah leaves behind a loving husband Jacob and three wonderful children…* but no names of the children. I gently folded it back up and looked at the next one, from 1953. *Samuel Mills, died of natural causes. He leaves behind three children.…* And, finally, *Rachel Mills Robins, died in a fire along with her husband Howard and their daughter, Elspeth.*

I dropped the book onto my lap. We had died in a fire? What the hell was this? Suddenly the dreams of fire were more terrifying than before. I knew there was a connection between my dreams and the death notices, but what it was, I still didn't understand. There was something there, something on the edges of my brain that flickered in and out, something just beyond my reach, and I tried to catch it, but it slipped away. I stood up from the bed and started pacing the apartment. My head was spinning, and I opened the window for a blast of icy air. This wasn't happening to me. It was bad enough that my mother and I were incapable of having a healthy relationship, but to have confirmation— hard proof—that I never even really knew her? It was too much. I took in a huge breath of cold air and tried to numb my face with the cold. My whole life I had wondered about my real father, wondered why we never went back to Africa, why Howard had so easily given up on me and moved on as my mother had claimed. But Howard hadn't moved on, he had died. Or had he? After all, my mother and I were alive, so why did we have obituaries? I walked over to the phone but stopped myself. I couldn't bother Ted again, especially not after he'd been right. Much like everything else in my relationship with my mother, for every hard-earned victory came several more bombs lying in wait.

I grabbed the album and took another look at my death notice. I peeled it off the page and saw a little note written in the margin on the back. *Thought you'd want to know.* I scanned the top of the page to see which newspaper this had come from, but any sign of publication had been removed. It could be from a local paper anywhere in South Africa. I wanted to go to Africa, to find that farm and ask someone about my mother, but where would I start? I never even had a proper birth certificate, although now I knew why. If it hadn't been for Ted hiring a lawyer to help us, I may never have gotten working papers, let alone a passport.

I picked up the box and shook it, half expecting a trap door to appear in its bottom, but there was nothing, just a box full of questions. I returned its contents, closed the lid, and used the rubber band that had been holding the photo album together to keep it shut. And there on the bottom of the box was an inscription.

For D, another place to bury the past...here's to the future.
Always,
Philippe

CHAPTER EIGHT

Philippe. It was a name that had started and ended many arguments I'd had with my mother. Long before I even knew the man, I knew what he meant to her, and that had been enough for me to decide he was somebody I wouldn't get along with. His name started coming up in conversations right after I'd first heard it on the phone at my mother's apartment. *Philippe had thought this*, or *Philippe had said that*, and whenever my mother and I were at a stalemate on some issue, it would be Philippe and his indisputable knowledge or unfaltering wisdom that she would quote to turn the argument in her favor. It was like getting in a boxing ring and discovering after eight rounds that your opponent has an extra set of hands, ones that were stronger and better than your own. He was her secret weapon. Somehow this man, who had traveled the world and had degrees in philosophy, psychology, and religion, had been able to pass on his infinite wisdom to my mother by osmosis, and his experiences had become hers.

I knew by the way she said his name that they were

lovers: a slightly affected French accent that pulled on the sides of her mouth when she said the i's, and the little exhale on the final e. *Fee-lee-puh*, her lips lingering a moment too long on the pronunciation of it. It made my jaw tighten every time she said it, and out of spite I insisted on referring to him as Phil. It wasn't that I didn't want her to be happy; it was that I didn't understand how she *could* be happy when she made my life so miserable.

When I was fourteen, I invited my mother to a recital for the dance company that I'd been working with, a small, casual event for family and friends. I thought she might like to see what I had been doing every waking hour outside of school and sleep, and to my surprise she agreed. My mother had always been an admirer of the performing arts, and I secretly hoped that when she saw me perform, that admiration would extend to me.

The recital was held on a rainy Saturday afternoon in one of the larger studios instead of the theater. I stood at the edge of the floor against the wall in my leotard and tights, hair pulled back into a bun, watching as the other parents came in slightly worse for wear from the downpour outside. Mine was the last group to perform, and with just two minutes left until we started, my mother was still nowhere to be seen. I tugged at my leg warmers and tried to stay loose and focused on the routine and not on the loud ticking of the wall clock. It wouldn't be the first time that she had stood me up, and I closed my eyes and tried to count backward to calm myself. When I opened them, my mother was entering, just as they were closing the door. The sound of her high heels clicked against the hardwood floor announcing her arrival, and all eyes turned toward her. She had on full makeup, and her hair was long and loose around her shoulders. She had donned her best well-heeled-patron-of-the-arts attire, and was so poised and trim in her pencil skirt and long-sleeve ballerina top that she looked like a dancer herself. And that was the point. As she made her way to the front row, one of the dads jumped out of his chair and gave her his seat. Once again, my mother had managed to take center stage, and I could feel the other dancers trying to figure out whose mother she was. My cheeks got hot, and when I refused to look at her, she whispered my name, just loud enough to be heard, and gave me a little wave. Just like that, everybody knew.

In spite of her grand entrance, I still managed to dance my best. Dancing was when I lost myself completely. The moment I started moving, the chatter in my brain would go quiet and every cell in my body would be absorbed into the movement. I could fly when I was dancing, unencumbered by the baggage of my daily life; I was pure energy, light, and emotion. Words would never come close to expressing what I could say onstage. In dance, I had a confidence and a calm that eluded me elsewhere. If I could've spent every waking hour dancing, I would have.

If my mother's entrance was dramatic, her exit was no less so. After taking my final bow and collecting my things, I found her holding court with some of the male dancers, boys much closer to my age than hers. She was making them laugh and blush with praise that she emphasized by placing a hand on a bare arm here or a wrist there. I could feel the disapproving gaze of some of the other parents, and I stormed past her and out the doors onto the street, where I waited for her to follow. After almost twenty minutes she joined me, saying only that after all the time I'd spent dancing with the company, she thought I'd have a larger part. It was the only performance of mine she ever attended. There was no need for her to attend any others; she had made her point.

As with all of the things my mother truly treasured, she had tried to keep Philippe to herself, but she still bragged about him every chance she got. He was like that one party that you missed in high school, the "best party ever," and you'd have no way of knowing if such a party really was true, as you had not been there. I'd even started to wonder if Philippe was real, and then the summer of my sixteenth birthday, I met him.

It was the weekend before I was to go on tour with the modern dance company I'd been working with during the school year. After all my hard work, I'd finally been offered a part in the company's summer tour. I accepted it without even checking with my mother, knowing that the two of us would welcome the chance to be away from each other for two months. It was a typical humid Toronto summer, the heat sticking to the back of my neck, my T-shirt always slightly damp at my lower back where I kept my messenger bag slung to one side. I was happier than I had ever been, knowing I was going away and bursting with the secret that I wasn't going to come back.

I believe it was because I was going away for the

summer, and because I'd turned sixteen, that my mother asked if I would like to accompany her to one of her meetings with the Seekers. It was a grand gesture, an opportunity to show me a part of her life, now that I was "old enough to appreciate it." And I knew that Philippe was in town for the weekend, and this way she wouldn't have to cancel her plans with him. She'd arranged for the three of us to go out to dinner after.

"Happy birthday, Elsie," said Vincent as I walked into the lobby of Dalewood.

"Thanks."

"Big plans?"

"Big."

"By the look on your face, I'm guessing really big. Make sure they're good ones."

"I leave Monday for my first dance tour." *And I'm not coming back*, I wanted to say, but I knew better than to burden Vincent with another secret. Who knows how many he was keeping about Dalewood.

"The first of many, I am sure."

"I hope so."

"Aren't you going up?"

"No, I'll wait here." I played with the little bit of crochet lace on the hem of my peasant skirt, flicking it up and down with my ankles as I sat on the edge of the lobby fountain. I'd bought the skirt with part of my first week's per diem money in Kensington Market. It was the color of lilacs and had rainbow-colored stitching around the waist and pockets. It was a little fuller than I would have gone for, but after living in cutoff tights and leotards it felt nice to wear something that didn't cling to my skin. It also concealed my tiny frame, which meant that I could get through a meal without my mother getting competitive with me.

The elevator button for the ninth floor lit up, signaling my mother's descent. I closed my eyes, took a deep breath, and counted backward, opening them only seconds before the door opened and she made her entrance.

"There you are." She waited for me to stand and greet her and I did, awkwardly touching my cheek to hers in what should have been a kiss.

"Sixteen, Vincent. Can you believe it? I mean, do I really look old enough to have a sixteen-year-old daughter?" She wore her long hair down for the occasion, and she tossed it back over her shoulders and held her chin a little higher.

"No. You barely look older than sixteen yourself." He smiled at her and then at me, raising his eyebrow ever so slightly.

"Well, that's because I take care of myself." She ran her good hand along the side of her body, stopping to rest it at her slender waist. She was wearing black cigarette pants that showed off her toned legs, gold beaded sandals, and a silk embroidered tunic that opened just enough to reveal her pronounced collarbones. Around her shoulders she had casually draped a soft scarf that looked beautiful against her honey-colored hair. The look was fashionable and slightly bohemian, without being too showy. I could tell that she was dressed to impress without wanting to seem so.

"Yes, ma'am."

"Exercise and diet, so important. After all my body is

my temple...."

"You look great, Mother." I knew this speech. It wouldn't end until she was complimented, and I wanted us to get along tonight.

"Thank you, Elspeth." She gave me the quick once-over and then clapped her hands together. "We better get going, we don't want to be late."

"See ya, Vincent," I said.

"You take care now," he said.

I nodded and smiled, meeting Vincent's eyes, and wished, as I had a thousand times, that I could read his mind.

The taxi dropped us off outside of an old brick building downtown. Large stone archways framed the entrance, and two gaslit lamps stood on either side of the heavy glass and wood doors. It wasn't a temple, that much I knew. The Seekers didn't use a regular house of worship; only a religion needed a temple or church. They were a philosophy, a collective of like-minded souls, holding their meetings in different places that were made available by their individual members.

"It looks like a law library."

"It is," my mother said. She used both hands as she pulled open the door and led the way inside, quickly crossing the marble lobby to the back of the building. I could hear people talking as we got closer, and it sounded like someone was strumming a guitar. My mother fussed with her hair as she walked and reapplied her lipstick. At the end of the hall she stopped and reached back for my arm, hooking hers through mine so we rounded the corner together.

"Brothers and sisters," my mother called out as the guitar strumming stopped.

"Sister," they called out, turning to face her. They were gathered around the library's reference tables, some seated, others standing among the stacks of books, leaning against the shelves. The room smelled of incense and was dimly lit by little study lamps that ran the length of the tables. There must have been at least a hundred people, men and women ranging in age from early twenties to late fifties. I was surprised at how normal most of them looked. For some reason I had always imagined that they'd be wearing robes, and here they were, some of them dressed casually, some clearly straight from work, but all of them looking like, well, regular people. They were all staring at me now, and I waited for my mother to say something.

"Philippe, I have a guest. My daughter Elspeth."

"Elspeth."

I found the voice at the head of the table and turned to see Philippe. The room went quiet and he placed his hands on the table and stood. He was shorter than I expected, but carried himself like a tall person, his shoulders pulled back and his spine erect. He looked me straight in the eye and smiled.

"Come," he said, motioning me closer. My mother nudged me forward, and I made my way down the table toward him. He was much younger and better looking than I'd imagined, and it made me uncomfortable, his salt-and-pepper hair and long dark lashes framing gray eyes. I gripped the sides of my skirt, resisting the urge to fuss with my hair or outfit. He stared at me intently, his smile widening slowly until I was close enough for him to reach his hands out and place them on my hips, turning his body to me as he did so. Everyone's eyes were on me as I held my breath and tried not to move my body under his hands. He leaned forward, pressed his forehead to mine, and whispered.

"Welcome."

"Welcome," the room replied in unison, and I exhaled as we turned out to face everybody. I looked across the room to my mother, but she was staring straight past me to Philippe, her eyes wide, her face plastered with a tight smile. I started to move toward her, but he gently touched my wrist and motioned for me to sit next to him.

"As a guest of your mother, and not a member, I ask you not to participate, but to observe." He motioned for those who were standing to sit. "Any questions you may have, feel free to ask me after." He placed his hand on my shoulder and gave it a little squeeze. "All right?"

I nodded, speechless. A current ran through my body, and my heart beat faster. I'd never felt this way in someone's presence before, and looking around the room, I saw by the adoration on the faces of those present that I wasn't alone. Like flowers finding the sun, they had all turned their bodies in their seats to find him.

"Let's begin."

He clapped his hands together, lowered his head, and started chanting in a low voice. The chant was in something other than English, so I didn't know what they were saying, but it sounded nice.

When he was done, he clapped his hands one more time and everyone whispered, "To the light," opened their eyes, and waited for him to speak.

The evening's talk was about karma, and how one's karma in this life was pre-determined by one's actions in past lives. *Karma* was a word my mother had been bandying about recently whenever she wanted to justify rather than deal with some inadequacy of hers, and now I knew why.

"The laws of karma that shape our lives are very complicated. Sometimes our karmas are created by us in this life, and sometimes we inherit them from the actions of our past lives."

"*Samskaras*," said a young man sitting near the front of the room.

"Yes, *samskaras*. Impressions and desires in us that are a result of actions in our previous lives. These too shape our karma. It's cause and effect, if you will. No one can escape the consequences of his actions. We all have to reap what we have sown."

"Sadhu?" asked an older woman, raising her hand.

"Sadhu? Please, sister, I am no monk. I am just like you and still live very much as a man, tempted by all the things that men are tempted with." A small smile flickered on his lips, and he shrugged his shoulders as if to say, *What can you do?*

"Maybe that is my karma, sister. I just try to do good work, spread the light, and bring together those who want to live their lives striving toward being better, kinder, more godly people. I am no better than you."

There were murmurs of disagreement about this last statement, and Philippe hung his head in embarrassment and shushed the room quiet.

"Please, continue with your question, sister."

"All right, brother." She paused after the word *brother*, and shook her head to show that she clearly found Philippe to be more than that. The room glowed with smiling faces, a room full of disciples, flattered that their leader felt he was just like them. It was hard not to notice how much it endeared Philippe to them, and I would be lying if I didn't admit that I felt the same way.

"What I was wondering was," she continued, "what if I don't know what I've sown? If I didn't commit my past actions, how can I know what they are?"

"Well, sister, all one has to do is look at the situations that we keep finding ourselves in. The good ones we don't worry about much, do we? Health, happiness, wealth—we don't worry about what we did to deserve these. No, it is the bad ones, misery, illness, conflict with others, that we want to understand and know how to stop, and who can blame us? But let's say you are in a bad marriage, or you're always finding yourself in bad relationships, maybe that is your fault. Maybe you were the one who was the cause of unhappiness in your past relationships. Or maybe you have money troubles; maybe you had so much money in your past life and weren't generous with others who needed it, and so now you know what it's like to always want for more. Maybe you have acquired so much bad karma over the years that it has made you physically sick, so that you have to take stock of your life and right the wrongs you have committed. You see, there is always a lesson to be learned. There is always payback, but there is always redemption, too."

"So what do I do?" asked the woman.

"Well, first you must accept this is part of the plan that is set out for us, and then you must work to overcome it. You must try to see what the lesson is and rise above it, and in some instances simply endure it, for that is what you are meant to do. With enough devotion and meditation, you will know what is right, and you will be able to right your karma. It may take a whole lifetime, it may take many, but it is possible to pay off your karmic debt."

I saw my mother nod her head and wring her hands at the back of the room. I had no idea what her karma was. I wondered what my own karma might be and what I had or hadn't done to deserve a mother like Rachel. Maybe I'd been too blessed in my past life. Maybe I would be rewarded for my suffering later. Unlike the people in this room, I'd never really thought about it before.

The rest of the talk continued with people offering their own stories and theories on how karma shaped their destiny and questioned whether or not their destinies could actually be changed. Of course, Philippe felt it was always best to remedy bad karma through good deeds and service, but that could take an entire lifetime, and sometimes even that wasn't enough time. To my surprise, it was a fascinating and intelligent discussion. I was amazed at how knowledgeable Philippe was and how quickly he was able to reference different philosophies and religions to support his arguments. At the time I was impressed at what I thought was the breadth of his knowledge, rather than suspecting that he might actually only know a little about a lot of things. A man who knows a little bit about everything is not an expert, he is a danger. But I was too young to see that.

Philippe was confident in his role as guru, more confident than anyone in the room. And his confidence in himself was infectious. Whenever a question was asked, everyone leaned forward and waited to see how he'd respond before nodding along with him or murmuring their own agreements. If he disagreed with someone, it wasn't long before they'd be apologizing for what they'd said, or changing their mind once he'd finished arguing his point. He was a charismatic talker, making eye contact with people as he spoke, often reminding them that it wasn't his opinion that they should defer to, but the teachings of the great spiritual thinkers who came before him. It made him appear humble, which only added to his appeal.

Somebody made a joke about karmic debts having a higher interest rate than credit cards, and when I laughed along with everyone else, he reached over and held my knee. Without thinking I reached out and touched his hand, and he turned to me and smiled, and then gave my knee a little squeeze before removing his hand as he continued talking. I looked out into the group to find my mother. I caught her looking at me just as she averted her eyes and fixed them on Philippe. I waited for her to look back, but she was committed to pretending she hadn't seen me. Her face was strained, and she held her mouth in a thin line that barely turned up at the corners. I recognized this look instantly. Jealousy. She was jealous that I was the one sitting next to Philippe, a man easily three times my age.

The sermon, for lack of a better word, lasted about an hour and a half, and at the end of it, Philippe asked everyone to close his or her eyes and reach out and touch the person one seat over. This time it was my hand on Philippe's knee, and I couldn't help but smile. I like to think I was simply captivated by Philippe's charm, but deep down I knew my surprise at his taking notice of me had escalated into delight when I realized it had been noticed by my mother.

I had never garnered attention. I was constantly outshone by my mother's gift for directing everyone's attention to her. It hardly mattered who was in the room, as long as it was clear she was at the center of it. It was something I'd resigned myself to, and we both had an understanding that this was the way things would always be, although lately I had begun to suspect, by the way she'd been looking at me—and the way the straight guys in my company stayed behind after rehearsals to praise my dancing and walk me to the subway—that I was no longer as plain as she had often told me I was. I'd suspected it but had yet to test it in her presence, and that night I was proven right. I felt more alive than I ever had, knowing I had a secret, knowing I wasn't coming back, and for that reason, I believe, I gently squeezed his knee and ran my thumb back and forth ever so lightly along it.

As soon as we lifted our heads from the little prayer that ended the service, people came rushing up to Philippe to try to talk with him further. Some asked him to transfer his good energy onto them, and he obliged, closing his eyes and chanting *om* as he ran his hands over the outlines of their bodies without touching them at first, and then ending the chant by opening his eyes and holding them in a tight embrace. I watched as these members dissolved into tears and laughter, thanked Philippe profusely, and rushed to find the Seeker who held the donation plate at the door. Eventually someone from the group led Philippe out of the room through a side door, and the meeting came to an end.

I found my mother waiting outside, surrounded by members, and was hoping to get a chance to speak with her about the meeting. Like everything with her, my feelings of anger and hurt were won out by my deep desire for her to notice and like me. No matter how many times she'd shown me that she wasn't interested in being my parent, let alone my friend, I still attached too much hope and importance to her actions. And so I foolishly let myself think that maybe this meeting was more than just a way for her to keep her date with the Seekers and celebrate my birthday—maybe it was an invitation to join the group and be a part of her life, now that she thought I was finally old enough. Maybe Philippe was just being friendly, maybe I was just being treated like a grownup, and maybe my mother would see that, and this night would be a turning point. I was planning on telling her how fascinating I thought her group was when she was joined by Philippe and some of the other members. I saw that we would be a party of six, although who the three other people were I had yet to find out. I doubt anyone knew we were supposed to be celebrating my sixteenth birthday. We wound up at a Moroccan restaurant that was a favorite of Philippe's. He said the owner was an old friend, and he liked to visit whenever he was in town.

"Philippe!" a large, dark-skinned man with slicked-back curly hair called out and grabbed him in a bear hug.

"Maurice. *Mon ami*, how are you?"

"How do I look?" He rubbed his hands over his big belly and laughed.

"Well. You look well."

"Too well! I am fat, but rich, and the two often go together, no?" He laughed and playfully slapped Philippe's flat stomach, making him wince.

"I see you've brought friends." He took my mother's bad hand and, surprised by its distortion, hesitated for a moment before he kissed it. "Madame."

"Monsieur," my mother smiled, her cheeks flushing.

"And Mademoiselle, you must be sisters, no?" I could hear the relief in my mother's fake little laugh that he hadn't said that I was her daughter.

"Elsie," I said.

The others in our group were a couple who looked to be in their early forties named Danielle and Simon and a good-looking man is his twenties named Henri. We were led to a private alcove and seated at a low, round table with cushions on the floor. The stone floors were covered in Persian rugs, and the place was warm and smelled of toasted spices and cinnamon. The ceilings and walls were draped with swaths of brightly colored fabric that had little ribbons of gold running through them, making them shimmer in the light of the colored glass lanterns that hung from the ceiling.

"This is just like it is in Morocco," said Philippe, raising his voice above the din of the packed restaurant.

"You've been?" I asked.

"Sure, that's where I met Maurice." He called over the waitress, who was dressed as a belly dancer in a long, gauzy pink skirt and a bra top fringed with gold beads. As she approached, I heard the little coins around her waist and ankles chime with each step. She arrived at the table and shook her hips and breasts seductively for a few moments before striking a pose and snapping her fingers. The table burst into a round of applause, and she laughed and tossed her hair back. "Tea, please," said Philippe as he reached his hand up to her waist and ran his fingers along the coins so that they sounded like wind chimes, and a moment later she returned with hot mint tea and a bottle of wine. "From Maurice."

Philippe blew a kiss across the room to Maurice, who bowed slightly.

"Wine?" asked my mother.

"Yes, wine," he said. He turned to me. "As members of the Seekers, we are not supposed to eat meat or drink, but...."

"But?" asked Henri, as he arched his eyebrows. "Don't worry, no one is going to card you here," he said, leaning in close and filling my glass. He winked at me, and I blushed, even though I was sure he meant nothing by it. Good-looking guys like Henri, who were sexy and okay with everyone knowing it, liked to flirt with girls like me, girls they knew would welcome the attention and give them the audience they were looking for, but whom they weren't actually interested in.

"But today is a special occasion. It is Elsie's birthday, is it not? And besides, nobody is going to order the lamb," said Philippe. He smiled at me and then took my mother's hand and lifted it to his lips. "Everything in moderation. Even moderation." She blushed and smiled back.

"Yes, but still she's only…." said my mother.

"Only what? What is age anyway? Our physical age means nothing. It is the age of our souls that really matters. And I can tell just by looking at Elsie," he reached up and placed his hand at the back of my neck, his fingers hooking ever so slightly into my hair, "she is a very old soul." He turned to look at my mother. "You were the same."

Her face went red, and I wondered whether it was because Philippe had acknowledged that she wasn't young anymore, or if it meant something more.

"How long have you known my mother?" I asked.

"In this lifetime, or all together?" he asked, smiling at me.

"Oh no, not this lecture again," joked Henri. "I for one do not have enough lifetimes to listen to it."

"Did you know my father too?"

"Elspeth." My mother sat up straight and clenched her jaw. "This isn't the time for another round of your twenty questions."

"It's all right," said Philippe, placing a hand on her leg and turning to look at me. "It's good to have questions. I can tell you this about your father. Wherever he is, I am sure he would be proud to see what a bright and beautiful young woman you are." He placed his hand against my cheek and raised his glass.

"To Elsie, happy birthday!"

"Happy birthday!" Everyone chimed in, and we all clinked glasses.

It wasn't my first glass of wine, but it was the first one I had in front of my mother. Ever since she had become serious about the Seekers, she'd tried to refrain from vices. These included meat, drugs, coffee, of which she still allowed herself one cup a day, and alcohol. But these apparently did not include lying, vanity, selfishness, and gossip. It came as no surprise to me that Mother would alter the tenets of her faith to suit her. I raised the glass to my lips and took a sip of the red wine. It was warm and sweet and made my lips tingle, and I quickly took another sip. I'd drunk half a glass before I set it down, and the room felt hotter than before. I leaned back on my hands and took a deep breath.

"So, Elsie, tell us, what did you think of the meeting?" asked Philippe.

"It was interesting. It wasn't as weird as I thought it might be," I said, looking at my mother.

"Well, that's good." He smiled and looked at my mother, who didn't seem amused.

"I mean, I didn't know what to expect. We haven't talked about it too much, but I'm really glad I got a chance to come. Thank you for bringing me," I said, looking at my mother. I heard the words come out of my mouth, and my heart started to race. I was doing it again. Hoping. Extending an invitation to my mother in the hope that she might take it. Never mind that I was running away, never mind that I'd told Arden I couldn't stand one more day of living with my mother. If she accepted my invitation, I'd forget everything and stay. I waited for her to say something. That she'd been waiting for the right time to introduce me to the group, that she always knew I'd be a good fit, that she was glad I was at last going to be a member of this family of hers, and finally, after an uncomfortably long silence, she spoke.

"Elsie is still concerned with all things earthly; the time isn't right," she said to the table. "She still has so much evolving to do."

I felt the room start to close in around me, and my heart sink. I thought I was going to cry. "I'm only sixteen." The way I said it, I sounded like a ten-year-old.

"And yet, our real age means nothing, right?" my mother said, shrugging her shoulders.

The table got quiet, and then Danielle, who'd been silent until that point, exclaimed, "Well, in that case, everybody forget that I turned forty this year!" She laughed at her own joke and smiled at me.

"Does that mean I get to take back your birthday present?" asked Simon, holding her hand and eyeing a large amethyst ring on her finger.

"No way, a gift is a gift." She swatted his arm playfully, and he leaned in to kiss her.

I looked at my mother and reminded myself to see her as the person she was—vain, selfish, and cold—and not as the person I wanted her to be. And I did. And just like that we were back to our respective corners of the ring. She had won this round, but I wasn't going to be back for more.

"I remember being sixteen," said Henri as he filled up our glasses. "It was incredible. I lost my virginity. To a woman twice my age."

I felt my jaw drop open as I quickly did the math, wondering what thirty-two-year-old woman would want to sleep with a sixteen-year-old boy.

"But as we have all agreed, age has nothing to do with it. I mean," said Henri, his face widening into a full-blown shit-eating grin, "she had a very, very, young soul, Papa."

"Papa?" I asked, turning to Philippe.

"Yes, that rascal is my son."

"And that saint is my father."

"If anyone has evolving to do, it is Henri," said Philippe warmly.

"And I am okay with that," said Henri. "But I am not okay with running out of wine, and can we please get some food? Elsie is going to blow away if we wait any longer!" I laughed at his joke, flattered that he'd even noticed my body and grateful that he was trying to make me feel welcome. I liked that he was able to laugh easily and include others in that laughter; it was a skill I had never known, but admired.

Philippe ordered an abundance of food for everyone, and it was delicious. There were hot and cold salads, and vegetables in clay pots, and couscous with raisins and apricots, and stewed chickpeas with tomatoes, and eggplant turnovers, and warm bread to wipe up all the sauces. It was more food than I would normally consume in a week—at least that was something my mother and I had in common—but I was so light-headed from the wine, and I knew there'd be nothing like this on our tour, so I sampled everything, savoring the flavors as I did so. I lost track of how many bottles of wine we ordered, as there always seemed to be a fresh one on the table and my glass never got empty.

My mother, on the other hand, barely touched hers, sipping her tea instead and picking at her food. There was a lot of talking, laughing, and vying for center stage as Philippe and Henri told stories of their travels. What I learned was that Philippe and Henri lived most of the year in Paris, and that Philippe had met Simon and Danielle in England ten years ago when the young couple had gone through their initiation ceremonies, becoming full members of the group. They credited the teachings of the Seekers for showing them how to use their wealth for a greater purpose than just their own pleasure. They had donated a lot of money to the group, and there was talk of building a center in Paris where members could study or work in exchange for room and board. It sounded like some sort of ashram with a much more fashionable address, perfect for my mother. But first they needed to spread the word. Henri was taking a year off school to help his father with this task as he toured the world and lectured.

The Seekers were fairly new to North America, and it seemed that most of their members were in Europe and

Africa, which explained the Moroccan connection, but what about South Africa? I wondered if that was where my mother had first met Philippe, and how long she had actually known him. She'd gotten upset when I asked, and I wondered what she was afraid of him saying. I wanted to ask, but everyone was talking over each other, and the belly dancers had started to do their show, and the wine had now officially gone to my head, which was spinning. It was too hot in the restaurant, and when I reached my hand to my forehead, it was wet. I knew I had to get some air. I carefully placed my hand on the table to steady myself and stood up. Henri got to his feet and pulled me straight as I started to lose my balance.

"Are we okay?" he asked.

"*Oui, oui.* We are fine, we just need to use the ladies' room." I turned to the table, "If you'll excuse me...." but nobody was listening. Danielle and Simon were kissing, and my mother and Philippe were flopped on the cushions. She was leaning on her side, and he was propped up on one elbow talking close to her, his hand on her stomach. The room felt close, and my legs were unsteady. I took a few wobbly steps and then placed my hand along the corridor wall that led to the back exit and the parking lot. The door was open, and I snuck outside and sat on one of the milk crates the dishwashers sat on during their breaks. I leaned my back against the wall and exhaled deeply. The air was warm, but it was at least ten degrees cooler than in the restaurant, and even the warm breeze was a relief against my skin. I piled my hair up on top of my head and wiped the sweat running down my neck with the back of my hand. I had no idea what time it was, but I knew I should be getting home. Arden was going to be picking me up in the morning, and I'd have to get up extra early to pack, as I didn't think I'd be in any state to do it tonight. In spite of my mother I'd had fun, but I didn't really belong in there with those people. They were interesting and captivating, but I had no idea what they were talking about most of the time, and I was pretty sure my birthday had just been an excuse for everyone to cut loose, and for my mother, an easy way to keep her plans and still supposedly celebrate it.

She was right: I had a lot of evolving to do, and I was going to start tomorrow by going away and not coming back.

"Mind if I join you?" Henri appeared in the doorway holding his glass of wine, an unlit cigarette dangling from his mouth.

"I was just getting some air. It's hot in there."

"Hot air? Are you saying I'm full of hot air?" He laughed a little too loudly as he lit his cigarette, took a drag, and exhaled the scent of cloves.

"No. Are you?"

Henri continued smoking and kicked a milk crate hard with his foot, startling me. He positioned it opposite me and sat down. The music from the restaurant filled the silence between us for a few moments.

"Yes."

"Yes, what?"

"Full of hot air, or full of shit, as you like to say over here. But at least I admit it. Unlike some people." While he took another long drag, he smiled at me sideways. I could tell he didn't mean me, but I waited to see if he'd go on. He passed the cigarette to me, and even though I didn't smoke, I took it, its sweet filter wet and sticky against my lips. I took a drag and immediately my head started to spin. I passed it back to him.

"You don't believe?" I asked.

"In philosophy, sure. In gurus, not so much. But then again, people want to believe in someone, don't they? And if someone is smart enough to give them what they want, then who am I to say that's wrong?" The smile was suddenly gone, and he stared at me intently.

"I see."

"Do you? He's married, you know." He fixed his eyes on me and waited for an answer. They were gray like his father's, but darker.

I wondered if my mother knew. I also wondered what kind of woman Philippe would be married to. An older version of my mother, or the complete opposite? After watching him flirt all evening, it was hard to believe he was married at all. I decided not to ask and stopped talking. Henri was staring off into the distance, and I could tell his thoughts were somewhere else. I stood to go.

"It was nice to meet you. I should get going." *I'm leaving tomorrow, to go dance for the summer, and I'm never coming back*, I wanted to say, realizing nobody had even asked me anything about myself all night. I had been a conversation starter and a witness to the evening's festivities. I recognized the feeling of being a prop, once again.

I walked back inside, and this time I did use the restroom. I splashed my face and used a paper towel to dry off my neck and underarms. I looked at myself in the mirror and said aloud, "Tomorrow—your life begins tomorrow." I walked back to the table and saw it had been cleared of all but the glasses and yet another bottle of opened wine. Simon and Danielle were wrapped in each other's arms facing the show of belly dancers, and my mother and Philippe were kissing. It was the first time I'd ever seen her kiss someone so tenderly. Her eyes were closed, her cheeks were flushed, and her hand rested gently on his chest. From the way she spoke about him, I don't believe she'd ever kissed Howard that way, and I wondered if that was how she'd kissed my real father. For a moment I felt sorry for her that she'd spent all those years not being able to kiss like that, and I longed to know for myself what a kiss from a lover must be like. I had never been in love, never had a kiss that I had lost myself in, oblivious to the stares of those around me.

"Are you going?" said my mother after breaking her kiss with Philippe.

"Yes. Arden's getting me in the morning. The tour starts tomorrow."

"Of course. Well.…"

"You should stay," I said, although she made no move to go anywhere. "I'll catch a cab."

"Good luck. Let me know how it goes."

"Sure. Uh, thanks for dinner, everyone, it was nice to meet you." I made a little wave to Danielle and Simon, who smiled back, and turned to Philippe. "I appreciate your.…"

"I'll walk her out and make sure she gets a taxi," said Philippe to my mother, and led me through the restaurant and outside with his hand on the small of my back. My shirt was damp, and I tried to walk quickly so his fingers wouldn't get wet from my sweat.

"You don't have to wait with me, I'll be okay," I said once we were out on the street in front of the restaurant.

"I know you will." He took a ringlet of my hair and tucked it behind my ear, tracing his finger down my neck and across my collarbone before tucking his hands in his pockets. I shivered at his touch. There was no one around us, and I felt myself wishing that someone would come outside.

"Aren't you my mother's boyfriend?"

"Yes."

"But you're also married?"

"Depends on your definition of marriage."

"Oh, I guess it's complicated." This was what my mother would often say rather than admit she was wrong.

"Only if you make it so. Otherwise it just is. Not everything needs a label."

"Convenient." I looked up the street for a taxi but didn't see one. I crossed my arms in front of my chest and kept my face forward. "I can keep a secret if that's what you're worried about. Can you?"

I smirked and tossed my hair over my shoulder. I had a secret, and the power of it bubbled up inside me and made me feel strong. I raised my hand for the taxi that had just dropped off its fare down the street and turned to face him.

He moved in close enough to me that our shoes were touching and I could feel his belt buckle against my belly.

"Can you?" he asked again.

"Yes," I said, barely able to breathe.

"Good. Because here's one," he said, and he wrapped his hand around my back, closing the space between us and putting his mouth on mine.

I was too stunned to move my mouth and kept my lips shut until he whispered, "Kiss me." And I did.

I snuck a glance back at the restaurant, and when I saw that no one was looking, I lowered my hand and let it rest on his chest while kissing him back fully. My heart was pounding, and I told myself that I was drunk and I should stop and this was wrong and what if my mother found out, and yet I couldn't stop. I didn't owe her anything. He'd said to kiss him, and when he had, I knew that I had wanted to all night long; I just never believed that he would want the same thing, that he would want me and not my mother.

If the taxi hadn't pulled up I don't know that I would have stopped. But I was glad it did.

"Get home safely," he said, opening the car door just as my mother appeared on the street.

I hurried in and heard him say as he closed the door, "Devedra, I thought you said it was easy to get a taxi in this town." He swung his arm around her waist, and out of the corner of my eye I saw my mother turn to look at me, but I didn't look back.

"Dalewood," I said to the taxi driver, and I placed my hand on my mouth, which still felt warm from the kiss. The driver headed back into the street to do a U-turn when there was a thud on the hood of the cab. I jumped in my seat and screamed.

"What the hell do you think you're doing?" yelled the cab driver.

"Elsie, wait!"

It was Henri. He took his hand off the hood, came around the side where I was sitting, and got in next to me, a bottle of wine tucked in his jacket.

"What are you doing?" I asked.

"Drive," he said to the driver. "Sorry, but you can't leave me with them."

I wondered what that must be like. Knowing your dad was cheating on your mom would be hard enough, but watching it take place must be even harder. I thought again about what Philippe had said about "labels" and couldn't help but think that those labels—mother, father, husband, wife—were supposed to mean something. I bet they meant something to Henri's mother, and judging by the dark look on his face, I was sure they meant something to him, too.

"Let's take you home first. I'll take the taxi from there," he said as he rolled down his window and let his hand hang out, catching the wind. He was sitting far away, and he made no attempt to close the gap between us.

"Henri, are you okay?" I asked, but he didn't answer. He just continued to stare out the window, opening and closing his hand as we drove back to the apartment in silence.

"Sixteen dollars," said the cab driver when we arrived at Dalewood.

I reached into my purse, but Henri put his hand on my arm.

"I got it."

"Thanks. Well, have a good night." I started to get out. But Henri was already out, opening the door for me.

"Elsie. I want you to know I'm glad we met. You are...

nothing like your mother," he said, looking me the straight in the eye.

But I was like her in some ways, wasn't I? I had just kissed her lover, his father, or rather he had kissed me, but I had let him and now I felt terrible. The cab was still running, but Henri hadn't made a move to return to the car, and I hadn't made a move to go inside. We just stared at each other, waiting.

"Do you want to come up?" The question was out of my mouth before I had time to consider it. He nodded, gave the cab driver twenty dollars, and followed me inside.

We rode the elevator up and didn't speak until we were in the apartment.

"This is it," I said. I was standing still in the dark, my back to him. He put his hand around my waist and kissed my neck. I let my purse drop from my shoulder as his hands moved across my breasts and over my belly and between my legs. My body had been like a live wire all evening, and finally it had an outlet. Henri's breathing was ragged. I could hear myself gasp, and when he slipped his hands under the waistband of my skirt and into my underwear, I gave myself over. My knees felt weak, and he held me up against him, pressing himself into me until I thought I would collapse. Then he gently lowered us both to the ground and turned me to face him.

Quickly we removed our clothes, and then he was naked against me. His skin was hot and sticky, and his hair smelled like nicotine and spices. The whole room was spinning; it was happening so fast, and I felt lost and wonderful all at the same time, and when he wrapped my legs around him, I pulled one leg back and placed my foot on his chest.

"Wait, I...."

"Shit, of course." He fished in his jean pockets on the floor, pulled out a condom, put it on, and before I knew it he was inside of me. I felt the carpet burn against my skin but didn't want to say anything, so I grabbed my skirt and put it under me. He was fast and intense, and I closed my mouth around his arm to stop myself from screaming out.

When he was done he collapsed onto his side, and I listened as his breathing slowly returned to normal. It felt like ages before either of us said anything.

"Are you okay?" he asked.

"Uh-huh."

"Are you sure?"

"Yes." I lay still and moved my hand around the carpet, trying to find any piece of clothing to cover myself. I found my shirt and placed it on top of me.

"Elsie, was that your first time?"

I cringed in the dark. "Yes."

I heard him sigh heavily. As I moved to get up, he pulled me back down and spooned me tightly toward him.

"I didn't know. I wouldn't have...."

"Why? There has to be a first time sometime."

"Yes. But...."

"What?"

He turned me to face him. "But...but I hope it's not the last time," he said quietly, his forehead against mine. It wasn't a question, it held no promise of anything, and yet something inside me told me that whatever this was, it wasn't over.

CHAPTER NINE

The doorbell rang and I nearly jumped out of my chair, dropping Shadow out of my lap in the process. I needed to post a sign somewhere that read, *I've just been through a traumatic experience, please exercise caution with loud noises and sudden movements.* It was probably Ted, coming by to check up on me. I'd gotten him worrying again, although I'm not sure that he ever stopped. The ringing continued, and I wondered why he didn't just use his key to the front door to come inside. I looked out the window, but it gave me only a view to the side and back of the house. I waited for the ringing to stop and when it didn't, I went downstairs.

"Who is it?" I asked.

"Elspeth? Elspeth Brennan?"

I froze. Someone had my first name right, but I had stopped using Ted's last name when we got divorced.

"Are you Elspeth Brennan?"

"Who wants to know?" I asked, my shaky voice betraying my nerves.

"Your taxi's here."

I opened the door a crack, wishing it had a peep hole, and peeked through, keeping the chain on. A man in a dark wool hat stood on the front step, and a yellow cab was parked in front of the house.

"I didn't call a taxi."

"Well somebody named Elspeth Brennan did. I just go where the dispatch tells me." He shrugged his shoulders, keeping his head tilted downward.

"You've got the wrong person and the wrong house."

"Shit, I'm sorry. It's probably just a stupid prank. Could I come in and use your phone for a second?" He moved toward the door, and I could make out the color of his pale skin and his sharp chin and cheekbones.

"Sorry, but I can't let you in."

"Please, it's freezing out here. I'll just be a minute." He smiled widely, placing his gloved hand in the doorframe. "If I don't call dispatch, they'll kill me."

"Why can't you call from your car?"

"Radio's broken."

Our eyes met, and the smile slipped off his face. If it was broken, how could he get the call with my address? He shot his gloved hand through the door and up toward the chain, but I slammed it hard and heard him scream. I slammed it again and again, and when he pulled it out, I bolted the door and ran upstairs to call the police, my whole body shaking as I asked for Officer Dixon.

"We won't find any prints, 'cause he was wearing gloves,"

said Officer Dixon after taking my statement, "but we got a pretty good description, so we'll do our best."

"It doesn't sound promising," I said, standing in the doorway to see him out.

"It's not. But the good news is, not only did you see his face but you crushed his hand, so it's unlikely he'll be back."

"You think the two incidents are connected?"

"Don't you?"

I nodded.

"It seems to me that someone is looking for something…do you have any idea what it could be?"

I shook my head. What could I say? That there was a box of secrets, and apparently my mother had died not once but twice, the first time in a fire? Or should I tell him about the ring that was appraised for $150,000? If it really was a family heirloom, I didn't want to risk having to give it up.

"You might feel better if you have someone come and stay with you. Is there anyone you can call?"

Ten minutes later I was dialing Ted's home number. I told myself that I wasn't just calling about me; someone had tried to break into his home, and I was sure he'd want to know.

"Hello? Anyone there?" I asked.

Somebody had picked up the receiver but hadn't said anything. I looked at the clock on the wall. It was past 1:00 a.m.; too late to call, but I needed to talk to him.

"Stop it." Julie's voice came in a whisper.

"Julie? It's me, Elspeth. I need to talk to Ted, someone—"

"I said, stop it." She spoke slowly, her voice stern. "Do you have any idea how long it took him to get over you? Years. Not weeks, not months, years. He's finally getting on with his life, we're finally moving forward, and then you reappear and act like you need him. And just like that, he's back where he was, wondering if he made a mistake letting you go."

"I'm sorry, I didn't mean to—"

"Honey, who is it?"

I heard Ted in the background, his voice groggy and far away.

"It's no one. Go back to bed babe, I'll be there in a minute." She was silent for a moment. "You can't do it to him again, Elspeth. You can't," she said and hung up.

Until recently Ted and I had only stayed in touch with the occasional letter and well-timed phone call that would go straight to our answering machines. I'd talked to him more in the last few weeks than I had in the last few years. My mother's death had opened up the floodgates that I was normally able to keep closed and, with them, the door to my heart that I had shut when we broke up. I missed him. But Julie was right, it wasn't fair to come back into Ted's life.

I put on the kettle and picked the sympathy card off the top of the fridge that Arden had dropped off at Dalewood for me. We hadn't been in touch in decades, but she had seen the obituary notice in the paper and wanted to extend her sympathies. She knew how hard it was to lose a parent, no matter what the relationship. Her own mother had died of pancreatic cancer when she was seventeen, and Arden had never stopped missing her. She wrote in the card that I was in her thoughts and signed it with love. There was no phone number to call her if I wanted to talk, no false insistence that we should get together when I was in town, and I was grateful. Although I would have loved to talk to the Arden that was my best friend the summer I turned sixteen when we planned to run away, I was smart to enough to know that those days were long gone. Too much had happened on that tour to pretend we could ever go back. And too much had happened to me since.

The kettle boiled, and Shadow hissed at the noise and jumped out of my arms. I made myself a cup of instant cocoa with marshmallows from a packet that I found at the bottom of a tea tin and sat in the chair by the window. It was snowing again, and everything was covered in a soft blue-white blanket that glowed in the dark under the city's lights. I tried to imagine what Arden might look like now, but I couldn't. I'd even stopped myself from asking Vincent, deciding it was better to remember her the way she was that morning she picked me up. The morning we left Toronto with the intention of starting our lives over together.

Arden got herself a boyfriend within the first week of our tour. And although she always tried to include me in their late-night drink fests back at his room with the other dancers, I'd excuse myself and stay up late writing to Henri. I'd started writing him wherever I went. Nothing much at first, just little postcards I picked up in the lobby of whatever motel we were staying at. I found myself thinking about him, about the night we had spent together, about how much he was able to say and how few words it had taken him to do so. In the silences we shared, I felt as if full conversations existed that neither of us needed to voice.

I'd look for the cheesiest postcards, pictures of the cities we were in with rainbow writing on the front that said things like "Greetings from Sunny Buffalo," and on the back I'd write something like *It really is the sunniest! Until next time.... Cheers, E.* The only problem was that I had no address to send them to. Like me, Henri was on the road, traveling with his father. But that didn't stop me from buying them and writing on them, and soon I had a little collection that I tied with an elastic band and kept at the bottom of my suitcase. After the first few weeks of touring, the postcards turned into letters, and it wasn't long until I was using up all the cheap stationery found in every room.

The boys on the tour were fun, but there was something about Henri that was different, older, sadder—something in him I recognized as being the same as me, that I didn't see in the other boys. Arden was like us too, but she seemed determined to drink and fuck the sadness over losing her mother out of herself, and who was I to tell her not to? I wished I could, but something in me was different now, and besides, drinking too much always gave me the blues the next day. Under the polyester coverlets that were on the bed of every budget motel, I'd sit with my knees to my chest and pour my heart out on paper. I wrote to Henri about my mother, how I wished I knew who my father was, how I was excited to be running away, and scared, and how one day I wanted to have my own dance company and be a choreographer. And after every show I'd give him a review of our performance. His letters became my unofficial diary, and I often caught myself simultaneously experiencing something and crafting a sentence in my head about it that I could use later.

"We're at the halfway mark, can you believe it?" said Arden, grabbing one of the little bottles from the minibar.

"No, I can't," I lied. It felt longer than halfway. I looked around the motel room and was reminded once again of how they all looked the same: cheap wall-to-wall carpeting, multicolored polyester bedspreads, and poorly framed pictures of sunsets and flower arrangements. I'd planned to use my mother's camera to take pictures of the places we stayed, but one room began to blur into another, so I documented the theaters instead. I thought Arden and I could frame them and hang them in our first apartment, when we got one.

I couldn't wait until we had a place of our own. Living out of a suitcase and sleeping in lumpy beds with scratchy sheets had lost its charm quicker than I thought it would. It wasn't that I wanted to go home, it's just I never felt settled in any bed and had begun to wonder if I would ever feel at home anywhere. It was an anxiety that was starting to grow in me, and I didn't dare share it with Arden, who was having the time of her life and already mourning the end of the tour, which was still a month away. I didn't want to do or say anything to jeopardize our plan of running away.

"Soon, we'll be starting our own tour," I said, peeling off my leotard and tights and heading for the bath. "Mind if I go first?"

"No, go ahead, I need a drink. My ankle is killing me."

I looked at Arden's ankle, which was still twice the size it normally was. Three nights earlier she'd gone over on it and there had been a loud snap. I'd watched her face turn white and beads of sweat form on her upper lip. She had kept dancing, and at the end of the performance, after taking her bow, she had hurried offstage and thrown up in the wings. She'd been icing it whenever she was offstage, but the swelling kept returning, and I worried she may have fractured it.

"You still don't want to get it checked out?" I asked while running the bathtub and filling it with Epsom salts.

"Nah, fuck it. It'll heal, just a pulled tendon, I'm sure. Besides, there isn't any time. We don't get another break for a week."

"You could take a night off and just rest it. Let me step in."

"Sorry, but I'm not giving up my solo," she said, downing the little bottle of vodka and going for another.

"It's just one night; if you don't take care of it, it could get worse," I said while easing my bruised body into the hot tub. It wasn't just that I was Arden's understudy and would love a chance to dance her part. I really was worried that she was going to do some serious damage.

"I'll be fine," she said, standing in the doorway. She

leaned against the frame, picking at the label.

"What is it?"

"I called my dad today."

"And?"

"And I could hear Marla in the background calling him to come watch some stupid show."

"Shit. Sorry."

"I know. Bitch really lives there now," she said, coming into the bathroom and sitting with her back against the opposite wall. "My mother would roll over in her grave if she knew Dad had shacked up with the neighborhood hussy." She took a swig out of the little bottle, nearly finishing it. "They should make these bigger."

"They do."

"Right."

"Maybe he's just really lonely, Arden. I'm sure that's all it is."

"We're all lonely," she said, tossing the empty bottle into the trash and pulling another out of her pocket. "What about you?"

"What about me?" I answered quickly, worried that she was going to mention Henri.

"You called your mom lately?"

"Nope."

"You should. She might be a twat, but at least she's still alive," she said, steadying herself against the wall. "Hurry up—we're all going out tonight and you're coming with us."

I ducked my head under the tub and groaned. I had told my mother I would call her every week on tour, but a week had quickly turned into two. I expected that I could go the whole tour without calling her and she wouldn't care. Shit. I was going to have to call her now. Arden wanted me to feel bad and it worked. What if she was worried? It didn't have to be a long conversation; I'd just call and let her know I was okay.

"Bathroom's all yours," I said, wrapping a towel around me and draining the tub.

I waited until Arden closed the door and I heard the water running before picking up the phone and dialing my mom.

"Hello?"

"Oh, sorry, I think I have the wrong number."

"Elsie?"

"Yes."

"It's Philippe. How are you?"

Philippe. My skin turned cold, and I pulled my towel closer around me.

"Fine, I'm fine." I could hear my mother in the background asking who he was talking to.

"It's Elsie, darling."

"What are you doing there?" I asked.

"I'm staying with your mother," he said, and then he whispered, "Why, does that make you jealous?"

My jaw dropped, but nothing came out. After a moment I heard my mother enter the room and take the phone.

"Hello?"

"Hi, Mom."

"Is everything all right?" She sounded irritated.

"Yes, I was just calling to check in."

"Oh. I see. Well, if nothing is wrong I have to get going; we're having a big meeting tonight with some new members."

"I didn't know Philippe was still in Toronto," I said.

"Well, he just got back. We were in Montreal before then."

"I didn't know," I repeated, realizing for the first time that my mother was off having adventures of her own while I was gone.

"Why would you?" She paused, leaving a silence that neither of us knew how to fill. "Well, we better go, we have to pick up Henri from the hotel."

"What hotel?"

"The Hilton. Why does it…I really have to go now, Elspeth."

"Sure, okay, well, take care."

"Yes, you too," she said, and hung up.

I sat on the bed, stunned. Jealous? What kind of game did he think he was playing? Jealous of my mother and Philippe playing house? The thought of it turned my stomach, and just for a brief moment I let myself wonder what it would be like if I was still there. Would he try to steal kisses when she wasn't looking? Would he sneak into the shower and watch me wash? Would he pull back the curtain, place his hands on me, and demand that I kiss him? My face turned hot and my heart started to beat faster. He'd never get the chance to find out. I wasn't going home. *I* was leaving *them*. If I was jealous, it was because my mother was acting like a teenager instead of a woman who was having an affair with a married man, when I was the one who was supposed to be having the adventure, not her.

I dialed the front desk and had the operator give me the number for the Hilton Toronto. It was thirty minutes from my mother's apartment; hopefully Henri was still in the room. I waited as the phone rang and rang and then just as I was about to hang up, he answered.

"Hello?"

"Henri, it's me, Elsie."

We talked right up until my mother and Philippe arrived and he had to go downstairs to meet them. He told me how the Seekers had been gathering new members and how his father was pleased with how much money the Toronto chapter had raised in donations and how he had insisted on returning, as there was more gold to mine. He said his father had found another girlfriend, a young one living in Montreal, and he was keeping her secret from my mother. He said he wondered if getting a real job wouldn't have been easier after all and if he'd ever get back home to Paris. He sounded similar to the way he had when we'd chatted in the alley out behind the restaurant, only faster, his words fueled with an urgency I hadn't heard before. He barely stopped to take a breath, and I wondered if he'd been drinking. I let him do all the talking, his angry rambling mirroring feelings of my own. There was company in our misery. I waited until he was done to tell him about the letters. He wanted to read them, and he told me to send them to a member of the Seekers, someone in charge of collecting Philippe's letters and forwarding them to Henri. I'd mail them with no return address, because we were still on the road. It was a one-sided correspondence, but I didn't think of it that way. As far as I was concerned, someone was out there, for a change, listening to me. I could pour my heart out without worrying how it was going to be received; there was no interruption, no fear of recrimination, just a journal that would be read by someone who I felt understood me. By the end of the conversation Henri's anger had subsided and his tone was reassuring and comforting, and we decided that when we got to New York, he'd come and visit me.

By the time we reached Washington, Arden had practically moved into her boyfriend Ramon's room. It wasn't that she'd planned to, it was just where she passed out from partying after each performance. Every morning she'd sneak back down the hall to our room to shower and change, and we'd walk to rehearsals together. If the tour manager knew what was happening, she didn't let on. It seemed everyone was expected to hook up with someone while on the road, and so far I seemed to be the only person who had chosen a one-sided relationship with a French pen pal who was roaming the continent. My alarm had just gone off when I heard Arden throwing up in the bathroom.

"Jesus, how much did you drink last night?" I groaned, turning on the light beside my bed.

"Not this much," she said, flushing the toilet.

"Gross, light a match or something, it stinks," I said, plugging my nose and going into the bathroom to get my toothbrush.

"Sorry," said Arden, grabbing a pack of matches.

"You look like shit," I said. It was true; this was the worst I'd seen her. I knew I should ask if she needed anything, but I was pissed. This wasn't what we'd planned when we talked about going on tour together, and yet I didn't want to be a total bitch about the fact that she had a real boyfriend and I didn't.

"No kidding," said Arden, retching again into the toilet.

"What's the matter with Ramon's room—you couldn't throw up there?" I said, brushing my teeth.

"Sorry if my being sick is interrupting your morning," she said, wiping her face. "Fuck, Elsie, what's your problem?"

"My problem is that you're only ever here to shower and shit, and the rest of the time you're off with Ramon, and it kind of sucks. We were supposed to be on this adventure together, remember?" I spat out my toothpaste and rinsed my mouth. My face felt hot, and I thought I might cry.

"I remember. I guess I just figured you were fine sharing it with Henri."

I turned around to face Arden, who was sitting on the edge of the tub, slumped over.

"Excuse me?"

"Come on. That's who you've been writing all those letters to, isn't it?" Her tone was more hurt than accusatory, and I suddenly felt bad that I'd kept it a secret from her. I'd done it on purpose, although I hadn't meant to hurt her feelings. It was just that I loved having something that was all mine. Henri wasn't like any of the guys I knew, and our relationship made me feel special.

"How did you know?"

"Elsie, it wasn't only your mom that you were talking to that day, and that's fine. I just don't know why you had to keep it from me. I guess I'm not as cool or mature as he is. I guess none of us are."

"That's not true. I just…I don't know." I sat on the toilet next to her. "I feel like he gets it, you know? I mean, we both have this thing with our parents. And I feel like no matter what I say or how terrible it is, he's not going to think badly of me, or tell me how lucky I am that at least I still have a mother." I looked at Arden, who looked down and nodded. "I'm sorry, I shouldn't have kept it from you."

"I shouldn't have ditched you for Ramon. I could've asked. I knew something was up with you, but I didn't want to deal with anything heavy. I just wanted to have fun."

"Well, it looks like you're doing a good job of that," I said, laughing slightly and reaching out for her hand.

"Yeah, well, that's about to end."

"Not for another two weeks. Then the world is our oyster. We can go anywhere from here."

"No, no, we can't Elsie."

"What do you mean? We're not going back, we're running away, remember? Look, Ramon can come too, if that's what you really want."

"I'm pregnant."

I let go of her hand and gripped the back side of the tub. I felt like I might fall backward if I didn't hold on.

"Oh my God. What are you going to do?"

"Quit drinking," said Arden, looking down.

"I'm serious, Arden." This wasn't any time to be joking.

If Arden was pregnant we needed to deal with it right away. If she was too sick to perform or if she started to show, she would get replaced, and how would she explain that when auditioning for new companies? I needed to come up with a plan for both of us. I started to pace the motel room while she went to sit on the bed. "I'll find a doctor, someone who can help us. How far along are you? Because if you can just finish the rest of the tour, then we can go back to Toronto and take care of it there and leave like we planned."

"Elsie...."

"Don't worry, we can do this. Ramon doesn't even have to know."

"He knows," said Arden, sitting down on the bed.

"Shit, okay, well it's your body, nobody can make that decision for you. I mean, you're only eighteen, you still have your whole future in front of you."

"I'm having it and I'm marrying Ramon."

I stopped pacing and turned to face her. My ears were ringing, and it was possible I hadn't heard her correctly, hadn't just heard my best friend tell me that the future we'd planned for months no longer included me.

"You're what?"

"I'm having the baby and I'm marrying Ramon." She was sitting on the edge of the bed, clutching a pillow and speaking softly.

"Really?"

"Really."

"So you're just going to throw it all away? Your whole career, everything we talked about, everything we planned?"

"I'm not throwing it away. I love Ramon, and I want to

have his baby." I could see that she was about to cry.

"Oh, now you *love* him? I thought he was just some guy you were fucking, but I guess now that you're knocked up, you love him," I shouted.

"Elsie...." Now she was crying.

"When were you going to tell me? The tour is over in two weeks. How do you know the thing isn't brain-damaged anyway? I mean, you drink like a fish!"

"I stopped when I found out. I'm not an idiot."

"No, I am," I said, grabbing my purse and heading for the door.

"I'm sorry," said Arden, crying as I ran out of the room.

The thought of going back to Toronto and playing second-class citizen to my mother, in the company of Philippe and his twisted mind games, was too much to bear. All those months of planning, counting down the days that I'd have to spend under my mother's roof until Arden and I could start our new lives together, it had all been for nothing. I hadn't had a breakup before and never thought that Arden would be my first. I assumed Ramon was a fling, and when the tour came to an end, she'd dump him and we'd go back to doing everything together. She knew how important she was to me. I'd never had a boyfriend, but I told myself that when I did, I wouldn't make the same mistake others made, that my mother made, and devote all my time to them and forget what was really important: my friendships. I believed that boyfriends come and go but girlfriends were forever. I'd made these decisions before I'd ever had to test them and had just assumed that my best friend, who loved me as much as I loved her, felt the same. And I was wrong. My mother never had any female friends; one time when I asked her why, she told me it was because women were competitive and selfish, and in the end they'd always just ditch you for some guy, so why bother? I hated it when she said things like that. And I hated it even more when I thought of her smugly singing *I told you so* at the way things had turned out.

Arden and I barely talked the last two weeks of the tour; she'd gone back to Ramon's room the day of our fight and had stayed there every night since. In two months some guy had managed to replace me, reducing our nine years of friendship to a placeholder in her heart. I was only there, it seemed, until someone more suitable and desirable came along. I'd been practice for the real thing. She sat with him on the bus and hung out with his friends, and when they weren't onstage, I'd see them holding hands in the wings. It looked like they were really in love after all, but I couldn't bring myself to tell her. I stuck to myself more and more, throwing myself into rehearsals and writing longer and longer letters to Henri that I mailed daily until I finally asked him to come out and see our last performance. He felt like the only person in the world I was still connected to, no matter how loose the connection. A well of sadness had begun to pool in me; it wasn't the first time it had happened, and I didn't want to talk about it, but I just wanted someone to recognize it. And I knew that someone was Henri. I left a single ticket for him at the box office and would meet him after. Some of the other dancers had friends or family members coming, but I never thought to ask anyone but him. I needed to see him and I needed him to see me, see what I did and who I really was when I was my best and truest self, dancing onstage.

Our last performance was at Judson Memorial Church in Greenwich Village, a beautiful stone building that had recently become a haven for artists and a home to some of the most innovative choreographers in modern dance. It was a huge honor to perform there and was supposed to be the highlight of the trip; it was also the end of the tour and, for Arden and myself, the beginning of our lives. We had talked about it for months. Imagining what our first apartment would be like, what we would do with our free time, and how it would feel to come home every day to a place that was ours. A place where we were appreciated and belonged. Looking back, it hadn't been a very well-thought-out plan, and I doubt that either Arden or I would have made it past a month or two; our money would have run out, and as Canadian citizens, we would have had to work under the table. But that still didn't do anything to lessen the sting of a dream crushed before it had even been given a chance.

We were rehearsing a few hours before our final performance when it happened: a loud crack, followed by a thud. I stopped mid-pirouette to see Arden go down. It was her ankle, the one that she hadn't had looked at since she first hurt it. She was writhing on the floor in pain and looked as if she might throw up.

"Arden!" Ramon rushed over to her side and held her. "Are you okay?" He looked at her, his face crumpling, and I knew that he wasn't just thinking about her ankle, but about the baby, and I felt terrible.

"It's only my ankle. I'll be fine," she said. She tried to stand on it but cried out and fell back down, her face white and slick with sweat.

I wanted to rush over, to sling her arm around my shoulder and help Ramon lift her, but my legs wouldn't budge. Ramon was in charge, and Arden wrapped her arms around him like a life jacket as he hoisted her up.

"What happened?" he asked.

"I lost my balance. I'm just really dizzy, you know?" she whispered as Madame Gitard, the artistic director of the company, came closer.

"Let's see how bad it is," said Madame Gitard. She turned it one way and then the next, and Arden screamed. "It looks like you've broken it. You'll have to go the hospital, you can't dance on this."

"But it's our final show," said Arden, crying.

"I'm sorry, Arden, but you can't even stand on it." She called over her assistant and told her to take Arden to the hospital. "Elsie, you'll have to do Arden's solo."

"What?" My mouth fell open. I had understudied Arden's part but had never performed it. Even though every time I had rehearsed it, I'd imagined myself standing onstage in front of a crowded house that leapt to its feet with thunderous applause when I was done, I didn't for a moment think I would ever get the chance. And now here it was, on our biggest night of the tour, in New York City.

"Come on, don't stand there, Elsie, let's get your understudy in your place and rehearse you in," she said, clapping her hands. "All right, everyone, no time to waste, we only have a few hours. Let's go!" Madame returned to her seat in the front row as we took our positions and the lighting and sound designers rushed to their booths. As the lights dimmed, I took a deep breath and took my place in the center of the stage, lunged deep, and opened my arms wide, just as I had seen Arden do every show for the last two and a half months. Looking down, I counted the bars of music until I heard my cue, and as the spotlight snapped onto me, I looked out and saw Arden watching me over her shoulder as she left.

It was our best show all tour. The house was sold out, and we got not one but two standing ovations. I danced Arden's solo knowing that it was the only chance I'd get, and everything I'd been holding in for all those months poured out of me and onto the stage. I felt electric; all rational thinking ceased when it came my turn to dance, my mind and body united by rhythm and movement and emotion. I moved with precision and abandonment, giving myself over completely to the dance, the music and me keeping time with each another. It was the closest thing to magic that I had ever experienced, and I was certain that not only was this all I'd ever wanted to do, but I was actually good enough to do it. At the curtain call as I held Ramon's hand for our final bows, I tried not to notice the despondent look on his face. I knew he was thinking about Arden, as I was. But the applause felt good and I let it wash over me, tickling my whole body. I scanned the audience for Henri. It was the first time I'd allowed myself to look out into the faces and see if his was among them. He was standing in the back row, applauding slowly, a sly smile on his face and a rose in his teeth. My heart began to pound, and if it wasn't for the hands of my company members on either side of me, I thought that I might float away.

Backstage, among hugs and kisses with the other dancers, we shook a bottle of champagne in the air and took turns passing it around. I didn't know what would happen for me next, but tonight I was really one of them, a member of the company who had earned their respect with the best performance of my career so far. I told myself to enjoy it, to savor it. It would all end tomorrow.

"Elsie, a moment," said Madame Gitard, signaling me over. I passed back the bottle of champagne and ran to her. I knew I wasn't supposed to be drinking.

"Sorry, Madame," I said, wiping my mouth and standing even straighter than I normally did around her. With her own ramrod-straight posture and broad shoulders, she had a way of making me feel like I was slouching when I wasn't. Even though she was in her fifties, Madame was all muscle and sinew. She was always dressed in a black leotard and wrap skirt, a shawl draped around her shoulders, her salt-and-pepper hair slicked back into a tight bun. Despite her age, she still looked every bit the dancer that she was once was. In her prime she had danced with Martha Graham and Merce Cunningham, and worked with just about every up-and-coming modern dance choreographer, and when her body failed her, as it eventually did every dancer, she moved into choreography and founded her own company. Hers was one of the few dance companies that managed to pay its dancers a living wage and was invited to perform all over the world. I idolized her, and yet I had barely said more than "Yes, Madame" the entire year and a half that I had been studying with her.

"You did great tonight, Elsie."

"Thank you Madame, I did my best," I said, trying to stand still under her piercing stare.

"I could tell. You still want it, unlike some others who have it and have forgotten what a privilege that is."

"I think we all want it, Madame," I said, looking down at my feet.

"But we can't all have it. That's the way it goes." She paused and leaned in closer. "I know you are only sixteen, and I would never tell you to quit school, but if you wanted to continue with this company in the fall, there may be a spot open for you. We'll have to see what happens with some of the other dancers."

"Do you mean Arden?"

"I know you're friends and she's been through a lot, but I'm afraid she has spent too much time having a good time this summer. But she does have seniority, so we'll have to see if she changes her ways this fall."

"She won't be around this fall." The words were out of my mouth before I knew it.

"And why is that?" Madame Gitard leaned forward, her gaze burrowing into me.

I stared back silently. I wanted nothing more than to be

a member of the company, but not like this.

"I asked you a question."

I was trapped: betray Arden or defy Madame? But hadn't Arden betrayed me first, when she decided to abandon our plans and marry Ramon?

"She's pregnant," I whispered.

I watched as she took a sharp intake of breath, stared off into the distance, and nodded.

"I see. Well, what do you know—we won't have to wait after all." She took a moment to compose herself and then spoke. "I really think you could be a principal performer if you did this full time, Elsie. You've got a gift, but the choice is yours. If you are interested, you could do your studies while on the road and get your diploma that way." She let the offer hang in the air for a moment and then put her hand on my shoulder.

"Think about it. I only ask once." And then she turned and left to go to the reception that was being held for us in the lobby.

I stood for a moment, letting it all sink in. The idea of going on tour full time and not going back to my mother and Philippe was a dream come true. I looked back at the other dancers for a moment and tried to imagine myself as one of them. Before tonight I would never have dreamed such a thing.

"Elsie, come on, we don't want to keep our fans waiting!" joked Antoine, one of the lead dancers. He waited for me to join their small group, and I rushed over to him. It was the first time I had been singled out to join the core group of dancers that made up the heart of the company, and it felt good.

"That's what I'm talking about, Two Shoes! Great show," he said, squeezing my hand and giving me a big smile.

I felt like I could burst with joy. Antoine was nice to all the dancers, but he didn't give out compliments easily, and when he did, everyone noticed. The most gifted dancer in the company aside from Arden, he was also the most popular. He had an easygoing personality and a quick sense of humor that made people like him instantly. But it was his talent that made everyone respect him. When I first started studying with the company he had affectionately given me the nickname Two Shoes, as in Goody Two-shoes, because I tried so hard and did everything by the book. *You're not gonna be great unless you let go a little and make mistakes. You got lots of time to get it right, but you only get a few chances to get it wrong.* It was the first piece of advice I'd ever gotten that wasn't from a friend like Arden or a teacher like Madame Gitard, but from a *colleague*. And the very idea that Antoine saw me that way opened up the possibility that I could one day be more than just another student of the company. I took his advice to heart and pushed myself to take risks in class where I could, so when the time came to prove myself I'd be ready. I'd been ready when Madame asked me to step in for Arden, and it meant a lot to me that he had noticed.

"Thanks Antoine."

"All right, people, we're in New York City. Let's celebrate!" he said, and we hurried offstage to get ready.

I changed as quickly as I could, peeling off my dance clothes and using baby wipes to wipe myself down. There were never showers at any of our venues, and we all did the best we could to wash in sinks with rough paper towels and cheap hand soap until we got back to our rooms and could bathe. Whoever brought perfume would pass it around, and we'd all spritz ourselves in whatever it was, whether it was intended for men or women. We laughed that we smelled like we all worked at the same cologne counter, and tonight I felt part of the laughter. I took my hair out of my bun, pulled a black slip that I wore as a dress over my head, and tied a scarf around my waist. A swipe of lipstick and I was out the door to meet Henri. My stomach must've done twenty flips from the change room to the lobby. A moment of ice-cold panic hit me as I wondered if Henri might have left. Surely something had to go wrong; the night had gone too well, and my mother had always taught me to be ready for the dark clouds that were on the edge of every blue sky.

I looked out into the crowd of proud parents and friends hugging the other dancers, arms full of flowers and faces full of pride, and tried to find the one face that I longed to see. Henri. He had stayed. He was leaning in the open doorway, his back to the crowd, smoking. He wasn't looking over his shoulder or glancing at his watch. He was just taking long, slow drags off his cigarette and staring into the night.

"Thanks for coming," I said, walking up next to him. I wanted to reach out and grab him. He was wearing all black, a thrift-store jacket and jeans and a button-down shirt that was opened low. His skin was tanned, and his dark gray eyes widened when he saw me.

"Thanks for the invite," he said, tossing his cigarette into the street and handing me a single red rose. He leaned in close and kissed my neck, and I smelled red wine on him. His face was warm, and his stubble tickled my skin and gave me goosebumps. "Congratulations," he said, picking his plastic glass of wine up from the front steps and raising it to me. "They'd only let me take one, so we'll have to share."

"I better not, not here," I said, looking back at Madame Gitard.

"Ah, right. Of course," he said, finishing half the glass.

"Did you want to meet the other dancers?" I asked, tugging at the scarf around my waist.

"Did you want me to?"

"No. I don't know. I just...." I had no idea what I'd been expecting, but it wasn't as awkward as this. I reached out and put my hand on his chest and was relieved when he wrapped his hands around my waist and buried his face in my hair.

"Elsie."

I felt my whole body sigh as he said my name, and for the first time since seeing him, I felt completely sure of my decision to invite him. I squeezed him back, and when we pulled apart we were both smiling.

"Let me say goodbye to everyone," I said, rushing inside.

"Well, well, well, looks like someone's been keeping a secret," said Antoine, sizing up Henri. Antoine pursed his lips and nodded appreciatively, making me blush.

"Oh, he's just a really good friend."

"Why?"

"Why what?"

"Why is he *just* a friend?"

My cheeks burned, and I heard myself start to stammer an explanation, but Antoine just laughed and threw his arm around my shoulder. I looked at the other dancers who stood around him, saw they were smiling at me too, and I relaxed. I was in on the joke. It was still a new feeling to me, to be included, and I liked it.

"Girl, I'm just teasing you. But I take it you've got your own celebration to attend to," he said, and he started swiveling his hips, making everyone laugh as I playfully swatted his arm.

I looked back at Henri, who gave me a little wave and smiled seductively. He really was sexy. I'd always thought so, but it felt good to have everyone else see it too.

"Okay, okay, have a great night everyone," I said, giving quick hugs and making my exit.

On my way out I promised Madame Gitard I would be back by curfew. The trip didn't officially end until tomorrow, and tonight I was still obligated to abide by the tour's rules. I saw Ramon on the pay phone, and knew I should ask about Arden but didn't want to burst the bubble the evening had created. Besides, if I accepted Madame Gitard's offer, it would be Arden's place I'd be taking. As Madame had said, the spotlight wouldn't accommodate everyone, and for each person who crowded to the center of its light, a few more would be pushed into the darkness. Arden was in the dark now, and I didn't want to be the one to tell her.

I grabbed Henri's hand and skipped down the steps with him and out into the Village. The air was thick and sticky, the night bringing no relief to the humid August heat. We'd been outside only moments and my dress was already sticking to my back and legs, outlining every inch of my body. Henri looked at me and smiled, and I felt naked and comfortable under his gaze. Dancing all summer and doing quick changes backstage in front of the other dancers had cured me of being self-conscious. Like every dancer, I was still critical of the way I looked, but my nakedness was much more matter-of-fact now than it had ever been, and it felt good to be in my body. There was also so little of my body to feel self-conscious about. I felt strong and light, and this newfound freedom from weight was dangerously intoxicating.

"You are at your happiest on that stage, aren't you?" asked Henri.

"I am," I admitted. "I am happiest when I am dancing, but you know that."

"I do," he said. "I got the letters."

The letters. I had shared so much with him through those letters, more than I'd ever told anyone. He knew about Arden and Ramon and the baby. He knew how upset I was that I was going to have to go back to Toronto and live with my mother. It was nice not to have to explain everything. He knew who I was, and even though our communication had been fairly one-sided, I felt like I knew him too.

"Madame Gitard offered me Arden's spot in the company. I feel terrible for Arden, but I want it so badly."

"It's good to want something."

"Even if it means that someone else loses something?"

"Isn't that usually the way?" He looked at me sideways, and I immediately thought of kissing his father and how I had to admit to myself that I had wanted to so badly because it meant that it would be one less kiss that my mother would get from Philippe. My face flushed, and I was relieved that I was shielded by the night.

"Do you think I should do it?" I asked. I wanted him to say yes. I mean, it wasn't as if I pushed Arden to break her ankle, and it certainly wasn't my fault she had gotten pregnant. But wasn't getting pregnant consequence enough? I told myself Arden would do the same thing if she had a chance. Opportunities like the one Madame had offered me didn't come around often. Still, I wondered what she'd say when she found out I was the one replacing her. I couldn't think about that.

"I think you are very talented and very lucky to have something you're so good at. Most people don't have that, but everybody wants to."

I knew we were talking about him now. He had spent the year following around his father, who was sure he'd found his calling. But what was Henri's calling?

"I think everyone has something they're good at. It might just take them longer to find it," I said, trying to keep my voice light.

Henri stopped, tilted his head, and looked me straight in the eye.

"This is what you believe?"

"Don't you?"

"No. Some people lead, some people follow, some people are seekers, and some wander life aimlessly, never knowing what they should be doing."

"I think that's sad."

"That's because you have found something you love, and you're good at it. And you should do it." He held my chin up and looked at me. His eyes were framed with dark circles that I hadn't seen before. "We should celebrate!" he said, slapping his hands so loudly that his whole body shook, and along with it, his somber mood.

"Okay."

"I want to take you somewhere."

"Anywhere. I've never been to New York."

"Well, then it will be easy to impress you," he said with a laugh, grabbing my hand.

I had no idea where we were walking, and I loved it. I thought of how only a few months ago, I had imagined exploring the city with Arden, and instead here I was with Henri. Nothing had happened how I pictured it, and I realized that I felt much older after a few months of being on the road. In truth I'd never really felt all that young. Philippe had been right when he called me an old soul. I may not have described myself that way, but I'd always felt that I looked at the world through older eyes. In my mind I wasn't sixteen, or twenty, or thirty. I didn't know what the correct age was to describe the weariness and caution with which I had always viewed my world, and it was always a shock to look in the mirror and see a young face staring back at me. Maybe it was because my mother had refused to mother me, or maybe it was because she had kept secrets and shared half-truths from the time I was young. Whatever it was, I always breathed easier around people who were at least a few years older than I was. Henri had eight years on me, and although he may have noticed it, I felt we were the same.

We found a table at a popular Indian restaurant. The place was tiny, maybe twenty tables, and all of them were occupied by couples sharing food and straining to see each other in the dim glow of twinkly lights and tea candles that lit up the place. The smells were wonderful, and the second we were seated I felt the bottom of my stomach open wide in anticipation. We ordered some naan bread and chutney right away and Henri had the waiter open the bottle of red wine that he'd bought at the corner store. Nobody here seemed to care that I was sixteen, and I wondered if that was because I didn't look my age or if it was because they just assumed that I was the same age as Henri.

"To a great ending and an even better beginning," he said, pouring us each a large water glass full of wine.

I smiled and sipped my wine, knowing how quickly alcohol went to my head these days. If I didn't eat something soon, I'd be drunk halfway through the glass. It was nice to be a cheap drunk, but I wanted the night to last, and I wanted to remember it as it was happening. Once again, we were together on a night when my whole life was about to change. I didn't know at the time that it would be the thing that would define us, these brief, intense encounters that would mark milestones that we would witness for each other. I noticed how much quieter Henri was without a crowd around to entertain. It was as if the Henri I had met that night, the life of the party, was a role he'd been playing. I had suspected as much that night he got into the cab, and later at my mother's apartment, but I saw it again now that I was sober.

He ran one hand through his hair and slouched over his menu while the other hand absentmindedly made its way across the table and intertwined with mine. I smiled and hooked my hand through his and allowed myself to just stare at him. His fingers were stained yellow from nicotine, and his nails were rough and dry. He had shaved fairly recently, although a shadow of stubble made him look even sexier. Unlike his father, who was intense and crisp in his appearance, his posture perfect and his movements direct, Henri seemed rough around the edges, his shoulders stooped, his clothes always slightly rumpled, and he looked like he could use a shower. I knew this look; it was the result of having an obsessive, domineering parent. You either competed with them for attention or gave up. I had picked the latter. I'd been hiding in my mother's shadow forever and had been lucky enough to find Henri there, although tonight I felt as if I had stepped out of her shadow and wasn't going back. It wasn't until the waiter arrived that either of us said anything, and when he did, I just told Henri to go ahead and order, as I was so hungry, I'd eat anything.

The food arrived quickly, a selection of curries, dahls, and chutneys, and I loaded up my plate. My hands shook as I stuffed forkful after forkful into my mouth, and it was a few minutes before I was able to take a deep breath, my blood sugar slowly returning to normal, my heart no longer racing.

"Sorry. I waited too long to eat," I said, wiping up the mango chutney with a piece of hot naan and taking a bite.

"The whole summer, it looks like," said Henri. "A few more weeks and you could've mailed yourself in a letter."

I laughed and took a sip of my wine. I had nothing witty to say back; I was too flattered that he noticed. There was no way I wasn't going to lose weight on the tour, dancing every day and rehearsing, but being in a leotard all day around other dancers had a way of resetting what was normal and what wasn't. It was normal to push your body to the limit on little more than fruit and coffee and cigarettes. It was normal to stand in front of the mirror and measure yourself before a performance and then after. In our world we needed to be strong, but we also needed to be light, and nobody was going to judge you for not eating or taking laxatives or throwing up. I hadn't done anything so far but skip meals and drink coffee when I was hungry, but it was working, and with each new bone that pushed a little closer to the surface of my skin, I'd receive a knowing nod of approval from one of the other dancers. I would have been lying to myself if I didn't admit I liked the growing attention. Tonight I'd received more attention than I had the whole tour, and it felt good.

"I'm glad I could see you before I left," said Henri.

"Where are you going?"

"Home," he said, refilling his glass.

"To Paris?"

"Yes."

"I don't leave until the morning Elsie," said Henri gently, laying his hand over mine.

I hadn't meant for him to see my disappointment. I was surprised, and yet a part of me knew that I would see him for just this one night. "Does your father know?"

"No. But he will tonight when he gets the letter I left him." He swirled his glass and smiled to himself, the smile of someone sticking it to someone else.

"Won't he make you go back to school or get a real job?" I pushed my plate a little farther away and drank more wine.

"Not if he wants me to keep my mouth shut about..." he stopped himself and shook his head.

"My mother."

"All the women," he said, looking at his plate and avoiding my eyes.

Although I didn't relish the idea of my mother being the mistress of a married man, I especially disliked the idea of her being just one of many.

"Why are you telling me this now?" I asked. It was a fair question: why now, if this had been their arrangement all along?

"Because..." he stopped, took a long drink of his wine, and sighed before reaching across the table and taking my hand. "Because although I can be and have been like him, I don't want to actually be him when I get older. I don't want to lie, and I don't want to keep his secrets anymore."

"You aren't like him." I squeezed his hand back with

one hand, and with the other I reached across the table and touched his mouth, letting him kiss my fingers.

"He is a powerful man, and he has the potential to bring the Seekers a lot of money with his followers, but a lot of power for one man is a dangerous thing, no?"

"Yes." I had never heard of my mother giving any money away, but then again, she wouldn't tell me if she had. I'd always had a part-time babysitting job so I wouldn't have to ask her for money when I needed it.

"What kind of money are you talking about?"

"The kind of money to travel around the world, dine in fine restaurants, and stay in nice hotels. It's still pretty small-time, but it's a good gig if you can get it." He saw my face and could tell I didn't find it very funny.

"What about the center?"

"Yes, the center. My father does believe in a center, with his name above the door, of course. He has that to live for."

I felt my chest tighten, the darkness of Henri's mood taking my breath away.

"You have a lot to live for, too," I said.

"I need to find that thing you have, Elsie," he said, leaning in close, "that thing that makes me want to get up each day. That thing that gives me purpose, and passion!" He slammed his hand on the table for emphasis, and I could feel the other diners looking at us. He was shouting, and it was making me uncomfortable. "You have it. My father has it. If I don't start looking, I may never have it. If I never find something of my own, I'm afraid I'll just follow him around, charming people, living off others, and making promises I can't keep." He pressed his mouth into my hand as if to stop himself from saying more, and I left it there until I saw him calm down.

"Henri...."

"Don't worry. He really cares about your mother, maybe more than my own." His eyes were sad, and he shrugged his shoulders as if to say, *What can you do?*

"Why do your parents stay married?"

"Because the great prophet's wife is Catholic, and she doesn't believe in divorce!" He forced a laugh and emptied the bottle into his glass.

"I would have thought she was a member, too."

"She is and she isn't, like me. I mean, we say we are because that's how he lives, but one has to actually be initiated to become a full member, and I don't think she ever was."

"Were you?"

"What are we doing talking about our parents? I mean, aren't we here to get away from them?"

And just like that he changed the subject and switched back to being the life of the party. "Come, I'll knock this back and we'll get another, yes? There's still a lot of celebrating to do and only one night to do it." He downed his glass of wine, paid the bill, and was on his feet lighting a cigarette and helping me out of my chair before I could say another word.

I glided out of the restaurant on my red-wine balloon, tethered to the ground only by the solid grip of Henri's hand. There was no way I could keep up with his drinking, and I didn't want to. Knowing that this was our only night together, I was hoping we'd end up naked and rolling around the floor. I also hoped I'd be better in bed than the first time, but as I hadn't had any practice in between, I wasn't sure how that was going to be possible. But I hoped so nonetheless.

We went to see a French torch singer at some little club in Soho, where he seemed to know the bartender and a few of the other customers, and over diet soda for me and another bottle of wine for him, I learned that he had actually lived in New York with a girlfriend one summer. He was supposed to be studying art at Parsons, but instead spent all his time at this bar where other Parisians gathered. He'd also taken a course in journalism, and one in business, and another at culinary school, but they never seemed to go anywhere. He told me about backpacking through Europe and nightclubs in Greece, and how he'd never seen anyone drink as much as Australians, which was saying something coming from him.

I missed my curfew, although I was less worried about that than I was about being caught sneaking Henri into my room. From the sounds of music coming from some of the other rooms, it was clear Madame Gitard had decided to look the other way on the last night of the tour and let everybody have their final night of fun. This time I was the one to make the first move, grabbing Henri and kissing him hard on the mouth once we were safely inside. My heart was racing as I pressed my body against his and ran my hands against his chest. I started to undo the buttons on his shirt, but he took my hands in his, pressed them together, and gently pushed me back.

"I don't want to rush this time," he said, placing one

finger beneath the strap of my dress and slipping it off my shoulder. He slipped my other strap down and my dress fell away, taking my alcohol-inspired confidence along with it. I stood naked except for my underwear, lit only by the light of my bedside table, and started to shiver.

"Are you cold?" he asked.

"No," I whispered back. "Nervous."

"Don't be." He held my face in his hands and began to kiss my eyelids, slowly working his way down my body. He paused just above my underwear and then slid them off and pulled me toward him, finding me with his mouth. My eyes widened as I inhaled sharply, and I started to reach down to pull him up. I was embarrassed and started to tell him that he didn't have to, to which he replied that he wanted to, and sometime after that I stopped thinking and started feeling until the whole room was a blur and I was gasping for breath. It was another first. When I called out, Henri stood up, lifted me onto the bed, and quickly tore off his own clothes.

I pulled the rough hotel sheet over my body and curled into Henri's side, listening to his heart beat loudly. I kissed his chest and smiled to myself as he twisted his fingers through my hair. The room was hot without the air conditioning on, and a thin layer of sweat covered us both. Before Henri, the most I'd done was make out with a guy at some of the parties that Arden had dragged me to. They were awkward, impatient fumblings, greedy hands grasping in the dark for a bit of breast or ass until they could make their way into my pants. I just assumed that like all the girls I knew, I'd do a little more each time, and eventually one day I'd lose my virginity to some equally inexperienced guy, because it would be time or it would be expected of me and it would be no big deal. I had heard that it wasn't great the first few times and that it was over before it really began. I didn't expect anything different, and I never thought I'd skip all that adolescent fumbling and be schooled by an intense Frenchman who took sex seriously and seemed as focused on my enjoyment as much as his own.

"Did you really lose your virginity to a woman twice your age?" I asked.

"I did, but I am not twice your age, Elsie."

"I know, I just…you are older and more experienced, and I just wonder what that must be like. What I must be like." I had told myself that I wasn't going to ask to be rated and ended up doing it anyway.

"What did you think it was like?" he said, turning on his side to look at me.

"I don't have anything to compare it to," I said softly.

"Who's talking about comparing? You know if something feels good, if it feels right, if it makes you happy. That's inside you," he said, pointing to my heart. "No one can tell you differently."

"Well then, for me…it's wonderful."

"For me too," he said.

I held his hand against my heart and looked into his eyes. Up close, he looked older than he was; his eyes appeared tired, and I wondered if they'd always been that way or if something had changed them. I felt a lump rise in my throat and tried to swallow it. I wasn't sure why, but holding Henri close like that, seeing him naked and spent before me, made me want to weep. I felt the sadness that I had sensed from him before starting to seep from his skin. It was a deep sadness that he managed to keep buried most of the time, and it was slowly leaking out now that we were alone and he was vulnerable. I had no words for it, only an idea of who had put it there, and it made me angry. I wanted to take it away from him, to replace it with something else, and so I took his lips in mine, pulled his body as tight to me as I could, and rolled on top of him.

CHAPTER TEN

I looked at Shadow sleeping curled up in my lap and scooped her up. I hated to disturb her, but I needed to hold her close, to feel her heart beat against mine. She indulged me a few moments and then hopped on the bed opposite me, stretched out, and immediately fell back asleep. I envied her for that. Every muscle in my body called out for sleep, and just shifting my weight in the chair left me exhausted. I knew I should snuggle up next to Shadow and try to rest for a few hours before the sun came up, but my mind was racing, reliving the past that seemed to be everywhere since I returned to Toronto. Too many memories called out to me, held me in their grasp, and demanded that I spend time with them, taking me back to those summer months when everything changed. I told myself that it was too dangerous to relive those two years leading up to my eighteenth birthday, and the traumas that I had buried in a box of my own, pushed down deep inside my body as far from my head and heart as I could get it. But in coming back to Toronto, my past threatened to find me, and if I wanted to stay ahead of it, I needed to go back to LA. As soon as the sun was up I called Diane and told her to list the apartment as is and take the first offer she got. Then I dressed quickly and drove back to Dalewood for the last time.

I entered the lobby and saw Vincent standing, like he had been expecting to see me.

"I take it this is goodbye," he said.

"It is."

I stepped forward and wrapped my arms around him, gave him a big hug, and sighed heavily as he hugged me back.

"I remember all the other times you left, when you went away to dance, when you got your own place, moved to LA. You came to say goodbye, but I knew I'd see you again. But this time feels different, doesn't it?"

"Yeah, it does."

"Sometimes, when a parent dies, you get that orphan feeling, like there's nothing left to connect you. It doesn't have to be bad. It can set you free, if you let it."

"I'd like that," I said. I smiled and touched his arm. "Please take care of yourself, Vincent."

"I have no choice. My wife and daughter say they'll kill me if I'm not around to see my grandkids graduate." He shook his head and smiled. It was the first I'd ever heard of them, and we both knew it.

"I'm really glad to hear it."

"You going up?" he asked, and we both smiled. It was what he'd to say to me when I used to hang around the lobby instead of taking the elevator up to see my mother.

"Yeah. I'm going to say goodbye." I gave his arm a small

squeeze and took the elevator one last time up to my mother's apartment. I had gotten rid of nearly everything aside from the largest pieces of furniture. These would soon go too, and someone else would make the apartment their own. I opened the door and took one last look around. Diane said she'd put a few things that I'd left behind from my previous visit in a paper bag by the front closet. I saw the neat package immediately, handles folded down, edges still crisp. Inside was a scarf I thought was gone forever, a brand-new book called *Spiritual Rehab* that I certainly didn't want to keep, and the book on dance I hadn't been able to part with. I also found the program from that final performance in New York City. I opened it, and the little slip of paper announcing *This evening the solo of Arden Douglas will be performed by Elspeth Robins* fluttered out. Flipping through the program, I fondly recalled the familiar faces of my dance family, remembering the morning after our last performance and the months that followed, when everything changed.

Henri left as the sun started to rise, and I held onto him at the door for a long time, clutching the little piece of paper with his address in Paris and promising to write the moment I got back to Toronto. As soon as he left, I showered, packed, and found Madame Gitard to tell her I was going to leave school and join the company full time. She was pleased, and instructed me to spend the next month training and getting in shape. I wasn't sure what shape she meant, but I knew that as the youngest member of the company, I'd have a lot to prove and that a summer spent dancing was not the same as doing it full time. She would wait until we were back home to tell Arden the news. I found a seat at the back of the train, and when Arden crutched on with Ramon, I pretended to be asleep so I wouldn't have to answer the question of how the night before had gone. By now, she'd know that it had gone great, and in twelve hours, she'd know that I had taken her place.

After two months of being away, I had the same feeling I always had when I came home, that it was someone else's place I was returning to and not my own. I felt like a visitor now more than ever. With the exception of my room, so little of me could be seen in this space. It was all my mother's: her art, her furniture, her books, and her magazines. Anything that was mine was in my room. I even had my own bathroom, and unless I needed to go to the kitchen, I rarely ventured out.

I dragged my duffle bag to my bedroom and dumped it in the corner. It was just as I'd left it, and the fact that so little had changed was more depressing than ever. I felt like I'd gone back in time, the post-show void growing larger inside me. I tried to recapture the feeling I had right after I'd performed Arden's solo and Madame Gitard invited me to join the company. I closed my eyes, replaying the moment over and over, trying to ignite the feeling I'd had, the one that made me feel special. It was still there, but fainter now that I was home, and I knew that when my mother came back it would be fainter still. I'd go to school first thing Monday morning and let them know I was leaving and would be finishing my education by correspondence. I wouldn't ask my mother's permission, but rather tell her what I'd done when she returned.

But she didn't return, not for weeks. I found the note on the dining room table, a single white piece of paper folded in half with nothing more than a few sentences written in her left-leaning, slanted handwriting, and several hundred dollars in cash.

> *Elspeth,*
> *Use the money wisely, it is to last for a month. I have gone with Philippe to share the light of the Seekers. This is important work that we are doing, and I hope you can understand and use this as an opportunity to grow. If you need anything, you can always ask Vincent.*
> *Mother*

Mother, what a joke. I read the letter over and over again, as if doing so would somehow make it different. I pictured her sitting at the table fully dressed with her bags packed, writing this note on her way out of the door, puffed up by the fact that she was accompanying Philippe on his mission. I thought it was no coincidence they left the day before I arrived, and I wondered if Philippe had been afraid of seeing me, or if he'd worried that if left alone with my mother, I may have told her about the night he told me to kiss him. *This isn't about you,* I could hear my mother saying, *this is important work.* She could be so condescending.

I slammed my hand on the table and yelled, "*I* am important!" while angry tears fell down my face.

Leaving school was easier than I thought. I didn't really have many friends except for Arden. We did everything together, and she was popular enough that I could always hang out with her crowd. I wondered what that crowd would think about her now, knocked up and getting married right out of school, but I wouldn't let myself feel sorry for her. After all, it had been her choice; she'd made it without me, and she'd have to get through it without me too.

Rehearsals for the company started a week after we returned, and with no distractions, I threw myself into them. It wasn't just any place that I was taking in the company, it was Arden's, and I didn't want there to be any doubt that I deserved it. I started a new routine: I'd wake at 6:30 a.m., make my way through half a pot of coffee and a protein shake as I did my classwork, and then jog to the studio. By 9:00 a.m. I'd be warming up for the company class, followed by our first rehearsal. At noon, I'd break for a lunch of salad and a hard-boiled egg, and then rehearsals would resume until 5:00 p.m., when we'd call it a day. After rehearsals I'd grab a big bowl of tofu and vegetable soup in Chinatown with the other dancers, then walk the hour home, no matter how tired I was, letting my legs turn to jelly and burning any calories I may have collected at dinner. I'd return to Dalewood around 7:00 p.m., have a hot bath, and then ice my shins and hips with bags of peas that filled my freezer, and tend to my feet. I'd learned how to soak them in Epsom salts to dry out blisters, and to carefully pumice and shape the callouses I needed to dance barefoot. Finally I'd complete my schoolwork for the day, do my sit-ups, and collapse into bed by 9:30 p.m. It was the same thing day in and day out, five days a week, and I loved it. When Saturdays came, I'd go by the studio and take the professional drop-in classes and push myself to the limit, inspired by the talent of the dancers who came by as a way to stay limber. Sundays were the hardest; with no classes or rehearsals, I'd find myself counting the hours until the weekend ended. And when my mother finally returned from spreading the word with Philippe, Sundays became unbearable.

My mother returned on a Sunday. "Thank you Vincent," she said, breezing into the apartment with her hands full of mail and Vincent carrying her luggage. She was tanned and glowing, her golden hair made even lighter by the sun. She kicked off her sandals and piled the mail on the entrance table.

"Welcome back, ma'am. Must be nice to be home, for both of you." He nodded my way and closed the door behind him.

"Yes, of course." She turned around to face me and managed a small smile.

"Hello, Elspeth."

"Mother. You're back," I said, en route to taking my clothes to the laundry room off the kitchen.

"For a few weeks, yes." She flipped through the mail

without opening it.

I walked past her and put my clothes in the washing machine. I wasn't going first this time. I waited for her to ask me how I was, how the tour went, anything.

"You really let this pile up," she said under her breath, but loud enough so I'd hear it.

We hadn't seen each other in months and she wanted to talk about the mail? What about me? What about the tour?

"In fact, there's a letter here for you, from your school." She emphasized the last word and waited for me to say something, and when I didn't, she tore the envelope open, cleared her throat and continued. "They want to remind you that you still have a lock on your locker and as you are no longer a student there, if you don't want them to cut it off, you should go by Monday and remove your things." She placed her hands on her hips and looked at me expectantly.

"They can cut it off," I said, continuing to put soap in the machine, my back to her. "There's nothing in there anyway."

"Elspeth. Look at me." She spoke slowly and clearly.

I turned around as she asked and walked into the living room.

"Do you mind telling me what they're talking about?" It wasn't a real question, or else I would have been tempted to answer yes.

"I dropped out of school," I said, stuffing my hands into my jean pockets. "Three months ago."

"And why didn't you tell me?" Her cheeks were getting

flushed.

"You. Weren't. Here." I let the words hang and stared right back at her.

"I see." Her mouth pinched and she inhaled sharply. "I was—"

"Doing important work. I know, I got the note."

"And the money." It was her turn to let her words hang. I felt like reminding her it was her job to support her child, but there was no point. "You know, you can't just drop out of school and expect that I'll support you the rest of your life while you dance part time."

"It's not part time. It's full time; they offered me a place in the company and a chance to do my studies on my own time, and I took it. I figured with all the *support* you're giving Philippe and the Seekers, there wouldn't be any money left for me." I was practically shouting, and I hadn't realized it until I saw my mother's eyes widen. Maybe she thought I hadn't noticed that the fridge was always full of his favorite fine foods when he stayed with us, or that I hadn't seen her writing him checks for the Seekers and their causes.

"What I do with my money is my business," she said, clenching her jaw.

"And what I do with my life is mine."

She stared at me for a moment as if she didn't recognize me. "And you never thought to tell me?"

"No, I didn't think you cared about my dancing. It's not like you came to our final show."

"It was in New York," she said, as if New York was halfway around the world and I was being ridiculous.

"The other parents came." I crossed my arms in front

of my chest and stood as tall as I could.

"Well, I guess I am not like other parents."

"I guess not," I said, and turned to leave.

"You have no idea!" she shouted, stopping me on the spot. "No idea!"

I slowly turned around and saw her standing up, shaking her bad fist. Her face was bright red and her eyes were wide and staring past me, like she was looking at something else, something that only she could see.

"Mother...."

She exhaled slowly, taking her bad fist in her good one and holding it tightly to her. After a moment she spoke. "As you seem to no longer need my parental guidance, then you won't mind that I am going to continue traveling with Philippe on behalf of the Seekers, and when we are not traveling, he will be staying here with me."

Her voice was even and robotic, and although she was looking at me, she avoided making eye contact.

"Okay...."

"And I do hope that you finish your studies, Elspeth. You are very fortunate to have found something you are good at and get to do, but life sometimes has other ideas; you never know what your karma is, so if I were you, I'd have a backup plan. Every woman needs one."

I wanted to yell that fortune had nothing to do with it, action did; not karma, not fate. I had worked hard to make this happen, and I deserved it. I was sick of hearing how things were the result of her karma, as if she had no control over her own future. But as much as it infuriated me, it troubled me that she believed it so strongly, and that made me worry that it was true.

"Are Philippe and the Seekers your backup plan?"

"No Elspeth, they are *the* plan. I don't expect you to understand."

"You're right, I don't understand. I don't care if you call them your brothers and sisters, they're not your real family. They're not even a real religion, you said it yourself. Just a bunch of lemmings following some guy nobody has ever heard of who thinks he's the second coming."

"That's enough!"

"What about me? Why can't we be a family?" Hot tears streaked my cheeks, and I wiped them away.

My mother stood still and looked at me. Her face softened, and she seemed older than her years, and sad. "We are Elspeth. We are. Not everyone's family looks the same."

She looked down and wrung her hands. "Philippe needs me. He's committed to building a center for the Seekers, and he needs my help. I owe him that."

"You don't owe him anything," I said bitterly. I thought of what Henri had told me about the other women, about the younger mistress in Montreal whom he wanted to keep secret. "How do you know he isn't just using you for your money?"

My mother stepped closer and surprised me by reaching for my hand. "Everything in life has a price. We wouldn't be here if it wasn't for Philippe."

"What's that supposed to mean?" I whispered. I couldn't remember the last time we had touched like this.

She opened her mouth to speak, but then shook her head and let go of my hand, and I watched as the softness in her face hardened back to the usual impenetrable mask.

"Finish your studies. You're young and you're beautiful now, but as you get older you'll see that life sometimes has different plans for you, and a woman needs to find other ways of keeping herself interesting."

Beautiful. It was the closest to a compliment she'd ever given me, and I felt my face flush with pride. My mother was beautiful. I had always known it and others had, too. It was a given. But I had never considered myself to be, and to think maybe we shared something, and she saw it, touched my heart. I wondered what her plans had been when she was young, and whether her studies of art and religion and philosophy were really for her, as I had always assumed, or if they were her way of making herself more interesting as she got older. I knew she feared aging. I'd caught her a few times looking in the mirror, holding the skin on her face back, smoothing out the wrinkles that only she could see. She wasn't just making herself interesting, she was making herself useful; traveling with the Seekers and supporting Philippe in any way that she could, be it with her body, her money, or a place to stay when in town. I suspected she was more concerned that I might cramp her style when Philippe was around than not consulting her about my decision to go on tour with the company. I vowed to make myself scarce during Philippe's visits and hopefully avoid his lecturing as well.

I had nothing to worry about. Philippe decided to support my decision, telling my mother I was in search of my destiny and the sooner I got started the better. Whatever. Outside his world of followers and devotees, his words seemed hollow, his presence oddly theatrical, like an actor who behaves as if he's onstage even when he isn't. He needed an audience, and I didn't plan on giving him one.

I placed the dance program inside my bag and took one last look around the apartment. *Go*, a voice inside me pleaded. *Just go, leave now. Don't look back. Don't think anymore about that summer. Leave this building and those memories behind.* I watched myself turn off the lights, close the door behind me, and move in what felt like slow motion down the hall. I opened the trash chute and moved to put the book *Spiritual Rehab* inside when I saw Henri's face staring back at me. I snatched it back and looked at the author bio. A father of three children, he was married to a loving wife, and he owed it all to his daily meditations with the Seekers, his yoga practice, and his healthy diet. When not traveling the world giving talks and helping others, Henri resided in Paris and oversaw the Wellness Center. The photo could have been of Philippe. Clean-shaven with a neat haircut and a deep tan, in a crisp white linen shirt, his eyes piercing, his face full of confidence, Henri looked just like Philippe did that fall when he moved in with us. My head started to spin, and I placed my hand on the wall and tried to breathe deeply, as if I could will the memories that were rushing forth to stay in the past. But it was no use. They were here, and I was naïve to think I could just throw them away and be rid of them.

I had just gotten out of the shower after my run one Saturday morning when I found Philippe sitting on my bed facing me.

"Elsie."

"Jesus Christ!" I shouted, quickly rewrapping my towel around me. "What are you doing in here?" I looked out into the living room, which was dark.

"Devedra isn't here. It's just me."

Devedra. I rolled my eyes after he said it. I had to hear it all the time now, and it got on my nerves. "You could try knocking! You scared the shit out of me," I said, pulling my towel tighter.

"I have something I need to discuss with you, something private," he said, patting the place next to him on the bed.

I ignored his invitation and continued to glare at him.

"You're right. I'm sorry. I just, well, it's important, and this was the only chance I had to slip away from your mother. She's getting her hair done."

Saturdays 9:00 to 10:30 a.m. It was a standing appointment she'd had for years.

"Can I change first?" I saw that he had a stack of postcards next to him. The postcards I had sent Henri.

"Where did you get those?" I asked, reaching for the postcards with one hand and holding my towel with the other.

"Please sit down," said Philippe, his shoulders sagging and his eyes heavy.

I held my ground and looked him straight in the eye.

"Those are private," I said, snatching them out of his hand. "You have no right to spy on us!" I started to shake, my wet hair dripping down my back and dotting water on the carpet. Philippe stood and took my robe off the back of the door and handed it to me. I put it on over the towel, tying it at the waist and letting the towel fall to the floor.

"Thank you," I muttered. It was hard to be indignant when half-naked and soaking wet. "Does my mother know?"

"No, of course not. This is between us." He sat back down and put his head in his hands, took a deep breath, and spoke. "I am sorry you think I was spying. I wasn't. Not on you, anyway, at least I didn't mean to. I didn't know you were the girl he was getting letters from."

"That doesn't make it okay. You still shouldn't be reading his mail. Some things are private; you of all people should know that." I thought about all the secrets Henri had been asked to keep of his father's, of the burden it had put on him and how his father had violated his trust. "After everything he's done for you, following you around, keeping your secrets, this is how you repay him?" I was shaking, my fists balled up at my sides.

"I don't have secrets."

"You're married."

"Yes I'm married, but we haven't been husband and wife for many years, and that's okay. We're still friends, and she knows about your mother. Did you know that?"

"What?" I felt like I'd been slapped in the face. His voice was low and calm, but his words shook me.

"Henri is not well, Elsie. He hasn't been for a long time. Most of the time he's okay, if he stays on his medication, but if he goes off of it, then, well, his mind gets the better of him and he starts to lose touch with reality, and he begins to imagine things."

"You're making this up," I said, my mouth getting dry. "It's not true. He cares about me."

"Yes, yes, of course he does. That is real. But so is the rest of it too, I'm afraid: the paranoia, the fear that people are out to get him. He believes it, but it isn't real. That's why I asked him to travel with me, so I could keep an eye on him and make sure he stays on track."

I leaned back against the wall, my knees weak, and looked down at the stack of postcards. I had told him everything about myself, believing him to be a kindred spirit. If Philippe was telling the truth, then what part of Henri's spirit had I connected with? Was it really the sick part? And if so, what did that say about me?

"How long has he been off his medication?" I asked, my voice barely audible above the growing lump in my throat.

"Months maybe? The night we went out for your birthday I started to suspect something had changed. He was acting strangely gregarious one moment, secretive the next, and I didn't make the connection. And then a few weeks later, I heard he'd been receiving letters, and that's when I figured out he must have a girlfriend. It's not the first time." He exhaled deeply and was about to speak, but then shook his head and stopped.

"What?" I asked.

"He has trouble getting an erection on the medication, so, if he has a girlfriend, he might stop taking it."

I dropped the postcards on the floor and watched them fall around my feet.

"Get out." My hands trembled with rage as I pushed my door open wide for him to leave. I didn't want to be talking about Henri's erections with his father. "If you're concerned about your son, you should be talking to him, not me."

"You're the one I am concerned about," he said, standing up and walking toward me. "He can be dangerous, and I wouldn't want anything to happen to you."

The word *dangerous* rang in my ears, and I tried to remember if I'd ever felt worried for my safety around Henri. I hadn't, or was it that I hadn't yet?

"I don't need your concern," I said, gritting my teeth. "I think I've been doing just fine without it."

"You really don't think I care about you? I do. Your words are so full of pain and loneliness. So much sadness for such a beautiful young woman, but then again with such an old soul, it's no wonder. Henri might be too young to understand what you're going through, Elsie, but I'm not. You are working through your karma from a past life. It's why you feel so alone, why you don't feel at home anywhere," he said softly, placing his hand on my cheek.

"Those postcards were private," I said, as tears of humiliation threatened to spill down my face.

"I don't need a postcard to tell me that you are special, Elspeth. Anyone can see that. Why do you think your mother is so jealous of you?" He lifted my chin and stared into my eyes, not blinking, and I felt the heat coming off his body.

My mother. He had compared me to my mother, and I had won. Hadn't Henri done the same thing? But now, suddenly, I was to believe that Henri couldn't be trusted. Slowly the tears started to fall.

"You should go," I whispered, steadying myself by leaning my back against the wall.

"I should," he said, taking a step closer, closing the gap between us until I felt him against me, "but I want to stay." He pressed his pelvis into mine, and I could feel him harden against me as he slowly lowered his hand from my face to my breast. "I want to," he whispered again, his lips on mine, "don't you want me to?"

"I... I...." The room started to move, and my body felt like it was unraveling. The well of sadness had opened up in me, and I was falling into it.

"You've wanted me from the moment you met me, Elsie. The way you touched my hand at the meeting, the way you let me kiss you on the sidewalk, even now half-naked in your robe, waiting for me to touch you."

"No, I'm not. I don't want to..." I said, pushing his hand away, and the second I said it, I knew it was true. I may have wanted a lot of things, an older man to find me attractive, my mother to be jealous of me for once, an experienced lover, and to believe that I was as old and mature as I yearned to be, but not this. I didn't want this. I cared about Henri, and as attractive as I may have first found him to be, Philippe wasn't who I thought he was.

"You do," he said, quickly kissing me and undoing my

robe, "you do." He reached between my legs with one hand and undid his pants with the other.

My hand shot up from my side and punched him in the stomach, but he caught my fist and pushed me down on the carpet. "Don't fight it, you wanted this, you've always wanted this, it was meant to happen." He raised my arms above my head and pinned me against the floor.

"Get off me," I said, as I tried to push against him, unable to free my body from beneath his weight.

"It's going to happen," he said, looking me in the eye, and I knew he was right. I wanted to cry out but wouldn't let myself. I didn't want to give Philippe anything. Not my body, not my voice, not even the silent tears that poured down my face as he forced my legs open and thrust himself back and forth inside of me. I bit down hard on my lip and tried to be as quiet and stiff as I could. His face swayed above me, and I squeezed my eyes shut. I didn't want to see Henri's features in his, didn't want to think of how he was erasing the memory of the first time Henri and I had made love on the floor of this same apartment. I heard a sob escape from deep inside me, and I hated myself for it.

"It's okay, let me heal you, I can heal you, I'm healing you," he said as he came inside me and collapsed his body against mine before leaving.

I don't know how long I lay on the floor after he left. I just remember hearing the door close and then going in the bathroom to throw up. I closed my eyes and tried not to see Philippe's face, but it was there, glassy-eyed and breathing heavily into mine; I leaned over the toilet again and heaved, the violent rush of vomit a scream that was unleashed from within me. With each hurl his face got a little bit fainter, the ringing in my head a little quieter, and when there was nothing left, a hard-earned calm washed over me, and I felt comfortably numb.

I thought about calling the police but was worried how it would sound: my mother's boyfriend, a man I'd kissed on my sixteenth birthday after a night of underage drinking, only an hour before I lost my virginity to his son, had forced himself on me. Hadn't I let him stay in my room? Wasn't I naked under my robe? What if they thought I was leading him on? After all, I hadn't screamed. Philippe had told me it was what I had always wanted, and what if they believed him? I thought about my mother finding out, I thought about how Henri would feel and was sure he'd want nothing to do with me, and I realized it would be best to try to forget it had happened.

After I vomited, I showered off the evidence of Philippe's crime and made myself go to dance rehearsal, and that night when I returned home, and my mother announced that Philippe had suddenly left on business for the Seekers, I got into bed with a fever and stayed there for days. I couldn't eat, I couldn't sleep, and my mother, who never worried about me and who didn't even believe in Western medicine, grew concerned and actually suggested we go to a doctor. But I didn't want anyone to examine me, I didn't want anyone to know, and when she started to insist, I got out of bed. I shampooed the carpet, threw out the robe I had been wearing that day, and tried to pretend nothing had ever happened. But every time I stepped out of the shower, I'd listen for Philippe's footsteps, my body going cold at the memory of that day, bile rising in my throat. Unlike the carpet, the stain on me could not be washed out. And so one day, I packed up my belongings and moved into the house where the other dancers lived.

"Elspeth, are you all right?" asked Mrs. David, who was coming toward me. My body was shaking, and the familiar feeling of saliva filling my cheeks returned. I was going to throw up. The first time I'd felt like this was the morning Philippe had forced himself on me, and I'd been grateful for the chance to purge him from my body. Throwing up had made me feel clean again, and it wasn't long until I began puking throughout the day, whether I was thinking about Philippe or not. I put my hand in front of my mouth now and willed myself to swallow.

"Yes. No," I answered, taking the hand she offered me and squeezing it tightly.

It had been years since I had vomited; Ted and a lot of therapy had finally cured me of trying to drown my sadness in a toilet bowl, but I knew I was never all that far from the porcelain's edge. I tried to talk myself down like my therapist and I had practiced, telling myself it hadn't been my fault, that I wasn't dirty and didn't need to clean myself from the inside out. I was good, I was clean, I was strong and whole and beautiful, and I didn't deserve to be raped.

Raped. It was Ted who first made me say the word, and after all this time, I still couldn't bring myself to use it. I still preferred to think that Philippe had had his way with me, forced himself on me, and as a result I developed issues with eating. Rape happened to innocent girls walking down the street late at night in bad neighborhoods, by depraved strangers who wanted to hurt them. It didn't happen in the safety of your own home by someone who tells you that they care about you and want to help you. That couldn't be rape, it had to be something else, a misunderstanding, an event better left forgotten. This is what I'd told myself whenever the "r" word crept into my brain. But Ted had made me see otherwise, and even though I tried my best to forget, there would be no forgetting. Eventually I found the courage to tell my mother, and she told me that my mind had been poisoned by my own jealousy, and I'd say anything to destroy her happiness.

As Mrs. David placed her hand on my shoulder and squeezed it, I shut my eyes tightly, trying to block out the memory of Philippe's twisted, grunting face, his hot breath on my skin, and his stupid chant about healing me. Even though I now knew what a manipulative prick he had been, I still felt ashamed, still worried that it had been my fault, that the signals I'd sent with that first kiss said yes even when I'd said no. It didn't matter how much therapy I got—a part of me would always blame myself.

"Breathe," she said. "Breathe. You're going to be okay."

"How do you know?" I asked. She sounded so certain, and looking into her face, I saw that she meant what she said.

"I don't know. I *believe*. You need to believe too." She leaned forward and placed her hand against my cheek, then turned and walked back to her apartment.

What did I believe? That I could actually move on without knowing the truth? My mother had said it was up to me to decide whether or not I wanted to open the box or bury it with her, but she must've believed that I would want answers, and she was right. I looked at the book in my hand and studied the photo of Henri. Father and son. Both of them had resurfaced in the past twenty-four hours, and now I knew that Henri was alive and well and working with the Seekers. He should be able to tell me why my mother, who was so important to the group, had died alone. And if he couldn't, then he could lead me to Philippe, the one person I believed knew my mother better than anyone.

CHAPTER ELEVEN

Ted and I had agreed to meet at the house. I waited by the attic window for his car to pull up and tugged at my sweater. I realized it was one he had given me many Christmases ago when we were still married, and had started to take it off, but then felt stranger about doing that than wearing it and decided to leave it on. I tended not to throw clothes out, but rather keep them as reminders of times and places and also as a way of measuring myself as I aged. My hair was loose around my shoulders, and I automatically fished the elastic off my wrist and started to twist it into a bun and then stopped. Ted had always loved my hair down, teasing me that my days as a ballet bunhead had never really left me.

I stepped back from the window as I saw his Range Rover pull into the driveway. I turned on the radio and checked myself in the mirror. The bags under my eyes were larger than normal. I'd dreamt of fire again last night, the dream now set against darkness instead of daylight. This time, as I watched Lafina go into the house, my mother took me off her hip, pushed me away from her, and yelled *run!* Her eyes were wide and full of fear, and as soon as her hands left my body, her heart burst through her chest and exploded into a million fireworks that showered down on me and set the ground alight. I turned and ran as fast as I could, barely keeping ahead of a trail of fire that snapped at my heels and tried to twist around my ankles and pull me back. My blood was pumping so loudly it rang in my ears, and in a panic I realized I had no idea where I was running to. And then I saw the giant tree that Lafina and I used to sit beneath extend its branches toward me, and I tried to move but the flames had caught up with me and were wrapping themselves around my legs. *Run*, I heard the tree yell, but it was too late, and I was consumed by the fire. I woke up when I accidentally kicked Shadow off the bed, my dream shifting to reality as the cat hissed and hollered at being thrown onto the floor. *Run!* Where was I running to? And why did I sense that it wasn't just the fire that I was running from? There had been no going back to sleep after that.

I pinched my cheeks and tried to put some youthful color into my face, but there was no denying that I looked my age. No matter how thin or genetically lucky I was, thirty-nine did not look like twenty-nine. I heard Ted open the front door and call out my name, and I slipped the ivory ring off my finger that I'd taken to wearing for safe-keeping and put it in my pocket. I didn't need to remind him that my mother had owned something so valuable and had chosen to consign it rather than leave it to me. I waited until he was just outside my door before opening it.

"Elsie." He had a way of sighing when he said my name that I loved, and today was no exception.

"Hi." I smiled back, my hands in my pockets, dying to fly out toward him and hug him. "Thanks for coming, especially after the other night. I shouldn't have just shown up like that."

He held up his hands to stop me from talking. "Yeah, you should've."

We stared at each other for a moment, neither of us moving or saying anything, until Ted broke the silence.

"It's good to see you." He closed the gap between us, his tall frame towering over me, and then wrapped me in his arms and lifted me off the floor, making me smile. "It's okay for divorced couples to do that, I hope," he said as he put me back down.

"Yes, it's okay. Come in. It's your house," I said, making us both laugh. "Coffee?" I asked, scooping a couple of teaspoons of instant into the two cups I'd laid out for us.

"Instant coffee, who can resist?"

"It's faster." I poured the boiling water into the cups. I added milk and sugar for Ted and pulled a stool around to the other side of the counter so we were sitting across from each other.

"You look good," I said. It was true. The lines around his eyes were a little deeper now, and there was gray in his stubble, but the worry lines I'd put in his forehead and around the edges of his mouth had been replaced with the kind of softness that one gets after a good night of rest. If Julie was helping him sleep better now, I was grateful.

"So do you," he said, reaching across the counter for

my hand and giving it a quick squeeze.

"It's not true, but I'll take the compliment anyway." I took a sip of my coffee and decided to get straight to the point.

"Ted, I'm going away."

"So soon? Julie was kind of hoping we could have you over to the new house for dinner. She'll be so disappointed."

"Not after the other night, she won't." I laughed knowingly. "She'll be relieved. Trust me. She's just too nice to tell you so." I tilted my head forward to look Ted in the eye, and he looked away.

"She *is* too nice," he said, staring at the table and fiddling with the sugar bowl.

"She's great. She's perfect." This time I reached over and held his hand. "And that's a good thing, you deserve it."

"So did you, but you didn't think so."

We were here again, Ted believing my leaving him was somehow more painful than my staying would have been.

"Yeah, but you weren't perfect," I said, squeezing his hand and hoping for a smile, and when I got one, my heart leapt in my throat and I had to stop myself from holding his face and kissing it.

"Ah, right. My mistake," he said, squeezing my hand back and not letting go.

"Not true. You didn't make any mistakes." I let my hand linger, intertwining my fingers with his.

"Sure I did, I let you go. I never should have agreed to the divorce."

I gently removed my hand from his and reached for the sugar bowl. I didn't actually want any, but I was afraid that if I let my hand linger in his any longer I would start to cry.

"Like I was saying...."

"You're going, I got it." He ran his fingers over his stubble and sighed. "Look, Else, I just got here, can we at least catch up before you run off again? I'm really worried about you."

"I don't want you to worry about me." I tugged at the hem of my sweater.

"It's a hard habit to break," he said, and smiling in the way that always told me that he was going to crack wise next, "and I got a lot of practice."

"You're welcome." I relaxed enough to laugh a little as I headed back to the counter and put the kettle on again. No matter how blue I got, Ted could always make me smile, and I was grateful. "Okay. But you talk first."

I heard about the new house outside of the city, with the extra room, the bigger backyard, and the safer streets. I heard what he didn't say. Ted was acting less now, having successfully made the move into directing episodic work and movies of the week. It was what we'd always planned, a more stable life with more income and time to spend with the family we never had. Ted was going do what he was doing now, and I was going to move into choreography after my dancing career ended. Our plan worked for a while, but it was a full-time job keeping my dance company going, and I was always applying for grants and hosting fundraisers like the one where I met Ted, and when I was no longer able to dance onstage from all the injuries I had acquired as a professional dancer, all the effort hardly seemed worth doing for someone else.

But I didn't go gracefully. I missed performing, missed losing myself in the movement and sound of carefully choreographed conversations. The inadequacies I had in my life offstage, I more than made up for onstage. I could live with my flaws and anxieties, and my bouts of depression, as long as I was able to express myself day in and day out in wordless flight. Without dancing I felt more exposed, unsure of myself in the real world. I was just like everyone else, only worse. I had hoped choreographing would fill the hole left by no longer being able to perform, but it didn't.

And then one day as I was leaving the studio, one of the dance teachers who rented space from me had a family emergency and asked if I could please cover her class. I'd had a rough rehearsal day already and began to say no, but she cried that it was too late to reschedule, her father was sick, and I gave in. I figured I'd wait until she left and tell her students that class was canceled and they'd be refunded for the day. But then they started to arrive in their little leotards and tights, faces bright with purpose and a desire to please, and I melted. Children. I had no idea that it was a class for children, and as they took their places on the bar, shoulders back, heads held high, waiting for my instruction, I was filled with a desire I hadn't had since leaving the stage. I wanted to teach them. I wanted to share with them and pass on everything I loved about dancing and communicating with my body. They danced with such focus and intensity, hanging on every word of my instruction, foreheads frowning when corrected and faces exploding into grins when I complimented them. I was gentle and patient, and I found myself encouraging them, as I had once been encouraged by Arden's mom. I attached imaginary strings to them at the bar, to raise elbows higher, and ran my fingers along the backs of their necks to the tops of their heads, leaving my hands smelling of honey shampoo. I raised their chins, marveling at the softness of their skin, and lost myself in their tender faces. When I finally ended the class, fifteen minutes later than I was supposed to, I wrapped my arms around every last one of them and didn't want to let go.

I walked home that day thinking about Arden and her child. With Ramon and I continuing to dance in the same company for years after she left, I'd see her at our performances with their daughter. Over time, we exchanged polite hellos and goodbyes, although our friendship never returned to what it once was. We both saw there was no going back. For Arden, that also meant her dance career. By the time she tried to return, she was too out of shape, too out of practice, and too old in comparison to the new dancers, who seemed to get younger and younger each year. I'd been right that she couldn't have it all, but I wasn't sure it really mattered. Every time I saw Arden's face light up at the sight of her daughter running to Ramon after a curtain call, I knew she was happy she'd kept the baby. With her jet-black hair, brown eyes, and long limbs, she was the perfect combination of her adoring parents. At the end of it all, Arden had a family. It was more than I had when my career ended.

That day in the studio with the children, I knew I was

done with choreographing. It was too hard spending my days working with dancers who had their whole careers in front of them, and I resented having to work overtime to provide them with the opportunity to do what I no longer could. I'd let myself become bitter about the one thing I'd always loved, forgetting the pure joy it had brought me ever since I was a child. The kind of joy those children had. It didn't matter if any of them would go on to be professional dancers or not. They did it because they loved the way it felt to spin around in a pirouette or fly across the floor in a grand jeté. And I loved it when they rewarded me with huge smiles and hugs on the way out the door after I recognized their efforts. When I got home and told Ted I was done with my dance company and I was going to start my own classes for children, he'd kissed me and hugged me tightly.

A year or so later, we moved to LA so Ted could work on his television show. I had just turned thirty, and we decided that with the money he'd be making, I could stay at home and we could start a family. I read countless books on parenting so I'd be ready when the time came. I bought a yellow cotton onesie with bananas on it that said, *Bananas for Mommy,* and I kept it in my dresser drawer. I taped a list of baby names to the fridge—Isabelle, Benjamin, Clara, Jack—and tried them out with Ted to see which one felt right. And at night we'd lay in each other's arms and wonder whose nose, eyes, and mouth the baby would have.

We started trying right away, and after two years we began seeing a fertility specialist. It wasn't that I was old, but after years of peeing on sticks and making love right when I ovulated, I wasn't pregnant. At thirty-three we enlisted the help of a naturopath, a doctor of Chinese medicine, and a positive visualization-coach; there was no shortage of people in LA to help us with my problem, for it clearly was my problem. My hormone tests indicated that I should be able to conceive, and yet I wasn't. So I drank alkaline waters, stayed off coffee and alcohol and wheat, built a baby shrine in the baby's room, wrote letters to my unborn child telling it how much I wanted it in my life and what a great mother I would be, and then, as I had been instructed to do, planted those letters in the garden next to the roses and watered them both to grow.

I turned thirty-four, and my hormone levels plummeted. I started hormone therapy, injecting myself regularly and watching as my body morphed into something I didn't recognize. Suddenly the skin I was in was not my own. It got acne and swelled, everything ached, and my once-moody self became volatile, my temper flaring with the slightest provocation. After years of being able to control my body, I was helpless.

At thirty-five, after our attempts to conceive via artificial insemination had failed, I wanted to call it quits. But Ted was sure there had to be another way. The first American test tube baby had been born the year before, and although our doctor warned that the rates of success were low and the chances of miscarriage high, there was always a chance. Ted heard "chance," while I heard "miscarriage." I couldn't do it. We'd used up all of our insurance and had started going through our savings, and I wasn't prepared to risk everything we had on one test tube baby. After endless hours of discussion, Ted agreed to a temporary reprieve on the question of in vitro fertilization, even as he continued to read every new article on the subject, and we looked to adoption. We got on the lists and waited. But we weren't exactly ideal candidates; we were both artists, without steady incomes and stable careers, Ted was now forty, and I had a history of bulimia and depression. But still, there was a chance. So I called the adoption agency every week for a year with no luck. There always seemed to be some family that had been waiting longer or that was a better candidate, and finally, I stopped. I couldn't risk any more heartbreak.

"Where'd you go?" asked Ted, reaching out and touching my arm.

"How far along is she?"

Ted hung his head down and exhaled slowly. He was quiet for a long time.

"She's not yet. But...we've been trying."

"It's okay Ted. I mean, you'll make great parents."

I saw his shoulders shake first and then heard him cry. He covered his face in his hands to muffle the sound, and I walked over and wrapped my arms around him and pulled him to my chest, rocking him slowly.

"I'm so sorry, Else, I'm so sorry. It should've been you. It should've been us."

"I know. But it wasn't."

And there was no reason that it wasn't. I had asked a thousand times. I had looked for answers, I had prayed, I had talked to doctors, I had consulted psychics, and nobody could tell me why our efforts didn't work. I drove myself crazy trying to think of a reason. My mother's twisted logic had me believing that I'd done something to deserve it, that I was being punished not just for events in this life but for events in past lives as well. I hated this way of thinking, but it was the only thing I could think of that made sense. I needed someone to blame, and years of living with my mother had taught me that the easiest person to lay the blame on was myself. But Ted wouldn't allow it; he refused to let me take responsibility for my barrenness, and then one day, I finally found a therapist who put it all in perspective and said what no one else was willing to say to me.

Shit happens.

"I'm sorry, I don't want it to be like this," said Ted as he buried his face in my chest and pulled me closer.

"I know."

"I don't want you to go," he said, running his hands up and down my back.

"Ted...." I was worried where this was going.

"I'll come with you. We can go wherever you want. I'll sell the house and we can travel, we can try again...." His voice trailed off as he lifted me on the counter and kissed me.

It was the most natural thing in the world, kissing him, and more than anything I wanted to be able to travel back, back to when our plans were laid out before us and we believed we could make them all come true. But that was never going to happen, and the only past I was willing to travel back into now was my mother's.

"Ted, please, listen," I said, gently pushing his chest off of mine.

"I've never stopped loving you and you've never stopped loving me," he said, holding my face in his hands. "We can do this, Elsie. We can fix this, we can find a way."

Ted had always been about finding a way. He was one of those people who didn't take no for an answer, who didn't believe things were impossible or insurmountable. To him life was full of opportunities to be taken and challenges to be conquered. It was an amazing way of seeing the world, and as it had always worked for him, he insisted on applying it to me. We could fix my eating disorder, we could work through my past, we could tackle and defeat my depression, and we could find a way to have a child.

At first his genuine belief that anything was possible inspired me, and at his urging I sought help, visited therapists, and worked on myself like the project I was. But over time his relentless optimism wore on me. I feared what would happen if things didn't get better, if I didn't stay better, and I worried about the day that Ted realized I was just a fucked-up mess and was always going to be a fucked-up mess. Would he still love me then? Would he know to just give up and accept me, and us, for who we were? Would he be able to embrace all the positive changes we had made and learn to live with the things we could not control? I didn't think so. I told myself I'd find a way to live with my depression, find a way to live without having children, but I would never find a way to live with the disappointment I saw every day in Ted's eyes when he looked at me, and the feeling he hid just below the surface that I hadn't tried hard enough.

I let him kiss me again. I had missed him. There wasn't a day that went by that I didn't think about him and wish we were still together. I wished I could just be enough for him as I was, without a child.

"Tell me one reason why we shouldn't do this," he said.

He wanted more, and I couldn't give it to him. I'd made a mistake in reconnecting; it wasn't fair to him. His eyes were pleading, and I knew I had to tell him the one thing that would make him angry at me.

"I opened the box."

"What?" He pulled away from me, his eyes wide.

"My mother's box. I opened it. She left me a letter, she wanted to explain, but she said it was my choice whether or not I wanted to know the truth. I could bury her secrets with her or uncover them. And I want to uncover them."

"Why?" He stepped back from the counter. "Why would you do that? You finally get a chance to bury that woman and everything about her and you can't let it go?" His face had turned red and he was clenching his jaw.

"Ted, she had relatives I never knew about, and there were obituaries for the two of us."

"What are you talking about?"

"People thought we had died, but someone knew the truth, someone who sent her notices in the paper, and pictures, someone who knows who she really was and can tell me what happened. I just have to find them."

"And how are you going to do that, huh? You want to tell me that?" His mouth was a tight line. He sat down, crossing his arms in front of his chest. It was a challenge.

We both knew there was only one way.

"I'm going to start looking," I said quietly, bracing myself for what was next.

"Really. And just where are you going to start?" He tilted his head and waited, daring me to say his name.

"With the one person who knew her the best."

"Jesus, Elsie. You really want to go down that road again?"

"Ted...."

"After everything he did, after everything he put you through? You know how long it took you—no, how long it took *us* to undo the damage that prick did? How many fucking therapy sessions, how many nights I held you in the dark when you woke up covered in sweat remembering how that asshole raped you and manipulated you?"

"A lot, I know. And I'm grateful."

"I don't want your gratitude. I want you to leave this alone. Otherwise everything we did, all the progress you made, you're just throwing away."

"I can't leave it alone. I need to find Philippe, and I think Henri can lead me to him."

"Henri as well. Wow. You really are hell-bent on destroying everything we worked so hard for."

"Ted...."

"Is that what I did wrong, Else? If I had been some crazy asshole like Henri, would you have stayed?"

Ted wasn't wrong to call him crazy. Henri had returned to Paris after New York, and judging by the letters he wrote me, he had rapidly unraveled. He'd enrolled in school for the fall, this time to study writing, but by winter he had lost interest in studying and wondered if writing could actually be learned or if one just needed to be born with the talent—a talent he didn't believe he had. A few months later he dropped out and was making money as a waiter. He was hanging out with a group of artists and talked about being a photographer, working in a medium that would allow him to tell stories, but without words, as he put it. I read his letters through a filter of doubts, wondering if Philippe had been telling the truth about Henri's mental state. I had once seen Henri as a kindred spirit, but now I read each sentence with more scrutiny, torn as to how serious his complaints were. I didn't know if his life with the Seekers was as bad as he said it was, or if he was exaggerating like his father said, seeing enemies where there were none. One thing I never doubted was how powerful and dangerous Philippe was, and I did my best to keep track of his whereabouts through Henri's letters, so I could avoid him at all costs.

Six months after we'd seen each other in New York, Henri began experimenting heavily with drugs. He'd started with pot and hash and moved on to mushrooms and LSD. He rationalized his drug use as an experiential way to get in touch with his more intuitive side and likened it to the religion that his father peddled, without the need for a guru and blind devotion. The more time he spent away from Philippe and the Seekers, the more he wrote me about them. And eventually he stopped writing about anything else, and would even forget to ask how things were going on my end. The summer of my eighteenth birthday, he sent me one of his last troubling letters, telling me that he'd finally realized what his calling was. I read that letter so many times, disturbed by its contents, that I practically committed it to memory.

Henri claimed to have experienced a breakthrough with some friends when they were taking mushrooms—it had allowed him to open his mind's eye and see the things that he normally couldn't see. He declared that it was his destiny as the son of the prophet to help all who were in darkness find the light. He was angry with his father and willing to challenge him and lead his disciples. He said he felt awake and alive in a way that he'd never known. No longer listless and wandering about, he was a man on a mission, like his father, but his mission was different; his mission was about salvation and the greater good, and he was devoting himself to it. Instead of his normal sign-off, *A La Prochaine*, he wrote, *Let all who seek, find the light.*

After that, when I didn't hear from him for months, I was more than a little relieved. His letters had started to frighten me, and I told myself that maybe he'd written them when he was high, and that his increasing drug use was just a phase. I wasn't a prude by any means; a lot of the dancers liked to smoke a little pot and I'd tried it, too, but this was different. I thought back to the times Henri and I had been together and wondered if the sudden shifts I'd witnessed, from joy to anger, had been more than just the mood swings of an angry young man. I remembered him urgently clutching my hands in the Indian restaurant and shouting about how he needed to find his passion. I thought about how uncomfortable I'd felt, the other diners staring at us. Was it more than just anxiety about finding his purpose? Was it madness as well? I didn't know what to think. But I knew what I wanted to believe—that the old Henri I had shared myself with would return.

It was the weekend of my eighteenth birthday when I finally saw him again. I'd been living at the house with the other dancers for almost two years, and they'd planned a small party in honor not just of my birthday but of my graduating from school. When Henri eventually reached out and told me he was coming to town and wanted to see me, I invited him to the party and said he could stay at the house. I wanted him to see where I was living. It wasn't that the house itself was so special; in fact, on the outside it was little more than a run-down rooming house. But on the inside it was a home. We'd painted every room a different color and decorated with furniture and pictures that we'd found at yard sales and thrift stores. The landlord was absent and the rent was cheap, so we didn't mind the inconveniences of sharing one bathroom and an old kitchen in which we did little more than make coffee. We all pretty much had the same schedule, and it was nice to be among people who understood the importance of living and breathing what you did. We were one big, incestuous, dysfunctional family, obsessed with dancing, working out, and staying thin. We overlooked each other's eating disorders, massaged each other's sore muscles, and provided each other with comfort when lonely. I was happy here.

Happier than I had ever been living with my mother, happier than I was the last time I'd seen Henri.

I was nervous about seeing him again but hopeful that he meant it when he said that all the traveling he'd done, all the soul searching, had paid off and he wanted to share that. His voice sounded calmer than it ever had, the crazy letters had stopped, and I found myself daydreaming about what life might be like for the two of us if he stayed put long enough. Of course, I didn't share these thoughts with anyone. I made it a point not to talk about my life outside the company. Not talking about my mother or Philippe or what had happened made it easier to forget.

The other dancers knew who Henri was; they had seen him at our performance in New York, and they'd taken his calls at the house, and every now and then they'd bust my chops about the older French dude who they said had money to travel the world but called collect. I let them think he was my foreign lover, and everything else about him I kept to myself.

On that weekend, thanks to a trip to the dollar store, the house was done up in streamers, paper lanterns, and balloons. There were big plastic bowls of chips and popcorn that would remain untouched until everyone was too drunk to remember they shouldn't be eating junk food, and in the kitchen some of the dancers were busy making a punch of cheap vodka, cranberry juice, and Sprite. Someone was playing DJ, uncoiling speaker wire so music could be heard on the front porch, and somebody else was setting out candles and ashtrays. I stood on the stairs and smiled. I had never had a birthday party, and even though I knew this party was also a great excuse for all of us to do it up before our week off from rehearsals, I was touched. I'd dressed up in honor of Henri's visit and was wearing a yellow and white shift with black tights and black flats. I'd ironed my hair straight, done my eyes in black liquid eyeliner, and put on pale-pink lipstick.

"Well, well, look at you," said Antoine as I made my way down the stairs. "Girl, you look just like a beautiful bumblebee; that boy better watch out you don't sting him!" He laughed and twirled me around.

"Too much?" I asked.

"Perfect," he said, giving me the once-over. "You're all grown up now—he's not gonna know what hit him." He took a sip of his drink and offered his glass to me.

"Oh no thanks." I stared at my watch. I was going to be late.

Antoine looked at me closely. "You all right? You don't seem too excited."

"I am. I just gotta take care of something first," I said, heading toward the door.

"Where are you going? It's your party."

"Not for a few hours still. I have an errand to run."

"She remembered it's your birthday?"

I stopped and turned to face Antoine as he raised his eyebrow and took another sip.

I didn't talk about my mother to the other dancers, but it didn't take a genius to notice I was the only person who never had any family at any of our shows, never mind the fact I was always available to attend someone else's Thanksgiving dinner. A few of the dancers had moved to Toronto and were away from family, so it wasn't uncommon for us to tag along on someone else's holiday, but I was the only one who was always solo. Antoine had noticed it right away. He said he figured any girl who chose to pay rent at the age of sixteen when she could stay somewhere else for free must have a pretty good reason to do so. He told me he'd left home when he was sixteen too, after his father had decided *no son of mine was going to be a fairy ballerina.* For a long time nobody came to watch his performances either. And then one day he looked out and saw his mother sitting in the audience. His father had died, and she'd decided she'd be damned if she was going to die without ever having seen her only son dance. It was the kind of thing I had secretly hoped for myself, my mother surprising me in the front row of the audience. And even though I knew it would never happen, I still left her name on the company's annual mailing list, just in case.

"She only has to remember it once a year." I took Antoine's glass and finished his drink. "I'll be back in an hour, and then we'll celebrate," I said, running out the door and down the front steps.

Antoine was right: the errand was my mother. She had called that morning and insisted we have dinner together. When I explained that I had plans, she took the birthday party being thrown for me as a personal insult, so I'd agreed to go by her apartment and hopefully get the fifty-dollar birthday check she'd given me every birthday since I turned sixteen. I promised myself I would just get in and get out.

I wouldn't take her bait about not calling, not visiting, and how nice it must be for me to be able to follow my dreams when she herself had sacrificed so much for that to happen. My mother had never been so interested in my life as when I decided to move out and absolve her of the one responsibility that she had, and resented me for: being my mother. And yet she still managed to avoid seeing me perform. I didn't bother to ask her why anymore, and she no longer offered excuses. We both knew the reason. I had something that made me very happy. Something she had no part in. And if it wasn't about her, she wasn't interested.

I looked for Vincent in the lobby, but he wasn't around, and I decided to go straight up and not bother signing the registry. I have often thought back on how if I had, I may have been able to stop what happened next. I would have seen Philippe's name on the registry, along with Henri's.

I entered my mother's apartment and felt the door quickly shut behind me. Henri reached behind my back, locked the door and ushered me into the room. My mother was sitting on the couch, her face frozen in fear, and Philippe was sitting as far back against the cushions as he could manage, his eyes wide and his skin white. Henri grabbed me in a hug and kissed my hair as he whispered, "I was waiting for you. I can do this now."

I pulled back from him and saw the knife in his hand.

"What are you doing? What's going on?" I looked at Henri, who was staring straight ahead, his eyes wide.

"Don't worry, you don't need to be afraid. Only liars and false prophets need to fear, and we are neither."

"He's crazy! He's crazy and you told him to come here?"

my mother spat out.

"I didn't tell him to come here. I thought it was just us meeting for dinner." I tried not to look at Philippe as I said it. I never would have set foot into the apartment had I known he'd be there.

"Henri, tell me what's wrong?" I asked softly. His eyes were wild and he was sweating. He was breathing quickly and tightening his hand around the knife.

"He's what's wrong," said Henri, pointing the knife in the direction of his father. "He's leading everyone astray. He's squandering the will of his people."

"He's off his bloody medication again," said Philippe.

"Henri, please give me the knife," I said gently touching his arm.

"Listen to your girlfriend," said Philippe. His tone was icy, and I felt him staring at me.

"Girlfriend?" asked my mother. "So you're a part of this?" She clenched her good hand into a fist.

"Come on, let's go," I said, inching closer toward him.

"Not all of us live selfishly, as if this was the only life we will ever know," my mother snapped. "Neither of you can stand the fact that someone can actually do something good with their life and make a difference." She adjusted her gaze to me alone. "He's a good man, and you're jealous that he makes me happy."

I stood glued to the spot, my mouth hanging open in shock. It all came down to the one-sided competition my mother had with me. A competition I had briefly participated in, the night I met Philippe. This wasn't about right and wrong, true or false; this was about who was the most popular girl in the room, and I was playing it with my mother.

"You've got to be kidding me. He's a fucking fraud! Your good man forced himself on me. Why do you think I left?"

The room was so quiet that I could hear my heart pounding. All eyes were on me, but my eyes were locked onto my mother's.

"What did you say?" she asked slowly.

"You heard me," I said, starting to cry, unable to tear my gaze away from her. I didn't dare look at Philippe or Henri. "Almost two years ago, in my room, when he showed me he had found my letters to Henri."

"Why didn't you tell me?" asked Henri.

"Because it isn't true, that's why," said Philippe quickly. "She's ashamed of the real truth, that she threw herself at me and I rejected her. Just like that night at the restaurant when she kissed me while we waited for the taxi. You remember that, Henri; you were across the street, watching."

I looked at Henri and saw it all over his face—he'd seen the kiss. That's why he was right there as the taxi was about to take off, that's why he was so quiet in the car. "You're nothing like your mother," he'd said. Had he been trying to make me feel better about what he thought was Philippe's attempt to make a pass at me?

"Henri, I'm telling the truth," I said.

"You thought it was me who kissed *her*, didn't you?" said Philippe to Henri. "But it wasn't. She was embarrassed and confused, and I should've helped her, and I didn't, and for that I am truly sorry." He took my mother's hands in his and kissed them. "I didn't want to hurt you," he said to her, and then he turned to Henri. "It was never you she wanted to be with, son, it was me all along."

"Henri, let's just go, please, let's get away from them." I reached for Henri's arm, but he tugged it away, staring at me like he had no idea who I was.

"There's a reason you two were drawn to each other," said Philippe. "You are both lost souls. Let us help you find your way back, let us heal you."

It was the word *heal* that did it. I felt the bile rise in my throat, and I threw up. I looked at my mother, standing there staring at me, silent, her jaw slack. And then I ran as fast and as far away from them as I could.

"Elsie, listen to me," said Ted, grabbing my shoulders and bringing me back to the present. "She's dead, okay? She's finally dead. Be thankful you don't have to deal with her shit anymore and move on. You're still young. Don't let her fuck up the rest of your life too." He touched his forehead against mine and I felt tears on his face.

"I'm trying," I said quietly. "That's why I need to do this. I need to know who she really was, and what she was hiding." I wanted to tell him about the dreams of fire. That I knew it was my mother who had brought them and until I figured them out, she wouldn't leave me alone. That just when I decided to move on, the scrapbook had appeared. But I couldn't. It sounded crazy, and if Ted thought I was losing my mind, he would never be able to walk out the door. I was never going to be able to explain what it felt like to be incomplete, to long for something and someplace you hardly knew, and yet were wise enough to know that its absence defined you. I was motherless, and homeless, and nothing Ted could say would change that.

He sighed heavily and stood up, letting me go. "Those people nearly destroyed you, Elsie. Henri, Philippe, your own mother. Is whatever she was hiding worth the risk of losing yourself? What if she is only trying to take you down with her?"

It was a terrifying thought, and I didn't want to believe it. But Ted was right. I had no idea what she really wanted, or what I would find.

"I know it's a risk. But it's one I have to take."

"Well, then you have to take it on your own." It was an ultimatum, the one I'd been waiting for and not the first one Ted had given me regarding my mother. I'd chosen my relationship with him over my relationship with her years ago, out of necessity. But we were divorced now, and I had no one to worry about hurting but myself. If Ted was finally going to have a family with Julie, we needed to let go, and this would do it.

"I know."

He shook his head and grabbed his coat. "I hope it works out the way you want it to, Else."

"I hope so too," I whispered, as tears ran down my face. I wished I could tell him I would always love him, that I knew I would never meet anyone as wonderful as him, and that I would always ache for him and the family we couldn't have, but I couldn't.

Ted slammed the door and left, and I watched from the

window as he pulled out of the driveway to go, this time for good. Once he was out of sight, I removed the ring from my pocket, slipped it back on my finger, and took a deep breath. There was no going back now.

CHAPTER TWELVE

I needed to keep moving, and with enormous relief I welcomed the fact that I was still capable of wanting to. One of the things about being depressed was my legitimate concern that a desire to do anything would never return. As terrifying as the thought of wading into my mother's life was, the thought of never wanting to wade into anything ever again was worse. Before her death, my days had become a series of events I moved listlessly through, marking time until I could safely retreat to my bed without too much reproach. I'd go to sleep early and get up late, all in an effort to shorten my daylight hours. I'd turned getting eight hours of rest into getting eight hours of waking time. I knew I could've taken medication, but the idea of feeling even less than I already did wasn't an option; the painful ache I felt in my whole body was the only thing that reminded me that I was still alive, a decision I sometimes wondered about. My mother's death changed everything. It shook me from my slumber and stirred up all that I had been trying to bury for so long. I was about to risk the safety of my carefully managed unhappiness for the possibility of something more. I didn't know if the truth would set me free or bury me, but I knew I had to find out.

"It's up here on the right," I said to the cab driver on my way to the airport. I told him to keep the meter running and got out to take a look.

Though the actual structure of the large Victorian on Brunswick Avenue was the same, little else resembled the rundown house I lived in when I joined the company full time and moved out of my mother's place. The home in front of me, with its freshly painted brick exterior, shale shingled roof, and manicured front lawn, looked like it belonged on the cover of a magazine. Small topiaries flanked the sides of the bright-red door, and a large sticker on the bay window displayed the name of the expensive security company that protected it.

I hadn't told the other dancers what happened at my mother's apartment on the night of my eighteenth birthday, but when I returned home hours after I said I would, finally too tired of wandering the city, Antoine saw me and knew something was wrong. He pulled me aside and asked if I was all right, and when I wasn't able to answer him, he wrapped his arms around me and held me as I cried. Then he brought me the entire punch bowl and suggested I get smashed, which I did. Hours later Henri showed up screaming *you fucking whore* at the top of his lungs, and I watched from the window as Antoine and some of the other dancers physically removed him from the property and threatened to call the cops. He didn't leave easily, and I felt sick as I saw him scream at me through the window. He looked like a wild animal, one that knew it was cornered and didn't stand a chance. There was no way they were going to let him anywhere near me or the house, and eventually he retreated.

Like the family I'd always dreamed of having, the other dancers had rallied around me that night and the days afterward. They brought me coffee in the morning and soup at night, and they walked with me to rehearsal. If I went into my room, they'd listen outside my door, opening it a crack to see if I was okay. They didn't pry; they didn't need the details of what had happened in order to have my back. I was one of them and that was enough. I had never felt anything like it before and would never really feel anything like it ever again. I don't think any of us realized at the time how rare and special what we had was. There was something so pure about the home the other dancers and I had built together. We weren't husbands or wives or parents to one another; we had no need for anyone to be anything other than exactly who they were. We all loved the same thing, and that was more than enough. We'd all move on, move in with boyfriends and girlfriends, and wish each other well, and promise to stay in touch, and we would try, but it would never be the same. Some of us would continue dancing and some of us would stop and find "real jobs," and without our common language there would be little to connect us but the unspoken bond that had formed over those years of sharing a common passion.

I did manage to keep track of Antoine, though. He'd

gone on to have the most successful career of us all, moving
to New York and becoming a principal dancer with the
Alvin Ailey American Dance Theater, his picture featured
prominently in their posters and programs. He'd still come
to Toronto from time to time, showing up in the audience
of a show that one of us was in and staying afterward to offer congratulations and a quick hug before leaving. Success
hadn't changed him, and I think all of us who knew him
shared the kind of hometown pride you feel when watching one of your own hit it big. He was the one dancer I
could never be jealous of, even after I stopped dancing. It
was impossible to feel anything but gratitude toward him,
especially after that night with Henri.

Twenty-one years later, I could still feel my chest tighten
as I stared at the lawn where he had fought Henri off, air
getting trapped in my throat at the memory of it. I reminded myself to breathe. I reminded myself that a lot had
happened since then. I told myself we were different people now and I had nothing to be afraid of and it was all
behind me, in the hopes I'd start to believe it. I needed to
believe it. In eighteen hours I would see Henri again, and
I was counting on him leading me to Philippe. I'd often
wondered what Henri looked like now. I pictured him still
wearing his hair a little longer than average, salt and pepper
by now, with the same slight build, stooped shoulders, and
haunted eyes that I'd known. A slightly older version of the
young man I had once loved, and not the slick version of
his father that the back of his book boasted.

I wondered if everyone remembered people the same way, frozen in the moment of time when we meant the most to each other. The Henri I saw when I closed my eyes wasn't the man who had gone mad that night at my mother's apartment; he was the man who'd held me in the dark and reassured me that what I thought and felt mattered. I'd held out hope that he had gone on to become a painter or poet, something that provided him an outlet for all that tormented him. I chose to believe that he had realized over time that his father had been lying and that he'd forgiven me for not telling him what happened. I used to dream about it—a different ending to our last night together than the one we had. And I'd started to let myself believe that maybe after all these years, we'd see each other again and it would be right between us. But in spite of his rebellion, and in spite of my wishes for him, he'd ended up exactly where his father had wanted him to, following in his footsteps, firmly entrenched with the Seekers. I'd read the introduction about the Seekers in *Spiritual Rehab* and was amazed at how much the organization had grown in the last twenty-five years. It still wasn't mainstream by any means, but it was definitely more organized. The Seekers had a list of their other titles inside the book's cover, and the locations of their meditation retreats in places like Hawaii, Belize, and Cape Town on the back.

No longer an angry skeptic, Henri detailed his transition from manic-depressive drug addict to spiritual advisor and wellness practitioner. He wrote openly about losing himself to drugs, about trying to discredit the Seekers and his father. Everything he'd been through, including that night at my mother's apartment, was in there, with the exception of myself. The little details about his father's rape, or him yelling "whore" in front of my house after wielding a knife, weren't mentioned. Instead he described the night as an emotional confrontation between a father and son, and the story was their road back to mending their relationship and strengthening their bond through their faith. It was history reshaped to drive only one point home: the Seekers had saved his life, and if you became a member and paid for their services, it could save yours too.

Once the plane took off, I pulled out the hardcover and lay it face down on my tray so no one could read the title on the front. I didn't want the flight attendant to think I was actually reading it. Having never flown first class before, I was fully expecting I would have to read the book in secret, hunched over its pages in an attempt at privacy while sandwiched between the kind of people who looked at an eight-hour flight as an opportunity to vomit their personal life onto someone who had no choice but to listen, mistaking stunned silence for interest. But I was spared by an upgrade from a flight attendant who was sympathetic to the fact that my mother had just died, and I was able to stretch out, take up two seats, and numb myself with the free wine that kept appearing before me. There was no one peeking over my shoulder or making conversation; it was just me and a few businesspeople who busied themselves with their documents.

I tilted my chair back and closed my eyes. I was

exhausted and wide awake at the same time, fueled by my
desire to solve this mystery and get on with my life. And if
it hadn't been for my landlord breaking into my apartment
and finding me lying on the floor next to an empty bottle
of antidepressants, I might never have had this chance to
do so.

It had happened in LA two weeks earlier, before my
mother died. I'd been having a bad bout again, triggered
in part by the fact I had just turned thirty-nine, a birthday
I celebrated alone with a trip to my gynecologist. I'd been
sitting in one of those pale-blue regulation cotton gowns
that tie up in the back when she once again delicately
broached the topic of trying IVF. She said it was now or
never, as I was at an age where my already-compromised
fertility would soon begin its descent into menopause. I
burst into tears. Something about the finality of it and the
fact that the only person to comfort me was my physician,
a woman the same age as me with four beautiful children
displayed proudly in a picture frame on her desk, was just
too much to bear.

"It's all right to cry," she said. "It's perfectly natural for
a lot of women to mourn the end of their child-bearing
years." She passed me a box of Kleenex, and I took one.

"What child-bearing years?" I asked, sobbing.

Dr. Warner leaned against the counter opposite me and
folded her arms across her chest.

"I'm sorry, Elspeth. I know how hard you and Ted
tried." She paused for a moment, no doubt weighing
whether or not to say what was coming next. "You know,
I'm only saying this because I really believe you still have a

small window of opportunity. There have been significant advances with IVF since you started trying, and we've had success with women in your same situation. Look, there's never a guarantee, but there's still a good chance...."

"Don't," I whispered, shaking my head.

"Okay," she said with a sigh. "I don't want to nag, but have you been taking your antidepressants? I know you don't like the side effects, but they'll give you some relief, and it doesn't have to be forever, you know, just until you're feeling stronger."

I knew this was a lie. Nobody ever recommended coming off those things; why stop taking something that was working? I'd tried taking antidepressants a couple of times before, but each time I felt like a stranger in my own skin and stopped. I knew Dr. Warner was only trying to help, so I'd filled my latest prescription and carried it around in my purse, and whenever I didn't want to stick to my routine of things that kept me, if only loosely, connected to the world around me, I reminded myself that a life of pills was what awaited if I didn't. I hated to admit it, but my mother's belief that pharmaceuticals were only for the weak had stayed with me.

"Yes, I have," I lied. I looked at the suntan marks that the straps on my sandals had made on my feet, instead of making eye contact.

"And?" she asked, sounding hopeful.

"Oh, yeah, they're helping. Definitely." I tugged at the hem of my cotton gown.

"Good." She sounded unconvinced. "Well, I'll let you get changed then."

I took my time getting dressed and paid the nurse my co-pay on the way out. She checked my file, registered the date, and wished me happy birthday as she handed me the receipt. I nodded thanks, afraid if I opened my mouth I would cry again, and headed back to my apartment near the beach. It was the small two-bedroom apartment Ted and I had lived in when we were together. The second room had started out as an office, and then had been converted to a baby room, and when that proved to no longer be necessary we had painted over the murals of clouds and smiling suns and had closed the door. We had talked about turning it back into an office for Ted, or a darkroom for me, if I ever actually took the photography classes that I thought of taking, instead of keeping my crummy little bookkeeping job, but then we got divorced and the room stayed as it was, empty. The rest of the apartment was pretty much the same as when Ted and I were together, furnished from the pages of a Pottery Barn catalogue: classic Americana, all pieces bought and paid for by Ted's TV contracts. He had left me everything when we split, on the pretext it was more hassle than it was worth to ship furniture, but we both knew that I'd be sleeping on a futon if he hadn't.

It had been one of my worst birthdays yet, which was saying a lot. There were no birthday greetings on the answering machine. Not from my mother, which I expected, and not from Ted. He had Julie in his life now, and I had long stopped expecting to hear from him, even though at times like this, I still hoped he might call. I grabbed a cracker and a piece of cheese out of the fridge and forced myself to change into sweats and running shoes. I convinced myself that if I just took a walk, I'd feel better. With the exception of my doctor's appointment, I hadn't left the apartment for weeks, and the lows had been getting longer and deeper. I couldn't start my fortieth year like this, I told myself. I'd get through it, it would pass, and when it did, things would look brighter. And that's when the phone rang.

"Hello, Mrs. Brennan? Elspeth Brennan?"

"Uh, this is Elspeth, but actually it's Robins now. Who is this?"

"Oh, I'm sorry, ma'am. This is Marcy from Grace Adoptions. My files say the applicants are an Elspeth and Ted Brennan, is that correct, ma'am? Has there been a change in the marital status of the applicants?"

My hand slipped on the phone. My palms had broken out into a sweat the moment she had identified herself. I wiped my hands on my track pants and sat down on the edge of the couch.

"Um, no. Robins is just my maiden name. I use it professionally."

"I see. So you and Ted Brennan are still married, ma'am, is that correct?" She sounded young and Southern, and I thought to myself that she had probably been married and making babies all her life. I bet there wasn't enough space on her desk for all her baby-bragging photos.

"Could you please tell me what this is about?" I tried to sound busy and official, and take charge of the conversation.

"Yes, ma'am, you see, our records show your file has gone dormant but hasn't been removed, and we were wondering if you and Mr. Brennan were still hoping to adopt?"

My head started to buzz, and I swallowed before I spoke. "Should we be?"

"Excuse me, ma'am?"

"I said, should we be? We hoped for years, without any success. I was just wondering if we should keep on hoping, or if you are calling with some news."

"Well, uh, that all depends."

"Depends on what?" I squeezed the phone with one hand and my leg with the other.

"It all depends on whether or not you and Mr. Brennan are still looking, and if there have been any changes in the status of your application."

She said it as if she believed there had been, and even though she was right, I was angry at her for implying it.

"And if we were still looking and everything was the same? Then would you have news for me?"

"Well, I...."

"It's my birthday, Marcy, what do you say? Am I going to get a baby for my birthday? Is that why you're calling?" I could hear my voice go up in register, and I was aware that I was raising my voice.

"Well, uh, no, I don't have a baby. But we were wondering if you and Mr. Brennan might like to consider maybe looking to adopt an older child. Now that you yourselves are older."

She said that as if getting older was our fault, as if it was something we'd done on purpose and without the agency's permission. I wanted to yell at her that we got old waiting.

We hadn't been so old when we started.

"How old?" I asked.

"Excuse me?"

"How old would the child be?"

"Um, at least five."

I removed the phone from my face and held it to my chest as I caught my breath. Five, the age of those children that I first taught years ago. I inhaled deeply and spoke slowly into the receiver.

"And if Mr. Brennan and I are no longer together, how old would the child be then? Could I be a mother to a ten-year-old, or would I still not be good enough? Maybe you'd have a teenager for me, you know, someone who is already grown up and on their way to college."

"Mrs. Brennan, am I to understand that there has indeed been a change in the status of your application then?"

"Yes, indeedy, Marcy, there has!" I wanted to smack her. Smack her smug-sounding Southern hospitality right out of her mouth.

"I see," she said slowly, and I could hear her writing away.

"No Marcy, I don't think you do," I said, standing up and pacing the apartment. "Because if you did, you might not sound so fucking chipper. It's not like this is some service call about my cable. You're not asking me if I want the *Sunday Times* delivered, you're asking me if I still have that giant gaping hole in my heart where a child was supposed to go and if you can rip it open just a little bit further, and make me wait and hope for something that you are never, ever going to give me!"

"I'm sorry, Mrs....Ms. Robins. I'll make the changes to your application and we'll close it. Have a good day, ma'am."

"Fuck you, Marcy," I yelled, but she had already hung up. I threw the phone against the wall and started sobbing. I moved quickly through the apartment, unable to stand still, unable to stand being in my own skin anymore. I thought about calling Ted, but it was too much. I wished I had someone to talk to. I would've even settled for my mother, but it had been years since we had spoken. No husband, no parents, no friends. I had isolated myself with the shame of my failure, and it had worked. I was alone. And it seemed I was always going to be alone. It hurt to cry and it hurt worse to try to stop; every cell in my body screamed out *Enough!* until it was the only word ringing through my ears: *Enough, enough, enough!*

"Enough!" I yelled out, grabbing the bottle of anti-depressants from the bottom of my purse. I emptied the entire bottle into my hand, shoved all of the pills into my mouth, and downed them with a glass of water. The bitter taste of the medication burnt my throat, then I lay down on the edge of my bed, grabbed a pillow, and passed out.

I must've fallen on the floor, because that's where the landlord found me. In an effort to locate me and tell me my mother had died, Vincent called the last number my mother had on file for me and got Ted instead. When I didn't answer Ted's calls, he remembered it was my birthday and, suspecting that I was holed up in my apartment depressed, asked the landlord to go in and check on me.

When the landlord wanted to know what happened, I said I'd read the label wrong and accidentally mixed medications, and then I went to the bathroom and threw up for hours. By the way he looked at me sideways I knew he didn't believe me, but I didn't care. When I finally called Ted the next day, I lied about not feeling well and turning the ringer off. He offered to let me stay at his place in Toronto while I dealt with my mother's death, and I accepted. I packed my suitcase and left the landlord a note giving notice and telling him that he could take anything and everything in my apartment. I wouldn't need it anymore. Somehow, I knew I was never coming back.

CHAPTER THIRTEEN

I checked into my hotel in Paris's Latin Quarter and grabbed a map from the woman at the front desk. I did my best to ignore the sympathetic look she gave me when I told her I was traveling alone and didn't need the upgrade to a queen-size room, an admission I regretted immediately after being relegated to a room with a single bed by the elevator.

"Ah, the spinster suite," I said as she opened the door for me, unsure if she understood my English or not.

After years of being alone, I'd come to the realization that my being single bothered those around me much more than it did me, and I did my best to ignore the pitying looks doled out to the lone female traveler. Even the taxi driver told me that Paris was the City of Lovers, as if I should make that true to really enjoy my visit. It was also the city of liars and cheats and strange cults, I wanted to tell him, but just nodded as he turned up the radio and did his best not to look at the crazy lady in the back seat who was glaring at him and muttering to herself.

As I wandered along Place de la Contrescarpe, I pictured my mother walking these same cobblestone streets as a young woman, falling in love with the art and the architecture. She would have loved Paris's overwhelming sense of history, and that it had long been the stomping grounds of great writers and artists. Across from my hotel was a little plaque that marked the building Ernest Hemingway had lived and written in, and farther down the road were the homes of James Joyce and George Orwell. It was surreal to think of all those great writers, and many more, hanging out together in one of the numerous little cafés that I passed. My mother would have been right at home here, seated at an outdoor table, beautifully dressed, her long hair tied in a scarf, arguing passionately about art, philosophy, and religion. It was a perfect fit for her, all of the old coupled with all of the new. I couldn't imagine what would have brought her back to Canada when she could've stayed in Paris.

This wasn't how I hoped my first visit to the city would be. Who didn't want to come to Paris on the arm of a lover and roam the streets, stopping only to kiss and gaze at each other adoringly? I must have passed half a dozen couples who were doing just that, fingers intertwined behind each other's backs as they held each other close against the wind and warmed their lips on each other's mouths. I felt a pang in my chest as I thought of Ted kissing me back in Toronto, and I wanted nothing more than to have him here with me doing just that. I undid my scarf and let the cold hit the back of my neck where his mouth should have been, and did my best not to cry. I thought a lot of things would happen in my life, but being alone at thirty-nine wasn't one of them. How did I get here? And what would I have done for things to have turned out differently? It was a useless form of questioning, and I knew by now it got me nowhere. The answer was always the same. Nothing. Shit happens. Life happens, and we do our best to roll with it.

That's what I had always told myself, but lately I'd begun to wonder if it was true. What if I could have changed my fate by changing my karma, as my mother had believed? Where would I be now? I had never stopped blaming myself for being unable to have children. I thought of all those times I'd hoped not to get pregnant, looking at women who gave up their careers to be mothers with disdain. I had gotten my wish. It was dangerous for me to think like this, and I needed a drink before it went any further.

I stopped at a little café at the far edge of a fountain in the Latin Quarter. I chose a seat inside at the bar instead of at one of the little tables, made just big enough for two plates and just small enough for couples to hold hands across the table without leaning forward, their knees touching underneath. I thought how the restaurant looked right out of a movie, although whether it was truly Parisian or just tourist Parisian, I didn't know. The walls were a deep red, and the sconces that lined them were topped with little black lampshades. The tiny round tables had hammered-copper sides, and the café's name was written across the center of each, surrounded by gold stars. I ordered a glass of red wine from the bartender and then another when he came back with the menu. I wasn't hungry, but I knew I would be when I woke up in the middle of the night disoriented and jet-lagged, and by then it would be too late to do anything about it. I asked for a bowl of soup with some bread, laid out my map and pamphlets, and tried to locate the Wellness Center.

I wanted to go there first thing in the morning. I wasn't here to sightsee, and since deciding to come, I'd thought of little else. Sadly, the Eiffel Tower had little on Henri and the Seekers.

"Madame," said the waiter, placing down the food.

"Merci," I said, covering the pamphlet with my hand. Who knew what reputation the Seekers had. Until recently I'd assumed it was a disorganized group of old hippies that had all but faded away, but now I knew better. My poor attempt only attracted the attention of the bartender, who stopped by my elbow and raised his eyebrow at me.

"Um, do you know where this place is?" I said, in the best French that I could remember from high school.

He picked up the pamphlet, bit his lip, and in fluent English answered, "Yes, it is about fifteen minutes from here. It's very popular, lots of artists and drug addicts go." He lowered his chin and peered at me from under hooded lids.

"Oh, well, I am neither," I said, lifting my wine glass and awkwardly putting it down. "I'm just looking for someone." I pulled at a piece of bread.

"Someone, or something?"

"Never mind," I said, pulling the pamphlet closer and avoiding his gaze.

He walked to the other end of the bar and returned with the bottle of wine and topped up my glass. "My ex-girlfriend went there. They helped her a lot. They also took all her money, but then again, I suppose she would've just snorted it all away anyway." He turned the pamphlet over. "This guy. She always talked about him. Like he was Jesus or something." He pointed at the picture of Henri and shook his head.

Or something.

"And he fixed her?" I asked.

"For a while. She was in love with him, and when he didn't leave his wife, well, she went back to using drugs and...." His voice trailed off. "She left them all her money, can you believe it? Not that there was much to leave." He touched his finger to his nose, and I knew what he meant.

I wondered if the Seekers had expected my mother to do the same. They must've been very disappointed to learn she'd left all her unpaid bills and the responsibility of selling her apartment to me.

"My mother was a member," I said, surprising myself.

"Oh."

"Yeah. But she's dead now, cancer." It was the first time I said it for nothing other than the truth.

"Merde." He ran his hand over his stubbly chin and shook his head.

He seemed too old to be a bartender, but then again I'd heard that bartending in France was much more of a profession than it was in someplace like Los Angeles, where every server was a model, actor, or aspiring screenwriter. In LA it was the job people did in between rather than the job that people did. His fingers were stained with nicotine, just like Henri's had been the first time I had seen them, and for a moment I saw Henri standing before me, as he could've been.

"I'm sorry they couldn't fix her," he said, resting his elbows on the bar and leaning forward. "What with all their vitamins, teas, and special bathing waters. They say they can cure cancer, but you need to be ready for it to be cured; you need to have done the work. If you don't get cured, they say it's your fault." He shrugged angrily.

"You really know a lot about them," I said gently.

He looked around the restaurant. It was empty except for a couple by the window, who looked like they could use a room but seemed content to improvise with the small table and chairs. No one needed his attention, so he grabbed a glass from above the bar and filled it with wine for himself.

"Your mother was not alone. They couldn't fix me either," he said, taking a large drink.

"I'm sorry."

"Why? I am still here." He smiled, and his tired eyes broke into crinkly paper fans at their corners.

"True," I said, allowing myself to smile back and take in his long, thin face.

He was about my age, maybe a little younger, but I wasn't sure that mattered once you were over thirty. I didn't know. I hadn't been with anyone since Ted, and what's worse, I hadn't even imagined that I ever would be again. It seemed absurd as I sat here, a lonely woman in Paris, that I'd been with only a handful of men in my life, and after my divorce I'd assumed that was it. And it seemed unreal that in the first café I went to, I'd meet someone with whom I had less than six degrees of separation. But I had. I couldn't ignore it, and I didn't want to. I took a long drink of wine. I didn't want the last lips to have touched mine to belong to my ex-husband. I didn't want my former lover to see me as an old, lonely, divorced woman, even if I was one. I took a deep breath, undid the scarf around my neck and removed my jacket and draped it on the stool next to me. I shook my hair loose from its bun and twisted it in my fingers. I ate my dinner, and ordered another glass of wine, and when it came time to close the bar, I waited. I may have been a cliché, but I didn't care. *I am still here.* I had been elsewhere, anywhere, hiding for so long, and now for one night I needed to let someone else look for me.

"You make love like it might be the last time," said Luc the next morning. Sometime during the night, in between our lovemaking, I had learned his name.

"Oh?"

"It's a compliment."

I rolled onto my back, letting the sun that was starting to stream in through the window rest upon my face. I knew what he meant. For the first time in a long time, I felt wide awake.

"And what's your reason?" I asked, turning my head to see him resting on the pillow beside me.

"I'm French." He cracked a smile and I laughed out loud. The laughter rippled through my body, and as soon as it left, I felt a cry well up where it had been, and tears start to leak down my face.

"I'm sorry. I don't know why I'm crying."

Luc rolled on his elbow and placed his left hand on my chest. "It's okay. You're just relaxed. You're not wearing your armor right now."

"I'll need my armor later on," I said, placing my hand on his. "When I go to see the Seekers."

"No. You'll need your strength. It's not the same thing." He leaned down and kissed my hand. "And breakfast. You'll need that too," he said, picking up the phone and ordering us room service.

I couldn't help but notice the innkeeper's eyes widen at the sight of the empty wine bottle and glasses next to the dresser, the sheets twisted in a heap in the middle of the bed, and the tall, shirtless French man who took the tray of coffee and croissants from her and thanked her.

"Bon appétit," said Luc as we sat at the little table by the window overlooking the courtyard.

"Bon appétit."

I'd only wanted coffee, but it seemed crazy to go all the way to Paris and not eat a croissant. I tore off the end and reached my fingers down the middle of the croissant and pulled the sweet center out, like Lafina had shown me how to do. I'd dreamt of her again last night, the dream of fire returning to me in the few hours I'd slept. The flames had burned brighter this time, and I felt them licking my body as if real, the line between memory and dream harder to discern than ever. This time, when my mother told me to run, I went straight to the outstretched branches of the tree, which wrapped me in its embrace and held me tightly to its trunk. Exhausted, I cried tears of relief, which softened the trunk until it transformed into Lafina's belly, and for a brief moment, I believed I was safe. And then a chorus of voices rose up from the earth, and Lafina let out a howl so strong it shook the night sky and whipped across the ground. The force of her wailing threw me backward, and when I opened my eyes I saw she had grown large white wings that carried her up and into the flames that engulfed our home. I felt a hand grip my own as I screamed her name. *Lafina! Lafina!* And I woke up, drenched and shivering from the sweat on my naked body, my hand tightly squeezing Luc's, his fingers curled just as my mother's once had, against my palm.

"Can I ask you something?" I said.

"I should think so," said Luc, eating his croissant.

"Could you tell me about the initiation process? I was told you couldn't be a full member of the Seekers unless you were initiated. What does that mean?"

"It means you agree to devote your life to them. You can always drop in on meetings, but to really study with them and receive their counsel and blessings, you must agree to follow their ways, abide by their meditation practices…and donate your money."

I wanted to ask more about the actual process, but I could see by the way he tightened his jaw it wasn't a subject he wanted to talk about. I fiddled with the ivory ring on my hand, running my thumb back and forth along its smooth underside, and was surprised when he continued.

"They decide when you are ready to be initiated, and

they choose their members carefully. The more important you are, and by that I mean the more money you have, the faster you get initiated. The more you give, the higher up their ladder you go, and the more you believe you will be saved from whatever it is you're looking to be saved from." He paused and took a deep breath, and I reached over to his hand and held it in mine. He squeezed my hand back and then reached for his cigarettes, taking one out and lighting it. He took a long drag, threw his head back, and exhaled smoke up toward the ceiling.

"I watched Céline, my girlfriend, become a member. We were both in line for initiation, but that bastard Henri must've wanted her badly, so she was picked before I was. Céline was upset—she really wanted us to be initiated together—so at the last minute, he invited me to attend. He said that way I could see what was in store for me when my time came. The ceremony was held at night. Everyone gathered in a circle holding candles, forming a ring for the new members to enter."

Out of the darkness and into the light... that's how Henri had signed his letters after he had started acting crazy.

"We all stood in silence as they made their way one by one, taking their rites, and then it was Céline's turn. I watched as she walked to the center of the circle, slowly removed her clothes, and stood naked in front of the leaders. In front of all of us." He took another drag and stared down at the table, ashing his cigarette into the saucer of his coffee cup. "They had her turn in a circle, and as she did they counted her shadows. Each shadow represented a stain upon her soul."

"But the candlelight...."

"It casts a lot of shadows." He shook his head sadly and stubbed out his cigarette. "But it doesn't really matter, they could say two or they could say two hundred, and you'd believe them. By the time you are initiated, they know all your secrets anyway. It's part of the unburdening process. They make you believe that the greater your burden, the more you have to do, give, volunteer. You are literally *paying* for your sins."

I shuddered at the thought of my own mother naked before Philippe and the others, and wondered how many shadows they would've counted for her, and what they knew that I didn't.

"After that, everything and everyone else in your life comes second, and the group and its members come first. You're not who you were before, but you're working off your karmic debt toward who you want to be. They even give you a new name."

"They gave my mother one."

"How long was she a member?"

"A long time. I first heard her mention them about twenty-five years ago."

Luc sat up straight and turned toward me, his face serious.

"Twenty-five years?"

"Yes."

"That means that she was one of the originals. She helped build the center that you are going to see."

"I find that hard to believe. My mother wasn't very good at manual labor."

"This is not a joke. She must have been very important to them. What was her name?"

"Rachel. Devedra."

"Philippe's wife." He lit another cigarette. "Merde."

I felt my face get hot as I watched him drag on the cigarette and shake his head.

"She was not his wife."

"She was his *spirit* wife," he said, sighing heavily. "That is what they call it, when you're with someone in the organization, even if you're already with someone else on the outside. Convenient, no? They have a whole wedding ceremony, and the 'wife' signs over everything to her new husband. What a racket. My ex-girlfriend became a spirit bride of that asshole son of his. Well, she was one of them. She used to wear a little ring and everything."

I felt my flesh go cold as soon as he said it, and I instinctively hid my hand beneath the table. My mother must have promised whatever she had to the Seekers, and this ring proved it.

"Did you ever meet my mother?"

"No. But I did see her, and of course I'd heard of her. But I was too low, and too poor, on the ladder to mix."

"I'm sorry. I really didn't know much about them. And what I did know, I didn't like."

"And yet you travel all this way to meet with them?"

"My mother and I weren't close. I'm just trying to understand."

"Them or her?"

"Both."

"Be careful," he said as he lifted my chin and stared

into my eyes. "They won't tell you the truth."

"Oh yes they will, and I'm not leaving until I get it."
I closed my hand tightly around the ring and took a deep
breath. If anyone was actually watching me, or looking
over me, I needed them to pay extra attention today.

I decided to walk to the Wellness Center after having learned
it was just under an hour away. I left the hotel and headed
north to Cardinal Lemoine, my boots clacking along the
cobblestone streets lined with shops selling their goods out
front, stacked high in wooden crates. Bottles of wine with
beautiful labels sold for little more than a bottle of water,
and everywhere the scent of fresh bread was met with that
of cheeses and of crêpes being cooked at roadside carts. I
inhaled the cool morning air deeply and could almost taste
the Nutella being slathered onto the crêpes students were
grabbing for breakfast on their way to school. For once I
didn't hate the fact it was winter. Here life didn't seem to
slow down with the cold; the streets were full and busy,
the markets crowded with shoppers and vendors who were
bundled up in oversize scarves, their hands moving quickly
in fingerless gloves. I understood very little French, but I
loved the sound of it just the same. There was something
wonderful about not knowing what people around me
were saying, as if not understanding the language gave me
license to just stare and enjoy them. I moved briskly along
Rue Monge, past Boulevard St. Germain, until I came to
Shakespeare and Co. The famous bookstore with its green
and yellow façade was packed to capacity with locals and

tourists combing through the sale shelves out front. I could easily imagine my mother parked on the bench outside lingering over her beloved books. I checked my little map and made a left at quai de Conti. I was a long way from Los Angeles. I was a long way away from anything that I knew, and yet I walked with purpose, not sure what I was walking into, but sure of my reasons for doing so.

After another twenty minutes I arrived at the Musée d'Orsay and made a left down the rue de Bellechasse. It was just a name, until you separated it into two words, *belle* and *chasse*, translating into either "good hunting" or "beautiful search." Both were accurate: one described the greed of the organization, and the other the desires of its members. I stopped in front of what looked like a small museum, but then again most of the buildings here did. Even the government buildings were magnificent centuries-old sculptures with large wrought iron gates and private entrances that looked like they'd once been mansions of the incredibly wealthy. I ran my hand along the stone columns at the entryway and over the small gold plaque with the center's name. The age and stature of the building made it seem as if the Seekers had been here forever, but the dates on their pamphlets and in their books revealed they'd only been publishing since the 1950s. Still, the building was impressive, and impressions were important.

"I'm sorry, madame, but without an appointment, I'm afraid waiting won't do you any good," said the young receptionist from behind her information desk. "You are welcome to take some of our literature and come back at a scheduled time."

"I'm not going anywhere," I said, seating myself in the overstuffed leather chair in the lobby, next to the bubbling fountain full of floating lotus flowers.

"I'm going to have to ask you to leave," she said, coming out from behind her desk and walking over to me.

"Just give him this, and if he doesn't come out after he reads it, I'll go." I took one of the flyers off the table and wrote on the back, *A la prochaine…Elsie*, folded it in half, and handed it to her. "I'll wait."

She took the folded piece of paper and strode off down the hall.

This place felt more like a spa than a wellness center, with its organic-green-tea dispenser, pitcher of water with lemon slices, and plate of freshly cut oranges to enjoy while you waited. I looked at the pamphlets on the table advertising their meditation retreats. For thousands of dollars, a member could have one-on-one counseling sessions with Henri and the chance to meditate and do yoga with celebrity instructors. Their brochures were full of testimonials from CEOs and successful artists who claimed they had seen the light and realized their true destinies as members of the Seekers. Through loyal devotion they'd been able to reverse illness and change misfortunes into fortunes by paying off their karmic debt, just as Henri had.

Along the walls were a series of photographs in gold frames documenting the history of the center from twenty-five years ago until the present day. The original building looked more like a small schoolhouse than the grand structure I stood in now. It sat on a wide expanse of land, presumably outside the city, with a small wooden sign hanging off the center of the roof. In front of the building a few members of the Seekers stood close together and smiled at the camera. In the center was Philippe, strong and proud, his chest puffed out as the camera captured his moment.

I looked at the other faces in the line and saw my mother's. She looked to be about my age. She was wearing a cotton skirt that was belted across her trim waist, and a simple blouse with the Van Cleef & Arpels pin. So that's when she got it. It must've been a gift from Philippe.

The other photos were of this new building and its transformation into the Wellness Center: members holding paint brushes, putting up new walls, and tiling the entryway, their faces beaming with smiles. The final photo showed the completed center, with hundreds of people standing in front holding a ribbon being cut by Philippe. Henri was on one side of his father and my mother was on the other, holding his arm, the large ivory and gold ring on display for all to see. According to the date, it had been taken only two years ago, and I wondered if my mother had known she was sick at the time. She was extremely thin, and her hair, although completely gray, was tucked up at the nape of her neck in the same chignon she always wore. She was as put together as ever, but it was the look shining in her eyes that really struck me, the look of genuine pride. She was where she wanted to be.

I thought of all the time she'd spent at the sideline of Philippe's life, working with him to raise money for the Seekers, and it would seem it had all paid off, as she stood next to the man and the cause, front and center for all to see. I wondered where her spirit brothers and sisters had been as she lay in bed dying halfway across the world.

I looked down the hallway where the receptionist had gone, but there was little to see past the thick, frosted-glass doors etched with the Seekers logo. A logo, and a little trademark symbol next to it—that was new. They really had come a long way since gathering in loaned meeting places. I touched the ivory ring in my pocket and tried to still my heart. For a moment I wondered if Henri would even remember me, or if he'd just read the note, stare at it blankly, and send the receptionist back after telling her he had no idea what it meant. I didn't have to wonder much longer, as the young woman returned. She placed her hand on my shoulder and smiled one of those insipid smiles meant to convey sincerity. Instinctively I pulled back.

"You're Devedra's daughter. You should've just said so."

I cringed as she said my mother's spirit name. She tilted her head, then turned back toward the frosted doors. "Follow me."

I did as she said, and at the end of a long hallway we came to two more double doors that she opened for me. Henri stood with his back to me, facing the windows that overlooked the highly manicured French gardens with a mini-labyrinth, sculptures, and a fountain. Outside, members were reading, walking the garden, or sitting in meditation, all under the eye of the man who they lay their total trust in. I stood in the doorway and waited.

Henri slowly turned to face me, holding his palms upward and extended, as if I was to walk forward and take them. He looked exactly as he did on the back of his book, tanned and clean cut, no longer stooped at the shoulders; he stood tall and confident. "I am very sorry about your mother. We all are."

I said nothing. It wasn't the greeting I expected to hear after all these years.

"Please, Elsie, come in, come in."

He gestured to the seat in front of me, and I took it as he sat in his oversize leather chair, the desk separating us. "It's been a long time," he said. "Where to begin?" He opened his face into a wide smile, but the gray eyes, once so soulful I could get lost in them, remained guarded. Maybe it wasn't as easy to pretend in front of someone who'd seen all the crazy that you had to offer.

"How about here?" I replied, gesturing to his massive office. "This is a surprise."

"Only to you, and maybe me at first," he said, forcing a small laugh. "But this was always meant to happen."

"Fate. Karma," I said, hanging onto the last word.

"Yes. I take it you still don't believe." He folded his hands under his chin and leaned on them.

"Just not in the same way you do." It wasn't that I didn't believe in karma, or cause and effect, it was that I didn't believe we were powerless in our own lives and destinies. "You didn't used to believe either. You were on a mission to expose your father and the group. And me." I felt my voice break a little at the memory of Henri yelling "whore" on the street.

"That was a lifetime ago. So much has happened since. I understand you've been married and divorced, and I am married with three children. We are no longer the children we were when our parents introduced us, when we still lived at home."

"I haven't lived at home for a long time. You, on the other hand, look like you never left." I bit the inside of my cheek to stop myself from losing control.

He tightened his jaw and his face went red. "I can see you're still angry, and I suppose you're right." He took a breath and exhaled slowly. "I should have apologized for that night. I was sick and confused. I was lost and I needed help."

"And the group helped you."

"They did. And I realized if they could help me, just think of all the others they could help. But it would take vision, someone who was willing to do more than just spread the word and be adored by his followers, someone who was willing to devote himself to making the Seekers the refuge we are now. It may hurt you to hear it, but that night was one of the best nights of my life. I heard my calling and I answered, and it has brought me here."

"And judging from the photos I passed in the hallway, here is a long way from the original center."

"People have been very generous," he said, looking at me.

"People like my mother?"

"Yes. Thanks to people like her we are no longer meeting in conference rooms and public parks. She was devoted to the group, and she was determined to make amends. It was why she joined in the first place."

"Amends for what?" What else had she hidden from me?

"She never told you?" His face softened, and he stood up and came around the desk and sat in the chair next to me.

"My mother told me a lot of things; what was true and what wasn't, I'm still trying to find out."

"The truth about your father."

I felt my whole body stiffen. "What do you know about my father?"

"What your mother was afraid to tell you."

My heart was beating faster now, and I worried Henri would hear it. Had my mother really shared the secret of my paternity with him?

"She already told me Howard wasn't my real father, but his brother, Leo, was. What I don't know is why she told you." I crossed my arms and waited for his answer.

"We don't have secrets here."

"Bullshit."

"When members are initiated they unburden themselves to the group's leader."

"To Philippe you mean."

"Yes, and in turn to me."

I stared at Henri, my eyes wide in surprise. What happened to Philippe?

Henri hesitated a moment before answering. "What she didn't tell you was that Leo had drunk himself into a stupor at a party earlier in the evening and had embarrassed her in front of everyone. He was in no shape to drive, but Rachel insisted they leave and let him get behind the wheel. She was angry at the way he behaved, and he was furious she was criticizing him. They fought bitterly and were so busy yelling at each other that they didn't see the other car coming until it was too late. Rachel blamed herself. If only she hadn't let him drive. If only they'd stayed behind at the party until he sobered up, things might have turned out differently."

"Why are you telling me this?" The words came out in a whisper.

"Because you should know." He reached for my hand and gently placed it in his, putting his other hand on top. The gesture, together with the look on his face, made him seem almost vulnerable, like the Henri I'd once cared for. "She came to us for salvation, Elsie. To right her karma."

I pulled my hand back from him. "A death on her conscience. Tell me, Henri, what kind of karmic price tag does that carry?"

"Your mother did everything she could, but in the end it was clear by the way she died that her work wasn't done." He stood and walked back to the other side of his desk.

"You mean broke and alone?"

His eyes widened, scrunching the lines in his forehead. "I mean how she died. Cancer. We tried to cure her with diet, aura cleanses, and intensive karmic unburdening sessions, but she was still sick. It was clear she'd be back to try and make things right in another lifetime."

He spoke as if he was trying to explain it to a child, as if it was an answer as obvious as the color of the sky.

"Is that when you tried to get a down payment for her next lifetime's worth of karmic cleansing classes? Or did you just ship her back to Canada, where no one could see how you failed her?"

"She left us, not the other way around."

"She had cancer, she shouldn't have been alone." I grabbed the arm of the chair, digging my fingernails into it.

"Cancer was just a manifestation. She had unresolved issues."

"Sure. And what did you need her for anymore anyway? I'm sure you got everything she had."

His face turned hard, and he clenched his jaw as he spoke. "Is that what this is really about? Money? Because I'm afraid it was her wish to leave her estate to us, so there's no point in fighting it."

Henri reached into his desk and took out a file with my mother's name on it. He pulled out a faded document and handed it to me. I looked at the signature on the bottom of the first page; it was my mother's handwriting. I checked the date. She would have been twenty-five years old at the time of her initiation.

"It says she promises to give the Seekers twenty-five percent of everything she makes."

"Yes, and it says here," he said, flipping the page and pointing hard against it, "she willingly agrees to leave her estate to us." It was my mother's "marriage contract" to Philippe.

"Well, I can tell you that she made a new will just before she died, and according to her lawyer, it trumps any other preexisting wills or promises, this one included. But, really, Henri, what's the difference? Everything she owned came to me, and I promise you, you'd have little use for what I inherited. Her entire *estate* consisted of a heavily mort-gaged one-bedroom apartment and a pile of debt." I shook my head. I don't know why I was surprised—my mother had been telling lies her whole life, doling out pieces of the truth to different people, but never enough so they'd have the whole picture. Had she lied to the Seekers too, to make herself more valuable to them, more *interesting*?

"Don't play games with me, Elspeth. Your mother was a very wealthy woman, and we both know it. She obviously wasn't of sound mind when she wrote the new will. She always intended for her fortune to go to us."

"Are you even listening to me?" I threw my hands up, exasperated. "There is no fortune—my mother conned you just as much as you conned her."

He smiled as if he didn't believe me and suddenly stepped forward and wrapped his hand around my waist and pulled me closer.

"It's not a coincidence that your mother's death has brought us back together. This was always meant to be. We can be your family. Isn't that what you've always wanted? A family, a place to belong?"

I stumbled as I pulled myself away. "Stop it. You don't mean any of it." I felt physically ill and was shaking. "I want to talk to Philippe."

"You can't. He's on leave."

"When he is returning?"

"I haven't decided." He ran his hand through his hair and then reached for me. "Elsie, please...."

"Touch me again and I'll scream. I want to talk to Philippe."

"Listen to me...."

"Tell me where he is and I'll give you something."

His eyes widened and he bit his bottom lip. "Don't do it for me, do it for Devedra."

I reached into my pocket and took out the gold and ivory ring.

"Where'd you find that?" He leaned forward and stared at the ring.

"Not where you were looking."

His eyes met mine and he nodded slightly. He was caught. I'd been right, the Seekers had ransacked my mother's apartment, and now we both knew it.

"The ring is sacred, and it belongs to us."

"So you say."

"That ring was a gift and is supposed to go to the spirit wife of our leader. Whoever wears it has the blessing and respect of every member of the Seekers." He stared at me for a moment and spoke softly, "Why don't you try it on? I bet you already have. I bet it fits you perfectly."

"Give me Philippe," I said, tightening my fist.

Henri tore off a piece of embossed stationery from his notepad, wrote out the address, and handed it to me in exchange for the ring.

"He can't protect you Elspeth, only I can. Whatever assets you're hiding from us, we'll find them." Henri slipped the ring on his pinky finger and looked up at me, his mouth a tight line. He inhaled deeply, and his eyes were hard as he spoke. "No matter where you go. We'll find you."

I met his eyes and stepped forward until only a breath separated us. "Knock yourself out," I said, and turned and left.

CHAPTER FOURTEEN

I shuddered out loud once I was on the street. To think that the man I'd shared all my firsts with had turned into that. Were we all so easily corruptible? Or had Henri just grown up like he said he had, while I'd stayed stuck in the emotional landscape of my youth, yearning for a family that I didn't have, longing to be happy and loved but struggling to get there?

After Ted and I had divorced, I'd often daydreamed that Henri and I would find each other, and he'd be as fucked up as I remembered him, and all my failures and shortcomings would mercifully pale in comparison. He would look at me and know, just as he once had, where I was at and what I had been through. He'd wrap me in his arms, and I'd lay my head on his chest and wordlessly transmit all my heartbreak. And I wouldn't have to worry about disappointing him as I had Ted.

Instead Henri had become his father, and who knew what would become of me if I didn't get the answers I was looking for. I wasn't prepared to wait and see.

The landlady opened the door and let me into the flat to wait for Philippe. "Please, please come in," she said, pulling me inside and closing the door behind us.

It was an average-size home by North American standards, which made it large for the French. What cosmopolitan cities like Paris and New York sacrificed in terms of living space, they made up for with culture and vibrancy. People in big cities didn't expect to live in places where each room had a singular purpose and there were more bathrooms than inhabitants, and so even though this was clearly the home of a wealthy man, it wasn't the gilded mansion I had envisioned for a charlatan as gifted as Philippe. It felt more like a family home, a place where children once gathered around the big kitchen table and where guests lounged on the sofa reading from the stacks of books that lined the living room walls. The floors were made up of large wooden planks, and the white plaster walls were adorned with prints of flora and fauna that matched the heavy green and white toile curtains. It was obvious someone had spent a lot of time decorating this living room, and I doubted that person was Philippe.

"He doesn't get many visitors. I'm sure he'll be happy to see you," she said.

"I think I should just wait here," I replied, tugging my sleeve from her bony little grip and hanging back in the entrance.

"Nonsense. What did you say your name was again?" She wiped her hand on her apron and flashed me a big, toothless smile.

"Elspeth." I leaned back toward the door and wondered

if this was a mistake. Just being in the same house as Philippe made my legs feel wobbly. The old woman standing before me clearly wasn't all there. Her blue eyes shone in her wrinkled face, milky and blank as if I had just appeared before her a second ago.

"What did you say your name was again, dear?" she repeated.

"Who is it, Marie?"

I stopped and held my breath as I heard the voice coming closer.

"Um, she said her name was, um...."

"Oh, for God's sake, hang on, I'm coming."

I closed my eyes and exhaled as slowly as I could before opening them again.

"Can I help you?"

"Yes, I...."As he came into view, my mouth dropped open and my knees went weak: Philippe in a wheelchair. I hadn't been prepared for the sight of him as an old man, whose once soul-piercing eyes now rested behind thick reading glasses. Age had caught up with him, and his once-trim physique now curled and sagged beneath a ratty cardigan that hung off his sunken body. Marie shuffled over to him and placed her hand on his shoulder.

"I'll go put the kettle on, monsieur." She tapped him a few times, flashed me a gummy smile, and shuffled off back down the hall, leaving us alone.

"Philippe," I said, my mouth feeling like it had gone numb as I tried to find his eyes.

"Yes, who are you?" he asked, leaning forward.

"It's me, Elspeth. Rachel's daughter." My whole body

deflated as I spoke, and I leaned against the doorway to help me stay upright.

"Elspeth," he said, settling back against his chair. "Oh. Elspeth." He hung his head and wrung his hands. "I am so sorry about your mother. I loved her very much, you know." He wheeled his chair into the living room and parked it next to the window.

I didn't know what to say. I was sure he did, but that didn't take away from the fact that this man raped me twenty-three years earlier, then called me a liar and cast on me a shadow of shame that I had spent years trying to undo. I wanted to believe that I deserved the kind of happiness Ted dreamed for me. As far as he was concerned, I could have *thrown* myself at Philippe and it still wouldn't have excused what he did to me. He'd remind me that I wasn't much more than a child, only sixteen, and I had a right to feel safe, and nothing I could have said or done meant I deserved what happened. I knew Ted was right. I knew it, but never really felt it. It was why I could never fight as hard as he could for my happiness.

"What happened, Philippe?" I asked, following after him and standing next to the couch. If he really loved my mother as much as he said, then why did she die alone? People who were loved weren't supposed to die alone. It was a fate I expected for myself, but not for a woman who had willingly been the mistress of the same man for decades.

I wanted him to stand up and look me in the face, but instead he was so small in his wheelchair, with his curved spine and his skinny legs resting on their pedals. He fished into his cardigan for a handkerchief and wiped his eyes.

"I had a bad fall and never recovered properly."

"Not to you. To my mother." It came out harshly and I was glad.

"Of course. Devedra."

"Rachel. Her *real* name was Rachel. You don't get to abandon her and still call her that."

He took a deep breath and turned to face me. "Rachel." He said it deliberately and waved for me to sit down.

"I'm fine right here, thank you." I gripped the back of the couch and stood up straighter.

"You've come all this way. Sit. Please."

I sat on the couch, in the spot farthest away from him, folded my arms across my body, and waited.

"We did everything we could, but she was very sick," he said.

"I know, cancer. I found out after I returned to Toronto to clean up her affairs. What I don't know is, if she was such an important part of the Seekers and you loved her so much, why she was all alone when she died?"

"Why, indeed." He looked me in the eyes, and I felt the hair on my arms stand on end. "Where were you?"

"I had no idea she was ill. She never told me, but then again, I think we both know that she chose you over me a long time ago."

"Here you are, some tea for the mademoiselle and for you, monsieur," said Marie, returning with a tray. She set down a cup before me, placed some pastries in the center of the table, and took the other cup to Philippe. She waited until he tasted it, his age-spotted hands rattling the china as he did, and then she left again, humming to herself.

"Your mother wanted to make a difference. She was a smart woman who'd been trapped by circumstance and was full of so much potential that was just being wasted when we met. She had lost someone she loved very much and was trying to—"

"Make amends, I know. Henri told me she blamed herself for the accident."

"Your mother wasn't just some blind follower, Elspeth. She used to be a believer."

"Used to be?" I asked, leaning forward in my chair.

"Your mother stopped believing in me long before she died."

"What happened?"

"She learned the truth." He sighed heavily and continued. "That she wasn't the only one."

"I thought your group allowed that kind of thing."

"We do. But Rachel didn't. Just because it was allowed didn't mean she was okay with it. Still, I think she would have forgiven me almost anything. We went a long way back."

"To Africa." I stared at Philippe, wondering if he would deny it.

"Yes, to Africa."

"You knew her all that time and you never said anything."

"Some secrets aren't mine to tell."

"Not if they pay your way, right?" Philippe's eyes met mine and for a moment neither of us looked away. I was right, we both knew it.

"I loved your mother. I didn't plan on it. She was young

and heartbroken and rich when we met. Like the others. But Rachel didn't need direction, she needed redemption. And she would have given anything to get it."

"And judging by the state of her affairs when she died, she did."

"She may have lost faith in me, but she hadn't lost faith in the group's teachings. She still believed in karma, still believed that she could right the wrongs she'd done, but she was running out of time; she was sick, and I didn't want to see her suffer anymore. She needed to see a real doctor. I didn't want to be responsible for her death; I was already responsible for so much of her suffering. You were a part of that suffering. I begged her to go, but I knew the only way she would was if she lost total faith in the group, and so I told her about that day…in your room."

His voice cracked, and he reached for his handkerchief and gripped it tightly.

"I went to Henri first and told him I was to blame for what happened. I told him I was sorry and that I needed to tell Rachel before she died and it was too late."

"And?"

"He said it didn't matter anymore, and there was no point in drudging up the past. He said I should think about what was best for the group. He said Rachel had dedicated her whole life to the Seekers and learning this now might make her have second thoughts."

"Second thoughts about leaving you the money, that is."

"Yes. Your mother promised the organization a lot of money. She had property and assets, and she wanted us to have them. She had always been loyal to us, to me, even when I didn't deserve it. But after she learned about what I did, and that Henri knew but didn't want to say anything, any faith she'd had in the group was gone. But by the time she saw a doctor in Canada, there was nothing they could do, and I never saw her again."

"That's some karmic debt you have, Philippe—or don't you believe in that anymore?"

Philippe continued to stare out the window at the bare rose bushes. "I'm not sure it matters what I believe anymore. I have seen the future of the group, and it doesn't look anything like I pictured."

"You mean Henri. So he's punishing you for telling Rachel the truth, is that it?"

"It's my fault he is the way he is. I was young when I started the Seekers. I loved to talk, and people loved to hear me speak. And it felt good, discussing philosophy and religions and creating something that people could believe in. As long as I could give hope and answers, people would pay my way. And what's wrong with that? I was providing a service, and everyone wants to believe in something. We all need that. And they believed in me. And the more they believed, the more I believed."

"That you were more than a con man."

"That I was what your mother saw…special. But Henri saw it differently; he said I was small-time, that I was missing the potential and power of the group. He believed there was real money to be made. Classes and counseling fees, lifetime commitments and inheritances. He said the Seekers needed a real leader, that he'd been chosen to lead them. And as a devoted leader, he was entitled to the group's wealth. Your mother saw the changes coming long before I did, and was torn. She'd already invested so much. The center was a dream of hers, a place the Seekers could call their home. But it's not a home. It's a business. And I've been replaced."

"Karma's a bitch."

"Yes it is."

"You can confess all you like, Philippe, but I'm not here to forgive you. I'll never forgive you."

I knew how much my forgiveness would mean to him, especially since my mother had denied him the same thing, but I couldn't do it. I'd had to live with what he had done to me, and he would have to do the same.

"I know," he said, looking at me for a moment before turning away again and wiping his eyes. "Neither did your mother. That's why she left everything to you."

"An apartment the bank owned most of and a stack of debts and aliases to contend with. Some inheritance."

"Nothing else?" he asked, looking back to me.

"No."

"Are you sure?"

"Nothing but a box full of pictures and newspaper clippings. It's like a bunch of clues to a puzzle that I have no idea how to put together." I saw him smile and nod. "But you knew about that already, didn't you, Philippe? You gave it to her. *Another place to bury the past.*"

"Do you still have it?" he asked, wheeling toward me.

"Yes. But I don't understand what's in it."

"She will." He grabbed a piece of paper off the table and fished a pen out of his shirt pocket.

"Who?"

"Your mother's sister, Ingrid." With his hands shaking, he wrote carefully on the paper and handed it to me.

I stared at the address he'd written on the paper, too stunned to say anything. It was another secret he'd kept for my mother, until now.

"Go," he said. "It's what your mother would have wanted."

"How would you know?"

"Because it was the last thing she said to me, that you deserved to know the truth. And if you don't go, you'll never know."

"Why don't you just tell me?"

"Because I don't have all the pieces of the puzzle. Clearly your mother was smarter than that. It's up to you to put it all together."

I knew he was right. I looked at Philippe, at his small twisted body, his eyes full of tears. After all these years of hate, it had to come to this.

"And Elspeth...."

"Yes?"

"It probably means nothing to you after all this time, but I am sorry."

Seeing Philippe filled me with confusion and sadness I hadn't expected; his decades-late apology and admission of guilt didn't give me the satisfaction I'd always longed for. Maybe I should have forgiven him; maybe it would have given us both a sense of peace. But that's the thing about an apology—it's the responsibility of the wrongdoer to deliver it, but there's no rule that the one who was wronged has to accept it.

I walked back in the direction of the hotel as quickly as I could, until I came to the Seine, where I stopped to catch my breath. The city seemed sadder to me now. Steeped in history and full of stories that held no happy endings. I thought of my mother coming here for the first time, full of life and idealism, committed to the Seekers and their work, the very opposite of how she left.

In the end it seemed that my mother had finally chosen me, and she died alone as a result.

CHAPTER FIFTEEN

I had never believed in fate or that things happened for a reason, and yet my mother's death had saved my life. It had filled me with purpose and given me the strength to face my own past as I struggled to make sense of hers. I didn't know what fate awaited me at the end of this journey, but if I wanted answers I was going to have to go back to the place where it all began: Africa. I quickly packed my bags at the hotel and headed for the airport.

I asked the driver to go as fast as he could. Now that my mind was made up, I didn't want to waste another minute. I hadn't checked the flight schedules and had no idea what it would cost, but I didn't care. When we arrived, I headed straight for the ticket counter.

"Where to, madame?"

"Capetown."

"And the reservation is under what last name?" The attendant looked up from her screen and smiled.

"No reservation. I need a ticket on the first flight out of here. I don't care what it costs. One way." I shoved my credit card across the counter to her. I was breathing heavily from rushing, and she looked startled. "Please. It's urgent," I said.

She looked back at her screen and began typing. "There is a flight in forty minutes, but you'll have to hurry."

She swiped my card, checked my luggage, and handed me my boarding pass, and I grabbed it and ran. I couldn't remember the last time I moved so quickly. My chest was pounding and my legs ached, but I kept on running. People were moving out of the way and turning to stare but I didn't care—I was going to make that flight.

As soon as I landed in Capetown, I felt the heat from the earth go right through my feet and up my shins. The air was hot and dry, and I licked the dust from my lips, twisted my hair up, and stretched my arms high above my head. I'd gone from winter to summer in twenty-seven hours, and I could feel my muscles start to soften under the pulsing sun. I made my way over to the car rental agency, walking into welcoming waves of heat that made each of my movements feel as if they were happening in slow motion. The kid who worked at the rental agency said it was only a ninety-minute drive along Route 62 to Robertson Valley and suggested I get a convertible for the trip, so I did. After winter in three different countries, and a color palette of varying shades of gray over the last few weeks, I was grateful for South Africa's summer weather, for crisp blue skies that touched down on lush green fields, and for the striking pink king proteas, the country's national flower, that blazed along the

edges of the road. I gathered my thoughts, putting together
the pieces of my mother's puzzle and taking note of the
empty spaces that remained, spaces that had left their holes
in me. I hoped Ingrid would be able to fill in these spaces. I
was tired and wired all at the same time. Although I hadn't
slept for more than a few hours in a row since my mother
passed away, it wasn't sleep my body ached for, it was rest.
The kind of rest that comes with the peace of knowing, a
desire so strong it had brought me here.

I thought of Ted, another piece of me that was missing.
Ted wasn't Henri, he had never lied to me, and he hadn't
betrayed me like Philippe, but he had hurt me uninten-
tionally, and I needed to tell him so. I knew he was still
livid about our last conversation, and it might not change
anything between us, but if we never talked again, I'd feel
better knowing that I'd told him the truth. I found a gas
station with a pay phone and pulled over.

"Hello?" said Ted, sounding half asleep.

"It's me."

"What do you want, Elsie?" The sharpness in his voice
caught me off guard. He was angry, but he wasn't the only
one.

"I lied to you," I said, gripping the phone tightly.

"What are you talking about?"

"I lied to you. I didn't divorce you because I couldn't
stand what it was doing to you; I did it because I couldn't
stand what it was doing to me. I couldn't stand to see how
disappointed you were with me, that I wasn't pregnant,
that I wasn't fixed, that you hadn't made it all better."

"Elsie, I wasn't disappointed with you, I was disappointed

for us." He sounded irritated, as if he shouldn't have to explain anything so obvious.

"So was I, but you wouldn't *let* me be." I spat the words out as angry tears welled in my eyes. "I wasn't able to get pregnant, I wasn't able to control my body, I wasn't able to make a baby—not you Ted, me. I wanted to mourn that and accept that we'd done our best. But you refused to allow it. Instead, somewhere along the line, I became your project and not your wife and partner, and I couldn't take it anymore. I couldn't take you trying to fix me anymore."

"I just wanted us to be happy."

"We were always happy with each other, Ted, weren't we? I married you, not the father I thought you could be. You. And I wanted you to say the same. I wanted to be enough for you."

"And I wanted us to be a family," he said, exasperated, as if I didn't know that. As if I didn't understand, which I did. I wanted the same things. But I wanted *us* more, and I needed him to hear me.

"We *were* a family," I roared. "You're my family, Ted, and I'm yours, and that may not be everything we ever wanted, but you don't always get everything you want. And that has to be all right."

I pictured him sitting on the floor, his back leaning against the wall, knees tucked up against his chest. We had been here before. An ocean of hurt between us that seemed impossible to cross, until one of us reached out and touched the other. I imagined his hand in mine and sighed.

"Say something."

"What happened, Else?"

I leaned my head against the phone booth and exhaled deeply. "I saw Henri and he didn't apologize, and I saw Philippe and he did, and you know what? It didn't make me feel any better. It didn't undo what happened, nothing can. But it didn't destroy me either."

I'm still here, Luc had said to me in Paris. And he was right.

"I'll always be broken in some way, Ted, and I'll always wish that some things could have been different, and I'll always want the mother I never had, but I know I can't keep pining for the things I don't have, and missing out on the parts of my life that are wonderful...or used to be, anyway."

He was silent for a moment, and when he spoke his voice was low and gentle. "Look, I can't change what I want. I want a family, and I want it with you. And maybe it will still happen if we try again, and maybe it won't, but I don't want to do this life with anyone else, and I know that now."

I felt a calm wash over me, and my whole body softened. It was everything that I wanted to hear, but I needed to be sure. I needed to hear him say it.

"I need to be enough for you, Ted."

"I think we both know that you are more than enough for any one person." He sounded full of mischief when he said it, and warm, and I felt his smile traveling across the phone, giving me one of my own.

"What about Julie?" I felt a twinge of guilt as I thought of the phone call I'd had with her.

"Julie is a great woman who deserves to be with someone who isn't in love with someone else. After your visit to the set she accused me of still needing you. And she's right, I do. And no amount of time apart from you is going to change that, so she moved on."

We were both quiet, and as I closed my eyes, I could feel his body against mine, our arms and legs wrapped around each other. I wanted to reach through the phone, grab hold of him, and never let go.

"Where are you, Else?" he asked, and I felt a small piece of me return to where it was supposed to be.

"Africa. I'm on my way home. I don't know what surprises are waiting there for me, but I'm going to find out. And when I do, you're the one I want to share them with."

I stopped the car at the end of the property and looked at the little handwritten note Philippe had given me: *1421 Bowers Lane.* This was it. My mother's family farm. I recognized the small house behind the large metal gates from the photograph, and saw that a much larger house had been added onto the back. I felt like I had been here before, that some part of me was on the other side of the driveway ready to meet me. It was like I was returning, although to what and whom I didn't know. South Africa hadn't been my country for most of my life, and yet something in my very cells told me I was part of this place, that a piece of me had stayed here, waiting for me to return and reclaim it.

I tried my best to smooth out the wrinkles in my clothes from the car ride, and with my mother's box of photographs in hand, made my way to the security booth. I hadn't thought of what to tell the guard, but as I got closer he nodded and opened the gate, and that's when I saw the camera that had been watching me since I first pulled up. My heart was beating so strongly it was making the front of my T-shirt flutter. I took the three steps up to the front door and before I could knock, it opened.

"Elspeth."

"*Me....*" I whispered. The face was older, but I recognized the large beauty mark on her cheek. Here was the *Me* in the photographs, the younger woman who stood by my mother's side and held the baby in her arms. The woman who in the final photos was alone, without parents, and who, I was sure, had sent the obituaries with the handwritten note that said, *Thought you'd want to know....*

"Ingrid," she said, introducing herself and opening the door wide for me to come in. "She said you'd come home."

I remembered Mrs. David telling me about a phone call she had overheard my mother making from the hospital before she died. My mother must have spoken to Ingrid that day, and the conversation had been about me.

Ingrid was smaller than my mother, and darker, her skin weathered from the sun and covered in freckles. Her bare face was lined like dry earth, crackled and grooved around brown eyes that matched the long braid that she wore over her shoulder. I could tell by the thick, bare calves that stuck out from her knee-length cotton dress that she was strong and a walker like my mother had been, although judging by her flat bare feet, it was not from exercise, but from a way of life, from working on the huge property visible through the windows at the back of the house.

"Thank you," I said, walking ahead of her and straight

to the back windows. As far as the eye could see were rows of vines with green grapes being tended to by workers. "Vineyards?" I asked.

"Yes. If only my father had known that it wasn't strawberries these fields wanted but grapes, he could have been a very rich man." She came and stood next to me, and this time it was her turn to take me in.

"You look like your father, Elspeth," she said, studying my profile. "Same long nose and sad eyes."

"You knew him?" I asked, turning toward her.

"I knew them both. They used to have the farm next door, and their family would come up here on the weekends when I was a girl." She pointed to an area to the left of the vineyards that looked identical to the land in front of us.

"And now they're both dead," I sighed. "First, Leo in the car accident, and then Howard of a heart attack."

A strange expression passed over Ingrid's face and she moved toward the center of the room, where she sat on a large leather couch with her back to me. It was a magnificent room, with hardwood floors, stone walls, and wooden beams that ran the length of the ceiling. To my right was a fireplace and to my left a heavy wooden staircase that led to a wide landing and the second floor. I followed Ingrid and sat in one of the wingback chairs facing her as she poured glasses of iced tea for us from the pitcher on the table.

"I didn't know about you or any of this," I said, placing my mother's wooden box on the table and taking out the family portraits. "I only saw these after my mother died. She left them with a neighbor for safekeeping, along with a note. I don't know why she wanted me to follow her clues, why she couldn't have just told me what happened."

"I'm not sure I have a satisfactory answer for that. Perhaps she wanted you to walk in her footsteps? Perhaps she thought it would help you understand why she did the things she did? The Rachel I knew always believed she was right, even if others thought otherwise. I can only guess she hoped you would see things as she did."

Ingrid took the small stack of photographs and began to look through them slowly. Her eyes lingered on the picture of her and Rachel as children, standing with their parents in front of the original house that stood where we were now. She sighed heavily and held the picture against her chest.

"The Seekers seem to believe my mother was a wealthy woman, yet as far as I know, she died penniless and alone. I want to know why, I want to understand her." I took a deep breath and tried to calm myself down.

Ingrid leaned forward. I felt her eyes on me, deciding what she should say next. I didn't want her to sugarcoat any of it, so I pressed harder.

"Ingrid, please. Philippe said only you could tell me the whole truth. What was Rachel hiding? And why was she hiding it?"

Ingrid hesitated a moment. "My dear, she'd been hiding truths and telling lies from the moment she could talk. Our mother taught us to hide from day one."

"Hide what?"

"That we were Jews."

Ingrid told me that my grandparents, Samuel and Hannah, had fled the pogroms in Russia and started over in South Africa. Samuel was a farmer who had believed there were fields of strawberries there, and Hannah had agreed to go anywhere there was no snow and that Jews were safe. They'd been practicing Jews back in Russia, but when Hannah saw how blacks were treated in South Africa, she was convinced it was only a matter of time until the Jews were next and she would be hunted again. She saw apartheid coming years before it did, and it scared her. So she changed our family's last name from Milevsky to Mills, forbade Samuel from practicing the Jewish holidays, and tried everything she could to make the family seem like gentiles. Only it didn't work—Samuel no longer went to synagogue, but he still practiced at home, and no matter what the family name was, they still looked like Jews. Except for Rachel, who they called Ray. She was fairer than the rest, her hair lighter, and my grandmother made her take elocution lessons to sound British.

"Mother dressed Ray better than me," said Ingrid. "She sent Ray to a better school and told her over and over again how she could be different, have a better life, how her beauty would help her find a rich man and her body would help her keep him. Our mother was a fearful woman, always looking over her shoulder and full of doom. Rachel was her favorite. Although I'm not sure what was worse, being ignored by her like I was or being the object of her obsession."

She stood and walked over to a small bar next to the

fireplace. She opened a bottle of wine and brought it and two glasses back to the table.

"I think we're both going to need something stronger," she said, pushing aside the iced tea and handing me a glass.

"Thank you," I said. I drank half my glass in one gulp and refilled it. "I don't know what to say. I mean it's true, she always used her looks, but her own mother made her that way? That's unspeakable."

"Not everyone should be a mother," Ingrid said.

"I guess not," I said, feeling my eyes sting.

And the people who should be don't always get the chance. I thought of all those years Ted and I had tried, knowing in my heart I would have been a thousand times better at it than my own mother.

"No children?" asked Ingrid.

"No." I paused for a moment, taking note of a small flicker of hope inside myself. "Not yet. We'll see. You?"

"Not my own," she said, taking a drink. "I did raise my baby brother, though, after our mother passed away and Rachel left."

"Does he live here too?"

"No, Isaac died years ago. Polio."

"Polio. My mother told me that Howard had polio. Did he?"

"No." She was quiet for a moment. "But I don't suppose that would have been as interesting."

"And Lafina? Do you know what happened to her?" I asked hopefully.

Ingrid smiled. "After you left, Lafina came to stay with us. Isaac was just a toddler, and I was alone. There was so much to do and so much land to take care of; she needed the work, and I needed the help. After a few months, I convinced her to bring her son Welcome over to play with Isaac. We were both raising children on our own, and it bothered me that she had to be away from her son so much. We used to hide the two of them in the backyard, where nobody could see them together. Welcome was only a child, not an employee, so under apartheid, he wasn't allowed to be here. But we were careful. And over time more of her family came, and I found work for them so they could stay. We built that house for them, away from the road, and away from anyone who might be looking," she said, pointing to a ranch-style bungalow on the far end of the property. "And we raised the kids together, as a family. She died peacefully ten years ago, surrounded by love. I still think of her every day."

I smiled at the thought of Lafina being a part of this place and having a family of her own. I was glad that after everything I'd feared, she'd had a good life. "Thank you. I really missed her."

"And she missed you, very much."

"All these people I never knew," I said, looking at the photographs. "Did you know about me?"

"Yes."

I took a deep breath and looked her straight in the eyes. "And are you the one who sent the obituaries?" It came out like an accusation.

"I am."

"You knew I was alive and yet you never contacted me. Weren't you curious how we were doing, all alone and far away? Didn't you care?"

"Of course I cared," she said, biting her lip. "Rachel used to write to me when she was away on her trips with the Seekers. She'd tell me just enough to let me know that she was okay, and to update me on how you were doing. But I never allowed myself to reach out to you, and believe me, I came close to doing so many times over. But it would have been dangerous for Rachel." Ingrid stopped herself and shook her head. "My sister had a past, Elspeth. A past that you weren't supposed to know anything about. That was always the deal. And then about a month ago, just before she died, she made me promise to tell you the truth, but only if you asked. Now I wonder if it was wise of me to make that promise, if you wouldn't be happier not knowing. I'm not sure what good it will do at this stage. You can't go back and change things."

"But I can't go forward either. I'm stuck and I'm tired of it. Whatever it is, it's better than not knowing."

"Are you sure?" she said quietly, giving me one last chance to change my mind.

Ingrid saw the way her mother admired the wealthy family next door. Mrs. Robins dressed beautifully and spent most of her time at her home in Cape Town. It was the old man, Mr. Robins, who had first started growing grapes on the land after having made his fortune buying and selling diamonds. The farm was a hobby for him and his boys and a private place to take his mistress. Ingrid used to watch as her sister, Rachel, played with Mr. Robins's sons, Howard and Leo, and she could tell by the way they looked at Rachel and chased her around that they both had a crush on her. It was something Hannah encouraged as Rachel got older, eager for her prettiest daughter to marry well.

"Howard's the one you want as a husband," Hannah told Rachel one day as she combed her hair for her on the porch. "He's smart and a hard worker, and he knows he'd be lucky to have a girl as beautiful as you for a wife. He'll appreciate you more, and work harder to keep you happy."

At the end of Hannah's speech, Ingrid looked pointedly at her sister, who carefully cradled her bandaged hand in her lap. But Rachel turned away, and Ingrid bit her bottom lip to stop herself from saying anything. She knew her sister wasn't looking at Howard. She knew she was in love with Leo. Leo who drank too much, laughed too loudly, and, according to their mother, would never amount to anything. Ingrid had caught the two of them rolling around in the fields the week before, the week Rachel hurt her hand.

"She's going to kill you if she finds out about this," Ingrid said to Rachel when she found her at the side of the house trying to wash the blood of her lost virginity from her dress.

"Please don't tell her," pleaded Rachel, as she carefully fed her soaking-wet dress between the rollers of the wringer on the washing machine.

"Why?" asked Ingrid. "She thinks you're perfect. It might do her good to know the truth."

"Ingrid, please," said Rachel. Her hands were shaking, and her eyes kept looking to the driveway for their parents, who were due back at any moment.

"After everything she has planned for you, you just go and throw it away without thinking!" yelled Ingrid. It was just like her sister to think only of herself. If Rachel didn't do what their mother had planned for her, then everything that Ingrid had to put up with, every sacrifice she had to make so her sister could marry better, meant nothing. "I'm going to tell her. You can't do this!"

"Ingrid, don't! We're going to get married."

"She'll never let you." Ingrid could already picture her mother in one of her rages, and the thought of it made her stomach turn. She saw Rachel's eyes widen and followed her gaze to the end of the driveway, to where their parents had returned. Rachel started pushing her dress frantically through the rolling pins with one hand while working the crank with the other.

"Ingrid please help me, I'm begging you!"

Ingrid hopped up on the stool next to the washer and grabbed the hand crank, turning it over as fast as she could while Rachel shoved her dress through. Rachel didn't know how to wash clothes, that was Ingrid's job—she was the one who had to do the laundry, she was the one who had callused hands and sore arms from working the stupid machine, not Rachel. All she had to do was hang the laundry, that was easy. Ingrid was so mad at her sister, and so focused on trying to finish before their mother made it up the path, that she didn't know what had happened until she heard the scream. And then she saw Rachel's hand caught between the rolling pins.

"Ingrid," Rachel gasped.

Ingrid fought the urge to be sick at the sight of the

mangled hand, and as gently as she could, she rolled the crank backward and pulled it out. Rachel collapsed on the ground as Ingrid called out to their parents, who started running toward them.

"Please, please, promise me you won't tell. Promise."

"My mother was furious at me for hurting Rachel, and when my father insisted it was an accident, she blamed him for bringing home the machine. She was terrified that a less-than-perfect Rachel would be harder to marry off. I felt terrible—it was my fault, and I owed Rachel. So I kept her love for Leo secret, and when I discovered he'd gotten her pregnant, I kept that secret too. But maybe if I hadn't, the accident wouldn't have happened."

It was late September 1947, the year before apartheid, and Mrs. Robins was having her annual spring fling party at the family's vacation home in Muizenberg Beach. The queen had just completed her first visit to South Africa earlier that month, and all over Capetown, people were full of pride, as the British newsreels had heralded the city as glamorous and cosmopolitan. The country was filled with an optimism that had only been heightened by the queen's tour. In honor of the historic visit, Mrs. Robins decided to give her party a royal theme. Leo had complained to Ingrid about having to get fit for a new tuxedo, and how it angered his father, who was already annoyed by the extravagance of the affair, and accused Mrs. Robins of just wanting to show off. Rachel sat awestruck as she listened to each new detail that Leo shared about the decorations, the champagne, and the guest list, which included Cape-town's wealthiest families. After weeks of dropping hints, Leo finally asked Rachel to attend as his date. Hannah had insisted that Ingrid go along as well, worried that the Robinses would think poorly of Rachel if she was to attend unchaperoned. She bought Rachel long gloves and a new dress that they couldn't afford, and Rachel wore her hair up, with little white lily of the valley flowers arranged in front to look like a crown and simple diamond earrings that once belonged to their grandmother. Ingrid was wearing the one good dress she owned, and she tried to dress it up with a beautiful silk embroidered sash that Rachel had surprised her with.

"Howard insisted on driving with Leo up front," Ingrid recalled, "and Rachel and I rode in the back. Rachel was so excited. The Robinses' mansion was perched atop a cliff overlooking the ocean. It glowed in the darkness, lit up by tiny candles that lined the winding driveway to its entrance. As we got to the front door, Rachel squeezed my hand and said, 'We're here, we're finally here.' She was thrilled to be part of this night. And I worried that her wanting to belong would shine too brightly on her and make her an object of ridicule. But I needn't have worried. She was absolutely charming and breathtakingly beautiful, and that was all anybody noticed."

All night long Ingrid stayed on the edges of the party, watching how easily her sister was able to talk to Mr. and Mrs. Robins and their guests, how quickly she could put people at ease, and how readily they laughed at her jokes. While Rachel kept her composure and only drank water,

Leo seemed to have a never-ending glass of champagne and then moved on to hard liquor. His charm disintegrated into sloppiness with each drink he took, until he crashed into a waiter and landed on the floor. Howard took him outside and Rachel and Ingrid followed.

"You're leaving," said Howard, dragging his brother away from the house and across the garden.

"Oh I am, am I?" shouted Leo, pushing Howard away and falling down in the process.

"Stop it please, people can hear you," said Rachel. She turned to look back at the house, where a small group of guests were watching them.

"What people? I don't give a fuck about them. They're nobody, just a bunch of freeloaders!" Leo shouted back at them.

"Stop it, you're embarrassing Rachel," said Howard.

"How sweet, sticking up for your girlfriend."

"What are you talking about?" stammered Howard, his face going red.

"Please, we've all seen the way you look at her, it's pathetic."

"Leo, enough." Rachel walked toward Leo and helped him up.

"You know it's true, Rachel. Then again, maybe that's what you want, someone who'll follow after you. Maybe he's the one you should be with." Leo was stumbling on his feet, walking toward Howard, when Rachel stopped him.

"He doesn't mean it, he's drunk," said Rachel to Howard.

"He's always drunk, and he always will be." Howard

reached out and gently placed his hand on Rachel's shoulder. "But he's right, you deserve better."

Leo swung at Howard but lost his balance and caught Rachel in the stomach instead, knocking the wind out of her. Ingrid ran to her sister and screamed at Leo, "You spoiled brat, do you have any idea what you might have done?"

"Ingrid don't!" Rachel gasped. She gripped Ingrid's hand tightly and with her help, slowly got to her feet.

"Let's get out of here," Leo said, grabbing Rachel's hand and pulling her away.

Rachel looked back at Ingrid and Howard and said, "Howard, please make sure that Ingrid gets home safely."

Leo peeled out of the driveway, swerving as he did so, and Ingrid feared the worst. Rachel knew there was no way Leo could get them home safely, so she begged him to pull the car over and let her drive, and he did.

"Wait a minute! Mother was driving?"

Ingrid nodded and looked at me, her eyes wet, her face full of sadness. "Yes. She said they argued the whole way home. Leo was really drunk. He said he didn't want to be tied down and told what to do. He accused her of trying to trap him, of being after his money. Here she was, believing she would be his wife, and he was accusing her of being a golddigger. She reached over and slapped him, not seeing the other car coming until its lights flooded her windshield and sent her crashing into the side of the mountain. The couple in the car was killed instantly, and Rachel was sure that her life was over, but then everyone assumed that it was Leo who had been driving, and she let them think so. She was devastated and racked with guilt when they brought her home, and she refused to come out of her room for weeks. I begged her to tell me what was wrong, and that's when she admitted that she had been driving. I didn't know what to do. I didn't want my pregnant sister to go to jail, so I alone kept her secret."

I thought of all the times my mother had gotten upset when I'd tried to talk about that night. The terror she said the person driving the car must have felt, knowing they were about to take the lives of others. And all along it had been her, and only Ingrid knew. Not the Seekers, not Philippe or Henri. I wondered if deep down my mother feared that the events of that night were truly unforgivable.

"Right after Leo died, Mr. Robins had a heart attack, leaving the farm and everything else to Howard and making him a very rich man. Howard was a mess. He blamed himself for fighting with his brother that night and letting him leave the party. And he feared he had ruined Rachel's life. He vowed to make it up to her if it was the last thing he did. He would talk to me and wait on the porch to see her, and my mother would beg Rachel to come out, but she refused. Then suddenly one afternoon she announced that she would be marrying Howard, and two weeks later she left. She was finally going to do what our mother had always wanted her to: marry well and move to the city. Mother used to get dressed in her best outfit and sit on the porch with an overnight bag packed, waiting for Rachel to visit and take her with her. At first she'd come every other week by train with Howard. But it wasn't long until she started coming once a month and alone; Howard was busy at work, or there was so much to do at the new house they'd bought, and she had to get ready for your arrival. She'd share all the details with our mother, who would hang on every word, a dreamy look in her eyes as she imagined this elegant new home and this sparkling new life that she thought one day she'd be a part of, but she never was. Our mother had taught Rachel that she was better than us, and she finally believed it. We didn't see her for ages, then Isaac was born and mother died in childbirth. Lafina brought you to the funeral."

"And my mother?"

"She was in Paris with Philippe."

The whole room seemed to move, and though I knew it was the truth, I couldn't quite believe I had heard Ingrid correctly.

Philippe had met Rachel at a New Year's Eve party thrown by Mrs. Robins. Howard's mother liked to collect interesting people, and on a recent trip abroad she'd met Philippe and had been taken with him. She encouraged him to visit her in South Africa, where he could take part in the salons she'd been holding in her home for herself and fellow ladies of leisure who were looking for a little distraction. It was a distraction that was short lived, as Mrs. Robins, who tired quickly of her interests, moved on. But it was long enough for Rachel to catch Philippe's eye, and for him to gain several wealthy new members. And when he returned to Africa a few years later, Rachel was looking for something and someone to believe in, and Philippe was happy to oblige.

Howard's dreams of winning Rachel over hadn't played out the way he hoped. She'd been in love with Leo, and no matter how much she needed Howard, she never felt about him the way he wanted her to, and Howard knew it. He became paranoid that Rachel would leave him. He needed to know where she was at every moment and lavished her with expensive gifts of jewelry, trying to buy her love. Rachel started spending more and more time away from home, taking tennis lessons and art classes, studying philosophy and religion, anything she could do to distract herself, but nothing worked. And then she ran into Philippe on one of his trips, and he told her that she was able to change her own karma, and she desperately wanted that.

"How old was she?" I heard myself ask.

"She was twenty-two. I remember I had just turned sixteen, and Rachel took me out to a meeting and then to celebrate," Ingrid said. "At the time, I thought the Seekers was just some weird group, another thing that Rachel was going to experiment with and abandon. I had no idea they would become such a large part of her life."

My stomach clenched as I recalled my own sixteenth birthday and my first encounter with Philippe. I needed air and stood and walked outside to the back porch.

"Are you all right?" asked Ingrid.

I nodded. "I suppose you think I'm crazy for wanting to find out what happened."

Ingrid was quiet as she slowly undid her braid and let her long hair loose down her back. I ran my fingers through my own hair and noticed it had the same curl as hers. The resemblance we shared was startling. Family. This is what it feels like to look at someone and see parts of yourself reflected back. I'd never had that with anyone but my mother, and she did everything she could to make sure she didn't look like me.

"I don't think you're crazy. I think you're brave. To have never been burdened by your family and their legacy and to choose to take that on...I don't know if I would do the same." She looked at me closely, her eyes squinting in the setting sun.

"It's a greater burden not knowing," I said. "I feel like a half-finished jigsaw puzzle, and the pieces that are missing have been hidden from me. I've tried to fill them in, but it isn't the same. I remember some things and yet I don't know what is real and what is a false memory planted by my mother, a piece of fiction created to hide the truth."

"Sometimes the truth is painful, and knowing it won't change anything."

"That's not for you to decide." I held her gaze. "Please, tell me about the fire."

Ingrid's footing faltered for a moment, her knees buckling slightly. "You remember the fire," she said, regaining her balance and looking far off into the fields.

"I dream about it, but I don't know what it means." I told her about the dream and waited for her to speak.

"Walk with me." She reached her hand out and I took it. As we made our way through the rows of vines, Ingrid kept her eyes ahead of her and spoke softly and evenly.

"Rachel had gotten very involved with the Seekers, and Howard had discovered that she'd been giving them money. He was furious when he found out and forbade her from going to meetings. But Rachel wouldn't listen." Ingrid paused for a moment, a distant look in her eyes. "I remember the day she brought Philippe to the house," she said. "I was working right here when I heard her call my name. I looked back and there she was, standing next to him and waving." She slid her hand out of mine and raised it to her mouth, as if still surprised at the memory.

"She was standing too close to him and smiling, and it was the way she waved, so excited, her feet practically lifting up off the porch, that I knew."

"Knew?"

"Knew my sister had betrayed her marriage. She looked like a young girl in love that day, like she'd looked when she was around Leo. Her hair was loose, and she had on a sundress sheer enough that you could see the silhouette of her legs through it, and her body arced toward him as if they had been joined only moments ago."

Ingrid turned to me and spoke. "It wasn't that I didn't want her to be happy, it was that I knew there could be no happy ending if what I suspected was true, and it was. She told me she and Philippe were in love, she wanted to show him where she grew up, where she really came from. She was going to join him in spreading the word of the Seekers."

She rubbed her strong hands over her face and sighed. "It was impossible. She couldn't just leave Howard for Philippe. Without Howard's money, where could she go? I was furious that she wanted me to keep her secrets for her again, and she accused me of being jealous of her happiness. And maybe I was. After our mother passed away, it had been up to me to take care of Isaac. I was only fifteen when he was born and suddenly I had to run the house and take care of a baby. I thought my dad would come around, would find a way out of his depression, but he never did. Some days he never got out of bed, and I'd clean the house, make the food, and try to tend to the farm. I was in over my head. Sometimes he was so depressed he wouldn't say a word, and nights would pass without either of us having spoken to each other. It was like that for three years, until he died. You can't know how draining it is to live with someone who is always depressed, Elspeth."

But I did know. I thought about my own depression and the many times Ted had watched me shuffle listlessly in my pajamas from room to room, silent and full of despair and unable to leave the house. He'd felt helpless watching me, trying to get me to eat or bathe, propping me up in a chair by a sunbeam, like some wilted houseplant he was sure could be brought back to life. When I would emerge, sometimes weeks later, he'd confide in me how terrified he was that I was going to stay there in the dark, unable to find my way back through his voice and his touch. He was a grown man, and I could only imagine how hard it must have been for Ingrid as a teenager. I wondered if knowing about my grandfather's own battles with depression would have made those dark days easier for me to bear, if it would have helped me to not worry every time that I was losing my mind, and losing Ted in the process.

"When she came by that day with Philippe, saying she wanted to show him where she grew up, I wanted to scream. The farm meant nothing to her, but you could see Philippe's eyes widen at the possibility of it."

She shook her head and closed her eyes at the memory.

Ingrid told me that if Rachel was going to leave Howard, she needed money. She asked Howard for a bigger allowance on the pretense that she was sending some of it to Ingrid. She said it was the least she could do to help her sister, who'd been burdened with raising Isaac on her own. Then she started collecting jewelry, pieces that were one of a kind or from luxury brands. Things she could sell later on. They cost a fortune, but Howard was desperate to buy her love back, and as long as she stayed with him and away from the Seekers, he gave her whatever she wanted. For a while it was easy for Rachel to obey Howard's wishes. The group had been having trouble with outsiders who objected to them having black members, and Philippe had asked her to stay away until things calmed down. But things got worse. The Seekers were accused of being an anti-apartheid organization, and the police broke up a meeting, seriously injuring black members and anyone who tried to defend them, including Philippe. Philippe wanted to leave Johannesburg, and Rachel wanted to go with him. She started giving him her jewelry for safekeeping, and word got back to Howard when Philippe had shown off a couple of the pieces to his friends.

Howard was livid, and when he confronted her, she said she was in love with Philippe and was leaving Howard and taking her daughter with her. Howard said he wouldn't let some whore raise his only child, and that's when my mother told him that I wasn't actually his, but

Leo's. Howard slapped her hard, knocking her down. She belonged to him and him alone, he said. He threatened to go to the police and accuse Philippe of theft, of conning his wife out of her jewels. He was rich, people would listen to him over some foreigner who drifted in and out of the country and stayed at the homes of wealthy socialites. The Seekers were already in trouble with the law, and the police would be more than happy to arrest Philippe for fraud. Rachel panicked. She couldn't imagine her life without Philippe and the group; they had become everything to her, and she had to protect them.

"And that's when she decided to burn the house down, with Howard in it," said Ingrid gravely.

"The fire," I said.

I suddenly remembered my mother standing over me in the middle of the night, pulling me out of bed, and the two of us running so quickly we practically flew down the stairs.

"Go see Lafina," she said as she pushed me out into the night. "Now. Run!"

I ran past the big tree, all the way to Lafina's quarters at the far end of the property. I smelled it before I saw it, the rich aroma of wood smoke, pushing me onward, and when I got to Lafina's door she was waiting for me, standing in her nightgown and one of my mother's old bathrobes, belted underneath her enormous breasts. She grabbed me to her, and as I heard the sound of the fire crackle and spark, she shoved my face into her warm belly and held my head tightly so I couldn't look back.

And then Lafina was gone. Her white bathrobe flying

in the dark, like angel's wings behind her. I saw our house consumed in red and orange flames, and Lafina running toward it.

"Lafina!" I screamed in horror at the sight of her entering the house. "Lafina!" But she couldn't hear me. My whole body shook, my heart thrashed in my chest, and I gasped for breath until I passed out.

That was the extent of my memory, and Ingrid filled in the rest. She was the one who picked us up on the side of the road outside the train station, my mother carrying me in her scorched nightdress and sandals. Lafina had phoned Ingrid when she first heard the fighting, and Ingrid drove to the station as fast as she could.

As the flames grew higher, Rachel raced out and passed Lafina, who charged into the fire, determined to rescue Howard. She had agreed to help my mother escape, but not to murder. That was the image that always woke me up in the middle of the night terrified: Lafina running into the house and the fire raging. All these years I had feared that Lafina had died in the fire, but it had been Howard.

The house burned to the ground, and everyone believed that Howard and my mother and I had all died in the fire. There was no other way my mother trusted that we'd be safe. It was only a matter of time before someone figured out that the fire wasn't an accident, and that's when the police would come looking for her. She was also irrationally convinced that the police would find out that she lied about her role in the car crash, too. To those who didn't know the truth, it might look like she was some poor girl who'd worked her way into a wealthy family and stood to inherit a fortune when the sons were gone. So Ingrid wrote our obituaries and sent them to her friend at the newspaper, who had no reason to suspect they weren't real. And Philippe, who in many ways owed Rachel, used every connection he had to help get us out of the country and into Canada where we could start over. That was the debt she'd been talking about. Philippe knew what she had done, and he had helped her get away with it.

"I knew she was hiding something, but murder?" I stared at Ingrid in shock.

"She was beside herself that night, after her fight with Howard. She was desperately in love with Philippe and believed Howard was going to make good on his promise to put Philippe away—or that he might kill her if she tried to leave. She said the fire was self-defense."

"What do you think?"

"I think she would have done anything to save herself, and that meant saving Philippe and the Seekers. When Howard died, all his money and land went to Rachel, then you, and last to me, in the event that you were both dead as everyone believed you were. Rachel had planned it that way. I'd send her the money Howard willed to her when it was safe, and she would live off of it. It was more than enough for her lifetime, but she managed to go through it, thanks to the Seekers."

"And yet they're still convinced that there's more, that she had a large estate she was leaving to them. Were they right?"

"No." Ingrid smiled and put her hand on my shoulder, "the estate is yours."

"What?"

"Half this land is yours. We decided I would farm all of it, what my father left me along with the land he left Rachel, and I would own half. The other half she left for you. She never wanted it or tried to sell it, even when the money ran out and she had to sell her jewelry. She hoped that something good would come from all the suffering this land has seen. It was always meant to be yours, a place where you could put down roots."

"I don't know what to say." All those years thinking that I was alone, believing that no one cared, and here was Ingrid tending to my mother's wishes, nurturing the land in the hopes that one day I'd return. "Why did you do it?" I asked. Ingrid could have kept the land for herself, she could have lied or let my part of it suffer; instead she cultivated a fortune whose magnitude I couldn't yet comprehend.

"Because you're family," she said. She placed her hand on my cheek, and I reached up for it and held it. "My sister chose to take you with her. She could have left you here with Lafina and me. We were willing to raise you, but she insisted. She said she wanted another chance, wanted to do right by you, give you a better life by being a better mother than she had been so far. But I don't think she knew how."

Tears fell down my face and off my chin onto the earth below.

Family. What made a real family? People who guided you, loved you, and protected you as best as they could, no matter how damaged and fragile you were. Was that what my mother believed she had done? Had hiding the sins of her past been her way of protecting me, just as leaving me the box had been her way of guiding me safely to where I was now, overlooking the land that had been in my family for three generations? I chose to believe it was.

"Thank you, Ingrid," I said, holding both her hands in mine and looking into her eyes. "Thank you."

"I'm not sure it changes anything," she said gently.

But it did. I wouldn't get those years with my mother back, and knowing what I knew now didn't mean I could ever completely forgive or justify what she had done to all of us, not least to poor Howard. And yet, it was something. The anger that had lived in my heart for all those years turned to a deep ache as I thought of all Rachel and I had lost.

"It really is beautiful here," I said, looking out across the land, unable to believe half of it was mine.

"Yes it is," said Ingrid, standing next to me and hooking her arm through mine. "You know, in spite of everything and after all this country has been through, I have never wanted to be anywhere else. This land is real to me. Everything our family has suffered, all the heartache, it will come and go and come again. And like this land, we will sift through it and turn it over and bury it and plant new hopes and dreams and pray for them to grow, harvesting and celebrating and mourning them, then do it all over again. This is all there is. It will be here long after we are gone."

I'd always believed that I couldn't really know where I was going until I knew where I was from, and at last I did. I had a family whose branches were as twisted and fragile as the vines that grew on this land, but in spite of everything, they had endured and were determined to grow and bear fruit that would be transformed into something else. It gave me hope. I stared out into the night and felt the darkness wrap around me in a warm embrace, and in the stars overhead I could feel them: all the people who had been on this land before me, watching over me. I was home.

The house lit up behind us, and we both turned to see a man standing on the porch waving.

"Auntie! The kids are dying to see you."

"Is that Welcome?" I asked.

"Yes, Welcome," replied Ingrid. "Come meet the rest of your family."

ACKNOWLEDGMENTS

I'm forever grateful to UCLA Extension Writers' Program for changing the course of my life and introducing me to my mentor, the incredible Caroline Leavitt, who has championed this book from its first sentence and has been my cheerleader every step of the way. I wouldn't be a published author without you. Enormous thanks to my wonderful agent, Stefanie Lieberman at Janklow & Nesbit Associates, for believing in me and this book, and for working with me to make it as good as it can be. Thank you to everyone at Prospect Park Books, especially my dedicated editor, Colleen Dunn Bates, for reading my manuscript even when she was closed to submissions and taking a chance. To Kathleen Zrelak at Goldberg McDuffie Communications and Jennifer Lynch at Publishers Group Canada, thank you for talking this book up far and wide. And to my amazing friend Alexandra Watkins, thank you for giving me a home at Eat My Words, and always supporting me.

This book was on a long journey, and through it all, my friends, colleagues, and family listened, waited, and hoped, cheering me on from near and far, keeping faith when I had doubt and celebrating with me when it found the right home. Much love and gratitude to you all. Along the way were many drafts and insightful readers, and I'd like to thank Robert Eversz for giving one such read at a particularly critical time. Thanks to my husband, Jeff Clarke, for your love and support, and for years of walking and talking it out, and to my favorite person on the planet, Grady, who adores words as much as I do.

Thank you to my family members, who mean the world: Lisa, Stuart, Marc, Martine, Gabriel, Grace, Olina, Kayla, Anya, Eric, Jennifer, Matt, Alex, and Margaret. My parents have always loved a good story and have shared many over the years with me. A special thanks to them: my father, Denny Peressini, who has encouraged my writing since I was a young girl, and my mother, Leonie, who has lovingly supported me in everything I do, and who has served as a constant reminder that one must simply "go for it."

ABOUT THE AUTHOR

Gina Sorell is a writer who was born in South Africa and now lives in Toronto with her husband and son. After two decades as a working actor in Los Angeles and Toronto, Gina returned to her first love, writing, and graduated with distinction from the UCLA Extension Writers' Program. When she isn't writing fiction, she's the creative director of Eat My Words, a San Francisco–based branding firm. *Mothers and Other Strangers* is her first novel.